WAITING IN SÓLLER

ROBERT O'BRIEN

Waiting In Sóller

BY

Robert O'Brien

Copyright © 2024
Robert M. O'Brien

ISBN:

EBook: 978-1-963609-85-1
Paperback: 978-1-963609-86-8
Hardback: 978-1-963609-87-5

Robert M. O'Brien
21971 Blazing Trail
281-686-3631
guinnesslover@icloud.com

All Rights Reserved. Any unauthorized reprint or use of this material is strictly prohibited. No part of this book may be reproduced or transmitted in any form or by any means, electronic or mechanical, including photocopying, recording, or by any information storage and retrieval system without express written permission from the author.

All reasonable attempts have been made to verify the accuracy of the information provided in this publication. Nevertheless, the author assumes no responsibility for any errors and/or omissions.

CONTENTS

ACKNOWLEDGEMENTS 3
FOREWORD 4
THE STATION 6
PARIS 8
I INTO THE CRUCIBLE 16
HOLLAND 30
GOING HOME 45
THE SEINE 57
GEORGIA 68
PEGASUS 79
THE MARKET 89
HARRY'S 99
ANDREA'S STORY 112
MOURMELON 113
PALMA 140
WACHT AM RHEIN 142
JACK'S FOREST 150
FOY AND THE FALLEN 189
LETTERS 206
DESPERATE MESSAGES 215
RETURN TO MOURMELON 227
KAUFERING 241
THE PROMISE 252
BERCHTESGADEN 229

TRIUMPH	237
HOMECOMING	279
PREPARATIONS AND ENDINGS	288
SÓLLER	302

ACKNOWLEDGEMENTS

In dedication to my great uncles, Frank, and George O'Brien, two remarkable men whose bravery and sacrifice on D-Day left an indelible mark on history. As I embark on the journey of recounting the events of that fateful day, I am humbled and honored to pay tribute to their courage and unwavering commitment to the cause of freedom.

Frank O'Brien, a valiant glider pilot, navigated the perilous skies, soaring with determination and purpose as he embarked on a daring mission to land behind enemy lines. His skillful piloting and unyielding spirit exemplify the bravery and resilience of all those who took to the skies on that pivotal day. Frank's bravery and determination serve as an inspiration to all, a beacon of hope in the darkest of hours.

George O'Brien, standing tall on the beaches of Normandy, fought with unflinching resolve, facing the harrowing reality of battle head-on. His unwavering dedication to his fellow soldiers and his unwavering commitment to the mission epitomize the selflessness and courage displayed by the brave men who stormed the beaches that day.

May the memories of Frank and George O'Brien, and all the brave souls who took part in D-Day, forever be etched in our hearts and minds. Their legacy will endure, inspiring generations to come with their bravery, dedication, and unwavering spirit. This book is dedicated to their memory, a humble tribute to their heroism and the legacy they left behind.

FOREWORD

In the annals of history, there are countless tales of love and valor that have emerged from the history of war. The story you are about to embark upon is one such tale, inspired by the television mini-series "Band of Brothers," and the remarkable events of the 101st Airborne during World War II. This book weaves together historical fact and fiction to paint a poignant portrait of a young soldier, John, and a spirited Spanish woman, Mary, from the idyllic town of Sóller, Mallorca, Spain.

Set against the backdrop of war-torn Paris, this narrative unravels a tender romance that blossomed amidst chaos and uncertainty. John, a brave soldier of the 101st Airborne, found himself in the midst of the grand theater of war, his heart drawn to the charismatic charm of Mary, a woman far from her homeland, yet fiercely resilient and spirited.

Their love story unfolds against the backdrop of Paris, where the Eiffel Tower stood tall as a symbol of hope, even in the darkest of times. As the city's streets echoed with the footsteps of soldiers and the trappings of war, John and Mary's bond grew stronger, reminding us that even in the face of adversity, love can be a beacon of light.

As John's journey took him to the front lines, Mary returned to her homeland, Mallorca, where she grappled with the weight of uncertainty and the longing for her beloved. Their paths diverged, but their hearts remained intertwined, connected by the unyielding thread of love and the hope of a future together.

In the pages that follow, you will witness not only the indomitable spirit of the 101st Airborne but also the resilience of ordinary individuals thrust into extraordinary circumstances. John's journey through war, Mary's journey back home, and the trials they faced as they waited for each other will tug at your heartstrings, reminding us that amidst the horrors of war, love can endure as a powerful force of strength and solace.

While this tale draws inspiration from history, it also delves into the realms of fiction, allowing the characters to come to life and the emotions to resonate deeply with the reader. The lines between fact and fiction may blur, but the essence of the human experience remains true, transcending time and place.

It is with great pleasure that I present this narrative, a story of love, sacrifice, and the enduring power of hope. May the journey of John and Mary serve as a testament to the courage of all those who have faced the trials of war, and may it remind us that even amidst the darkness, love has the ability to shine brightly.

As we turn the pages of this book, let us honor the memory of those who lived through these turbulent times and cherish the timeless love that found its way amidst the chaos of war.

- Robert O'Brien

THE STATION

As the afternoon sun cast shadows upon the charming streets of Sóller, Mary stood at the train station, her heart pounding with anticipation. The air was filled with the scent of blooming orange blossoms, mingling with the faint aroma of freshly baked bread from a nearby bakery. The vibrant colors of the Mediterranean surrounded her – the azure sky, the terracotta rooftops, and the lush greenery of the vineyards stretching into the distance.

Clutching a worn letter in her trembling hand, Mary replayed the words etched upon her memory. "I will return to you, my love, after the war. We will build a life together in Sóller, surrounded by the beauty of this place that you call home." John's promise echoed in her mind, a beacon of hope amid the chaos of a world at war.

In the distance, a low rumble grew louder, announcing the approach of the train from Palma. Mary's heart leaped with a mixture of joy and anxiety, for this was the day she had longed for, the day she had dreamed of during the lonely nights when John's absence felt unbearable.

As the train emerged from around a bend, its wheels screeched against the tracks, stirring up a cloud of dust. Mary's eyes searched eagerly for a familiar face among the passengers. She held her breath, her heart pounding in her chest, but with each passing moment, disappointment began to overshadow her hope.

The train came to a halt, and passengers disembarked one by one, their faces etched with weariness and uncertainty. Mary's eyes scanned each person, her hope diminishing with each fleeting glance. She strained to see beyond the bustling crowd, yearning for a glimpse of the soldier who had captured her heart.

As the platform emptied, a sense of longing washed over Mary. Tears welled up in her eyes, threatening to spill down her cheeks. She clutched the letter tighter, her fingers trembling with a mix of emotions. The reality of the war's unpredictable nature settled upon her like a heavy fog, casting doubt upon John's return.

But amidst the twinges of disappointment, Mary resolved to remain steadfast. She wiped away a tear, straightened her shoulders, and whispered to the winds, "I will wait for you, John. I will wait in Sóller, amongst the vineyards, orange and olive trees, until the day you come back to me." With renewed determination, Mary took a deep breath, as if inhaling the strength of her surroundings, and prepared herself for the uncertain path that lay ahead.

For tomorrow, she would return once again to the train station in the hope that John would return.

PARIS

The year was 1944, as the Allied forces regained control of Paris after the exodus of the German troops, the city underwent a remarkable transformation. Spared destruction because of a German General who disobeyed Hitler's command who didn't want to be remembered in history as the man who destroyed the "City of Lights."

Despite the continuation of the war, Paris began to regain its enchanting allure in early September. The people of Paris, who had endured years of occupation and hardship, now felt a renewed sense of hope and freedom as the Allies approached.

The streets of Paris, once haunted by fear and oppression, now saw a resurgence of life and vibrancy. The city's iconic landmarks, such as the Eiffel Tower and the Louvre, stood tall as symbols of resilience and cultural heritage. With the German occupation gone, the French flag flew proudly once again, and the spirit of liberation filled the air.

As the Allied forces marched into the city, the Parisians greeted them with joyous cheers and tears of relief. The atmosphere was electric with excitement and gratitude. Allied soldiers, many of whom had traveled from far-off lands to liberate the city, were welcomed with open arms by the grateful locals.

The cafes and bistros, which had long been quiet and subdued under German rule, even with limited food stores, now bustled with life once more. The aroma of freshly baked baguettes and pastries filled the air, and the clinking of glasses and laughter of patrons echoed through the streets. Parisians and Allied soldiers alike mingled in these establishments, sharing stories, and toasting to the newfound freedom.

The city's cultural scene, which had been stifled during the occupation, now flourished once more. The theaters reopened their doors, showcasing plays and performances that celebrated the resilience and spirit of the French people. Artists and musicians, who had hidden their works during the dark days of the occupation, now emerged to share their creativity with the world.

As the sun set over the Seine River, the city was bathed in a golden glow of newfound hope and freedom. Paris, known as the "City of Light," shone brightly once more, and its enchantment could be felt by all who walked its streets. The war had left scars on the city, but Paris had proven that it was a city of indomitable spirit, capable of rising from the ashes and reclaiming its place as one of the most enchanting cities in the world.

Mary, a young woman from the idyllic town of Sóller in Majorca, found herself wandering the bustling streets, her eyes wide with wonder. She had ventured far from home, seeking refuge from the war's relentless grip, and hoping to experience the city's famed charm after liberation from Germany.

As she strolled along the Seine, Mary savored the crisp autumn breeze that carried whispers of fallen leaves and distant laughter. The city's spirit had not yet been extinguished, and hope lingered in the hearts of its inhabitants. Paris, recently liberated by Allied forces, was beginning to regain the luster, magic and mystery that was the City of Lights.

The aroma of freshly brewed coffee and warm pastries filled the air as Mary sat alone at a small, outdoor table in the quaint café. Her eyes scanned the bustling streets of Paris, taking in the ebb and flow of the city's energy. Lost in her thoughts, she was startled when a weary soldier, his uniform adorned with medals, took a seat at the adjacent table. Their eyes met, and an unspoken connection sparked between them.

John cleared his throat, breaking the silence. "May I join you?" he asked, his voice tinged with a mix of weariness and hope.

Mary's cheeks flushed, and she nodded, a soft smile playing at the corners of her lips. "Of course," she replied, gesturing to the empty chair across from her. "Please, sit."

John settled into the chair, his eyes studying Mary's face with a mixture of curiosity and intrigue. "Thank you," he said, offering a tired but genuine smile.

There was a momentary pause as they exchanged glances, a sense of shared understanding passing between them. In that instant, the weight of the world seemed to fade, and they were just two souls seeking solace in a turbulent time.

"I don't often get the chance to sit and enjoy a moment of respite," John admitted, his gaze drifting to the bustling streets. "This city, it has a way of whisking you away into its currents."

Mary nodded; her eyes filled with empathy. "I understand. It is as if the world outside ceases to exist for a while. We all need that escape, especially now."

A gentle breeze swept through the café, causing a strand of Mary's hair to dance across her face. John reached out instinctively, tucking the stray lock behind her ear. Their hands briefly touched, a spark of electricity passing between them.

"I can't help but wonder," John began, his voice tinged with vulnerability, "what brings you to this café today?"

Mary's gaze met his, her eyes shimmering with a mixture of nostalgia and longing. "I suppose, in a way, I'm searching for a moment of peace amidst the chaos," she replied, her voice carrying a hint of melancholy. "To find a connection, even if it's just for a fleeting moment."

He nodded; his eyes filled with a depth of understanding. "In this city, amidst the turmoil, it's remarkable how such connections can be formed. Like chance encounters that carry a lifetime's worth of meaning."

Their conversation flowed effortlessly, as if they had known each other for years. They spoke of their dreams, their fears, and the fragments of hope that still burned bright within them. They shared stories of home, of the places that shaped them, and the loved ones they left behind.

John grew up under the vast Texan skies on a sprawling cattle ranch just outside of Austin, Texas. His childhood was filled with the rugged beauty of the land, surrounded by the gentle lowing of cattle and the fragrance of wildflowers carried on the breeze. From an early age, he learned the value of hard work, perseverance, and the importance of family ties.

As the son of a rancher, John embraced the ranching lifestyle with open arms. He spent his days helping his father tend to the herds, riding horses across the wide-open plains, and learning the intricacies of cattle management. The ranch became his playground and his classroom, shaping him into a young man of resilience and resourcefulness.

Driven by a thirst for knowledge and a desire to serve, John set his sights on Texas A&M University. There, he eagerly immersed himself in the rich traditions and rigorous academic environment that the university and its Corps of Cadets offered. He embraced the camaraderie and discipline that came with being part of the Corps, recognizing the importance of teamwork and leadership in all aspects of life.

At Texas A&M, John's days were filled with rigorous physical training, demanding coursework, and a deepening understanding of honor, integrity, and duty. He studied diligently, his mind hungry for knowledge in subjects ranging from history to engineering, all the while knowing that his education would prepare him for a future filled with challenges.

Within the Corps, John found a sense of belonging. He formed lifelong friendships, standing shoulder to shoulder with his unit, united in their pursuit of excellence. The Corps instilled in him a deep sense of responsibility, fostering qualities of selflessness, discipline, and the unwavering commitment to serving a greater cause.

It was during his time at Texas A&M that the rumblings of war grew louder. The world was on the brink of turmoil, and John felt a calling to answer the nation's call to arms. With a heavy heart, he made the decision to pause his studies and enlist, driven by a sense of duty and a desire to protect the values and way of life he held dear.

Leaving behind the familiarity of the ranch and the hallowed halls of Texas A&M, John joined the ranks of the military, embarking on a journey that would take him far from the rolling hills of Texas. Little did he know that amidst the chaos of war, he would find an unexpected connection, a love that would anchor him through the darkest of days.

His experiences on the ranch and in the Corps would serve as the bedrock of his character, shaping him into a soldier who understood the importance of resilience, adaptability, and the bonds of brotherhood. And as he faced the trials of war, his Texas roots and the lessons learned on the cattle ranch and at Texas A&M would continue to guide him, reminding him of the values that he held close to his heart.

Mary's story began amidst the picturesque landscapes of Sóller, a charming town nestled on the island of Palma, off the coast of Spain. Her family owned a small vineyard, where the rich soil and Mediterranean climate lent themselves to the cultivation of grapes that produced exquisite wines.

From an early age, Mary learned the art of winemaking and the deep-rooted traditions that accompanied it. She worked alongside her parents, tending to the vineyard, nurturing the vines, and participating in the harvest season. The vineyard became not only a source of livelihood but also a symbol of the family's resilience and determination.

As World War II swept across Europe, the specter of conflict cast its shadow over the tranquil shores of Majorca. Under the rule of General Francisco Franco, Spain aligned itself with the Axis powers of Germany and Italy. Fear of invasion by the Allied forces gripped the island, and many families, including Mary's, made the difficult decision to flee.

With heavy hearts, they bid farewell to their beloved vineyard, leaving behind the treasured memories and the life they had known. Mary's family sought refuge in distant lands, hoping to find safety and solace in the midst of uncertainty.

Separated from the vineyard that had been her sanctuary, Mary and her family faced the challenges of displacement and assimilation in a world torn apart by war. They sought shelter in a foreign land, the south of France, virtually untouched by the war, carrying with them the resilience instilled by their winemaking heritage and the memories of the vibrant community they had left behind in Sóller.

As the sun began to set over Paris, casting a golden hue across the streets, Mary and John found solace in each other's company. Time seemed to stretch, suspended in that moment of connection, and understanding.

Mary smiled, her eyes shimmering with newfound hope. "Perhaps, amidst the chaos, we've stumbled upon something extraordinary."

John's gaze locked with hers, a flicker of something deeper igniting within him. "Yes," he whispered, his voice barely audible above the surrounding chatter. "Perhaps we have. And maybe, just maybe, this connection we've found can withstand the test of time."

Little did they know, in that unassuming café, amidst the clinking of coffee cups and the murmur of conversations, they had set in motion a love story that would transcend the boundaries of war and endure against all odds.

Hours turned into days, and then to weeks. Mary and John explored the streets of Paris together, hand in hand, finding solace in their shared moments of respite from the war's turmoil. Amidst the grandeur of the city, their love blossomed like a delicate flower in the midst of a battlefield.

But the fickle nature of war soon intervened. John, bound by duty, received news that he was to return to his unit in London, he was part of the 101st Airborne in the US Army. Their time together was abruptly cut short, and a bittersweet farewell ensued at the same café where their journey began.

Mary watched as John's figure grew smaller, disappearing into the distance. Tears streamed down her face, mixing with the raindrops that fell from the overcast sky. She clutched onto the memory of their time together, his promises resonating within her heart.

As John's truck transport carried him away from Paris, Mary made a silent vow. She would return to Sóller, to the land of vineyards, orange trees and olive trees that she called home. And she would wait. She would wait for the day when John would fulfill his promise, when he would step off the train in Sóller, and they could build a life together amidst the beauty that had witnessed their love's inception.

With a heavy heart and unwavering determination, Mary left behind the vibrant streets of Paris and embarked on a journey back to her homeland, Sóller, where her love story had taken root. The memories of their time together fueled her resolve, and she knew, deep in her soul, that her love for John would transcend the boundaries of war, time, and distance.

And so, as her train pulled out of the Parisian station, Mary's gaze fixed on the passing landscapes. Fields of golden wheat swayed in the breeze, a stark contrast to the turmoil that gripped the world. She marveled at the changing scenery; her mind filled with images of the soldier she left behind.

What did the future hold for her? What would her fate be? Will she ever see John again? All these questions raced through her mind as the train sped through the French countryside.

I
INTO THE CRUCIBLE

The United States officially entered World War II on December 7, 1941, following the Japanese attack on Pearl Harbor. Prior to this, the US had been providing support to the Allied powers, particularly the United Kingdom and the Soviet Union, through the Lend-Lease Act and other aid programs.

After the attack on Pearl Harbor, the US declared war on Japan, and subsequently, Germany and Italy declared war on the United States, officially bringing the US into the global conflict. The US quickly mobilized its resources and manpower to support the war effort.

In the early years of the war, the US focused on building up its military strength and contributing to the Allied efforts in various theaters. American forces played a significant role in the North African campaign, fighting alongside British and other Allied troops to defeat Axis forces in North Africa.

By 1944, the Allies were planning a massive invasion of German-occupied Europe, codenamed Operation Overlord, commonly known as D-Day. The United States, along with the United Kingdom, Canada, and other Allied nations, played a crucial role in planning and executing the amphibious invasion of Normandy on June 6, 1944.

D-Day marked the beginning of the Allied invasion of Western Europe and was a pivotal turning point in the war. American forces landed on Utah and Omaha beaches in Normandy, facing fierce German resistance. Despite heavy casualties, the Allied forces managed to establish a beachhead and begin their advance into France.

The events leading up to D-Day were marked by intense preparation and coordination among the Allied forces. The success of the invasion was a result of careful planning, bravery, and sacrifice from the American, British, Canadian, and other Allied troops who stormed the beaches of Normandy.

During the Allied invasion of Normandy on June 6, 1944, the American airborne landings involved approximately 13,100 paratroopers from the 82nd and 101st Airborne Divisions, carried out in conjunction with Operation Overlord. Among them were the Pathfinders, a select group of 300 men organized into teams of 14-18 paratroopers each. Their crucial responsibility was to deploy the ground beacon of the Rebecca/Eureka transponding radar system and set out holophane marking lights. The Rebecca, an airborne sender-receiver, provided directional information for the Eureka, a responder beacon.

Though the Eureka-Rebecca system faced some early setbacks, it had been used effectively in a night drop during Operation Avalanche in Italy to reinforce the U.S. Fifth Army during the Salerno landings. However, the system had limitations within a two-mile radius of the ground emitter, where signals merged, making both range and bearing difficult to discern. Nevertheless, it was designed to guide large formations of aircraft close to a drop zone, where holophane lights and visual markers would facilitate the completion of the drop.[1]

Each drop zone had a serial of three C-47 aircraft assigned to locate the area and deploy the pathfinder teams

---

[1] American airborne landings in Normandy - Wikipedia

to mark it. These serials were organized in two waves, with the 101st Airborne Division's pathfinder serials arriving half an hour before the first scheduled assault drop. These brave pathfinders were the first American and potentially the first Allied troops to touch down during the invasion. The three pathfinder serials of the 82nd Airborne Division were to begin their drops as the final wave of the 101st Airborne Division paratroopers landed, thirty minutes ahead of the first 82nd Airborne Division drops. Despite challenges, the Pathfinders played a pivotal role in ensuring the success of the airborne operations on D-Day.[2]

Two months earlier from when John met Mary, the air on the night of June 5th, 1944, was heavy with anticipation at the airfield in England. The men of the 101st Airborne Division, including John and his comrades in E Company, prepared themselves mentally and physically for the mission that lay ahead. Their mission was vital: to secure key objectives behind enemy lines on D-Day and pave the way for the amphibious assault at Normandy.

Under the watchful eye of Sergeant Holmes, the platoon in E Company checked and rechecked their gear, ensuring that every parachute was in perfect condition. As they gathered in the dimly lit barracks, Lieutenant Hobbs addressed them one last time before they boarded the C-47 transport planes.

"Men, tonight we embark on a mission of great importance. Our success here will have a significant impact on the outcome of this war. I have full confidence in each and every one of you. Remember your training, stick to the plan,

---

[2] Easy Company | World War 2 Facts

and most importantly, watch out for your fellow paratroopers. We're in this together."

The roar of the engines drowned out any other sounds as the planes took off one by one. The tension inside the planes was palpable, yet the camaraderie among the men provided a sense of comfort. John and his fellow paratroopers exchanged nods and reassuring smiles, each one silently acknowledging the gravity of the situation.

As the planes crossed the Channel, they hit pockets of turbulence, making some of the less experienced soldiers uneasy. The dark void of the night outside the plane was punctuated by bursts of anti-aircraft fire from the German positions on the ground. The men knew they were in the heart of enemy territory.

The time had come. The red light turned to green, and one by one, the paratroopers leaped into the inky blackness below. The sensation of freefall was both exhilarating and terrifying. The deafening winds roared in their ears as they plummeted towards the drop zones.

As John descended, he could see the faint outlines of the French countryside below. Flashes of tracer fire illuminated the night sky, as German forces on the ground unleashed a barrage of bullets in their direction. It was a baptism of fire, a true trial by combat.

The ground rushed up to meet him, and John landed hard, rolling to absorb the impact. He quickly gathered his parachute and moved to join the scattered members of E Company. The plan had been for them to regroup once they landed, but the chaos of the drop had disrupted that.

John found himself huddled with a few other paratroopers, and they decided to make their way towards their intended objective. The darkness of the night provided some cover, but the German forces were on high alert.

They moved cautiously, sticking to the shadows, and avoiding open fields. As they moved forward, the tension in the air was palpable. Each step felt like an eternity, the fear of encountering enemy soldiers lurking around every corner. John's heart pounded in his chest as he gripped the cricket tightly, ready to click it if the need arose. The cricket was a child's toy that made a clicking noise. Each of the paratroopers had one hanging from the front of their uniform. It made a distinctive sound. Two clicks and a response of two clicks was the signal you were communicating with another paratrooper.

John understood the importance of the cricket in this perilous situation. With their lives depending on stealth and coordination, this little device held the power to keep them united. Each man in the platoon received a cricket, and they were scattered across the French countryside, searching for their fellow soldiers.

In the darkness, John clicked his cricket twice, the distinct sound cutting through the silence like a beacon. He strained his ears, hoping to hear the response of another cricket in the distance. After a few tense moments, he heard two faint clicks in reply.

"There's another one of us nearby," John whispered to his unit. "Let's move towards that sound."

The platoon cautiously made their way through the shadows, following the intermittent clicks of the crickets. It was an eerie yet effective method of communication, allowing them to navigate the darkness without giving away their position to the enemy. As they closed in on the other group of paratroopers, they clicked their crickets in response, forming a silent bond of brotherhood in the darkness.

Soon, they encountered another group of soldiers from their division. The tension in the air dissipated as they greeted each other with silent clicks, their crickets becoming a symphony of unity in the night. They quickly exchanged information about their mission, enemy positions, and possible rally points.

Through the use of the crickets, the platoon was able to establish a loose network of communication, guiding them towards each other and their common objective. In the darkness and chaos of the night, the crickets provided a thread of connection, a lifeline for these soldiers who found solace in knowing they were not alone in this treacherous landscape.

As they moved forward, the platoon continued to rely on their crickets, using them to find and assist other scattered paratroopers. It was a testament to the resourcefulness and ingenuity of these brave men, turning a simple child's toy into a vital tool for survival behind enemy lines.

As intermittent moonbeams pierced through the darkness, the tension in the air was palpable. The platoons of the 101st Airborne had to tread carefully through the French countryside, knowing that the enemy was likely to be lurking nearby. Their hearts pounded in their chests as they moved with precision, each step taking them closer to the unknown dangers that awaited them.

Suddenly, a hail of bullets erupted from the trees, cutting through the peaceful morning air with a deafening roar. The platoon hit the dirt, seeking whatever cover they could find. The sound of machine guns echoed through the air, adding to the chaos and confusion. In the midst of the firefight, Sergeant Holmes barked out orders, directing his men to return fire and seek better positions.

"Stay low, keep moving!" he shouted, his voice barely audible over the deafening gunfire. "We need to push forward!"

Amidst the chaos, the platoon's medic, Corporal Jackson, crawled over to a wounded soldier who had been hit in the leg. Blood stained the ground around him, and he clenched his teeth in pain. Jackson quickly applied a makeshift tourniquet, trying to stem the bleeding.

"Stay with me, soldier," Jackson said reassuringly, his hands working quickly and efficiently. "You're gonna be alright."

As the battle raged on, the platoon continued to advance, inch by inch, towards their target. Bullets whizzed past, hitting the ground with sharp cracks, and the air was filled with the acrid smell of gunpowder. The soldiers moved with a mixture of fear and determination, each one relying on their training and instincts to survive.

"Keep pushing forward!" Sergeant Holmes shouted. "We've got to take that position!"

A barrage of machine gun fire rattled through the air around Cpl. Jenkins and Private Davies. A searing whistle filled the air and a burst of light flashed and thundered around them. Jenkins looked over to see Davies lying on his stomach facing him, his helmet shattered into pieces.

"Medic!" cried Jenkins, as he quickly rolled Davies on to his back exposing a massive wound to his chest pumping blood out through his stained uniform.

Jackson came running a slide down to a seated position only to look at Jenkins and say, "He's dead Jenkins, we will come back for him after this is done. Let's find some cover."

"Flank them and push forward," yelled Sergeant Holmes. "We need to clear out the front so 2nd platoon can move up."

The platoon responded with a renewed sense of purpose, pushing back against the enemy with all their might. The intensity of the firefight was overwhelming, and the toll on the soldiers was evident. Some were wounded, others were running low on ammunition, but they pressed on, fueled by solidarity and the knowledge that their lives depended on their courage and resilience.

In the midst of the chaos, the platoon's radioman, Private Anderson, frantically tried to call for reinforcements. The radio crackled with static, making communication difficult, but he persisted, knowing that their lives hung in the balance.

"Calling all units! We need backup!" he shouted into the radio, his voice tense and urgent. "We're pinned down and taking heavy fire!"

As the firefight raged on, the platoon slowly gained ground, inching closer to their objective. The sound of gunshots and the cries of the wounded filled the air, but they pressed forward, their determination unwavering.

Finally, after what felt like an eternity, the enemy fire began to subside. The platoon had managed to break through the enemy's defenses and secure their target. Exhausted and battered, they took a moment to catch their breath, knowing that the battle was far from over.

"Stay alert, men," Sergeant Holmes said, his voice steady despite the exhaustion in his eyes. "We may have won this skirmish, but the fight is far from over."

And so, the platoon continued to push forward, each step taking them deeper into the crucible of war. They knew that the road ahead would be treacherous, filled with more battles and sacrifices, but they were determined to face whatever came their way. United by their common purpose, they stood ready to confront the challenges that lay ahead in the pursuit of victory and the defense of freedom.

While moving to their next position, they bore witness to a haunting sight below. In the pitch-blackness of the night, amidst the tangled web of electrical wires and branches, the lifeless bodies of fellow soldiers hung suspended, victims of a merciless barrage of bullets that had cut their parachutes and sent them spiraling into enemy territory.

Their hearts sank at the grim reality before them – these brave men had landed nearly a mile off target, right into the clutches of the heavily fortified German positions. The chaos of the drop had scattered the paratroopers everywhere, leaving them vulnerable to the ferocity of the enemy's response. The eerie silence that enveloped the scene was broken only by the distant sounds of gunfire and the soft rustling of the trees.

Their training had prepared them for many things, but nothing could have prepared them for the heart-wrenching sight of their fallen comrades. With heavy hearts, they pressed on, knowing that they must move forward and complete their mission, lest their sacrifices be in vain. They moved with caution, sticking to the shadows, and avoiding open fields, determined to regroup and find their fellow paratroopers to bolster their ranks.

The journey through the war-torn countryside was fraught with danger at every turn. They encountered pockets of enemy resistance, forcing them to engage in fierce firefights as they pressed on towards their target. The deafening sound of gunfire echoed through the night, mingling with the distant cries of wounded soldiers. They moved with purpose, every step a testament to their resolve and determination to push forward.

As they pushed deeper into enemy territory, they encountered more fallen comrades, their lifeless bodies a stark reminder of the high cost of their mission. But they knew they had to keep moving, to honor the fallen by completing the objectives they had set out to achieve.

As morning broke, the platoon faced enemy fire once more, and they engaged in fierce firefights as they advanced towards their target, securing Carentan. With their training and determination, they overcame the odds, eliminating key enemy positions along the way.

As the day wore on, the platoon managed to secure their primary objective, and they took shelter in a nearby farmhouse to catch their breath and regroup. The intensity of the past hours weighed heavily on their minds, but they knew their mission was far from over.

Huddled in that farmhouse, the men of E Company exchanged words of encouragement and gallows humor, finding solace in each other's presence. Despite the fatigue they felt and the danger surrounding them, a sense of brotherhood strengthened their resolve.

"Who would've thought we'd be spending D-Day in this French barn, huh?" one of them quipped, eliciting a few tired chuckles.

"Ain't quite the beach holiday we were promised, that's for sure," another chimed in.

"We got more work to do, boys. Check your ammunition, and we'll move out again once nightfall hits," Sergeant Holmes ordered, steering the conversation back to the task at hand. "Get some sleep if you can."

As night fell, the platoon found themselves in a small village on the outskirts of Caraten. The battle had taken a toll on their spirits, and they were grateful for a moment of respite amidst the quiet streets. As they cautiously made their way through the darkened streets, the dim glow of a candle caught their attention.

Moving closer, they discovered a French couple huddled together with their young son in a small, modest home. The couple looked visibly exhausted, their faces etched with worry and fear from the ongoing war that had surrounded their peaceful village. Their son, a boy of about seven, clung to his mother's side, his wide eyes filled with uncertainty.

Sergeant Holmes approached them cautiously, but with a warm smile. He tried to speak in broken French, and the couple responded with hesitant English, forming a simple but heartfelt communication. The language barrier seemed inconsequential as the warmth of human connection transcended words.

Understanding the hardships the family must endure, one of the soldiers, Private Jenkins, pulled a small chocolate bar from his rations. He handed it to the young boy, who hesitated for a moment before accepting it with a shy smile.

The boy's eyes lit up with delight as he unwrapped the chocolate, his parents looking on with gratitude. The simple act of sharing a chocolate bar with the child seemed to momentarily erase the darkness of war, replacing it with a flicker of hope and happiness.

As the soldiers observed the scene, they felt a profound sense of fellowship and compassion. Despite the harsh realities of war and the devastation it brought, they were reminded that acts of kindness and empathy could still exist amidst the chaos.

In that fleeting moment, the platoon and the French family became connected by a shared humanity, transcending national boundaries and language barriers. It was a brief respite from the brutalities of war, a moment of unity that reminded them of the values they were fighting to defend.

Before bidding farewell, Sergeant Holmes reached into his pocket and handed the boy a small toy soldier, a gesture of friendship and solidarity. The young boy clutched it tightly, cherishing the token of friendship from these brave strangers who had momentarily graced their lives.

Sergeant Holmes's son had given the toy to him before he departed home and there was no more deserving person than this boy to have it from now on.

As the platoon continued on their mission to Carentan, they carried the memory of that encounter with them. It served as a poignant reminder that even in the darkest of times, simple acts of kindness and compassion had the power to bridge divides and bring a glimmer of light into the lives of those affected by the ravages of war.

As the battle for Carentan raged on, E-Company and John's platoon found themselves amidst the intense fighting and ever-changing frontline. The city of Carentan, nestled in the Douve River valley, had become a crucial strategic point in the Allied push to connect the lodgments in Isigny and Carentan. The German forces, though outnumbered and weakened, fought with tenacity and determination to defend the city "to the last man."

The causeway leading into Carentan became a focal point of the conflict, and it was here that John and his platoon faced some of their most harrowing moments. Bullets and mortar shells rained down on them as they advanced cautiously, using the cover of darkness to their advantage. E-Company had to crawl and crouch, relying on their training and instincts to keep them alive amidst the chaos of battle.

The platoon used their crickets to communicate without words, moved together as a cohesive unit, supporting, and relying on each other in the darkness. It was their bond and unity that gave them strength in the face of overwhelming odds. John found himself moving with his fellow soldiers, their clicks from the crickets resonating like a silent symphony, guiding them through the darkness and towards their objectives.

The battle for Carentan was not only about the strategic importance of the city but also about the survival and liberation of its civilian population. The once enchanting city had endured the harsh realities of war, and its people longed for freedom and peace. E-Company knew that they were not only fighting for their country but also for the hope of a better future for the people of Carentan.

Days of fierce combat followed, with the platoon enduring heavy casualties and the ever-present threat of German counterattacks. The 101st Airborne Division, determined to complete its mission, pushed forward relentlessly, facing enemy fire, and overcoming formidable obstacles.

Finally, on June 12th, 1944, the 506th PIR, together with the 501st PIR, achieved a significant victory as they captured Carentan. The city was now in Allied hands, and the German forces retreated, leaving a sense of liberation and hope in their wake.

However, the battle was far from over. The Germans launched a counterattack on June 13th, which tested the resolve and bravery of E-Company and the 101st Airborne Division. With tanks and assault guns bearing down on them, the paratroopers fought fiercely to defend their hard-won ground. American tanks from the 2nd Armored Division, called in by Lieutenant General Bradley, came to their aid and helped repel the German offensive.

The "Battle of Bloody Gulch," as it would be remembered, was a turning point in the fight for Carentan. The gallantry and courage of E-Company and their fellow soldiers allowed them to hold their ground and secure victory. The city was liberated, and its people were finally free from the yoke of oppression.

As the dust settled and the smoke cleared, E-Company and John's platoon stood victorious, but not without scars and losses. The battle for Carentan had tested their mettle, but their determination to fight for freedom and justice remained unshaken. The city of Carentan, once a battlefield, now held the promise of a brighter future, thanks to the sacrifices and heroism of the 101st Airborne Division and their unwavering commitment to the cause.

HOLLAND

John stood in front of the make-shift barracks, his heart pounding with a mix of anticipation and trepidation. The air was crisp, and a gentle breeze rustled the leaves of nearby trees, as if whispering secrets of the impending mission. The cool mist off the English coast painting the grass a glistening green. He adjusted the strap of his duffel bag, the weight of his gear a constant reminder of the task that lay ahead.

Around him, other soldiers milled about, their faces etched with determination and a shared sense of purpose. The 101st Airborne Division had gathered here, in a place just outside of London, where Operation Market Garden was about to unfold. The mission held the promise of a turning point in the war, and John felt a mix of pride and responsibility for being part of it.

"Corporal Reynolds," shouted Sergeant Holmes.

"Yes sir, Sergeant, "shouted John as he snapped to attention.

"Is your platoon loaded and ready?" asked the Sergeant.

"Yes sir," replied John. "All ready to pull out."

As the trucks pulled out, the sound of their horns echoing off the barracks, John felt a surge of adrenaline. He knew that his company was also making its way to the airfield in Membury, 71 miles west of London. They would parachute in under the cover of darkness, their mission to secure key bridges and pave the way for the Allied advance.

The truck ride had been long and arduous through the English countryside, but it had allowed John time to reflect on the enormity of the task ahead. He thought of Mary, the woman he had left behind in Paris, and the promise he had made to return to her. It was her love that had sustained him through the darkest days, and he held onto that love as a beacon of hope, even amidst the chaos of war.

As he disembarked from the truck, John joined the ranks of his fellow paratroopers, their helmets gleaming under the pale moonlight. The tension in the air was palpable as they received their final briefings and checked their gear one last time. Each man knew the risks they faced, but they were united in their dedication to the mission and the cause they fought for.

The night enveloped them as they boarded the planes that would carry them to the drop zones. Inside, the atmosphere was electric, a mixture of nerves, excitement, and an unwavering determination. The engines roared to life, drowning out any other sound, as the aircraft taxied down the runway, hurtling toward the uncertain skies.

John's heart raced as he felt the sensation of the plane ascending, the world falling away beneath him. The aircraft shuddered and vibrated, a constant reminder of the dangers that lay ahead. He clutched the strap of his parachute tightly, his mind focused on the mission, the objectives, and the lives that depended on their success.

As the time neared for the jump, John took a deep breath, his mind clear and his resolve unwavering. He thought of Mary, waiting amidst the vineyards and olive trees, and the promise he had made to return to her. It was her love that fueled his determination, her presence that gave him the strength to face whatever lay ahead.

The red light blinked, signaling the time to stand, and the sound of the jumpmaster's command filled the air. Without hesitation, John stepped out into the night, the rush of wind engulfing him as he descended towards the unknown. In that moment, he became part of something greater than himself, a soldier, a paratrooper, and a symbol of resilience in the face of adversity.

As he floated through the night sky, John's thoughts turned to Mary and the love that bound them together. With each passing second, he grew closer to the ground, closer to fulfilling his promise and returning to her waiting arms.

Little did he know the challenges and triumphs that awaited him in the Dutch countryside, but he pressed forward, driven by love, duty, and the unyielding spirit of the 101st Airborne Division. The winds of destiny carried him towards his destiny, towards a mission that would forever shape the course of history and his own personal journey.

As John's parachute gently carried him down, he marveled at the sight below—a sprawling landscape illuminated by moonlight and dotted with scattered lights. The countryside of Holland stretched out before him, and a surge of adrenaline coursed through his veins. He landed with a soft thud, swiftly releasing himself from the parachute's harness.

As he gathered his equipment and checked his surroundings, John's thoughts turned to his platoon. Spread out across the vast expanse, they were on a shared mission to secure vital bridges and pave the way for the Allied advance. It was a crucial operation, and the success of their individual tasks would determine the outcome of Market Garden.

In the distance, John spotted the faint glow of a village. It was there that he and his fellow paratroopers would regroup and coordinate their efforts. With unwavering determination, he set off, his boots crunching on the gravel path beneath him. The night was alive with tension and anticipation, each step a reminder of the weight of responsibility on his shoulders.

As he approached the village, John observed the signs of conflict—a scattered trail of destruction and the distant echoes of gunfire. The people of Holland had endured the harsh realities of occupation for far too long, and the liberation that the Allied forces represented was within their grasp.

Inside the village, the streets were quiet, a stark contrast to the chaos that lay beyond its borders. John moved cautiously, mindful of potential threats, but also aware of the people who watched from their windows, their faces reflecting a mix of hope and fear. He understood the significance of their presence, for they were the ones who would bear witness to the Allied forces' arrival and the liberation of their homeland.

Operation Market Garden was a daring plan to establish a pincer movement and encircle the heart of German industry. The objective was clear—to secure the bridges, overcome resistance, and project deeper into Germany.

John's division was tasked with capturing vital bridges, including the one over the Waal River at Nijmegen. Their mission was crucial to the success of the operation, allowing the armored ground units to advance and consolidate north of Arnhem. However, obstacles awaited them.

The initial stages were promising. Allied forces managed to capture several bridges between Eindhoven and Nijmegen, displaying the early signs of victory. But setbacks occurred. The bridge over the Wilhelmina Canal at Son was destroyed before John's division could secure it. British sappers swiftly erected a makeshift Bailey bridge, but the delay cost them precious time.

Despite the challenges, John's determination remained unyielding. He witnessed the 82nd Airborne Division's struggle to capture the main highway bridge over the Waal River, which resulted in a 36-hour setback. The clock ticked, and the pressure mounted as they had to push forward and seize the bridge themselves.

At the northern point of the operation, the British 1st Airborne Division encountered fierce resistance, hampering their progress. German forces, the 9th SS Panzer Division "Hohenstaufen" and 10th SS Panzer Division "Frundsberg," organized a counterattack. The situation grew dire, with the paratroopers at the Arnhem bridge being overrun on September 21. The remaining British forces were trapped in a small pocket west of the bridge, their evacuation necessitated by heavy casualties.

Though the Allied forces made gains, crossing the Rhine remained elusive. The failure of Operation Market Garden dashed hopes of ending the war in Europe by Christmas 1944. The river would stand as a formidable barrier until subsequent offensives in 1945.

Amidst these trials, John displayed unwavering resilience. He fought with valor, facing the enemy head-on, and witnessing the courage and sacrifices of his fellow soldiers. The dream of a swift victory had faded, but the spirit of resilience burned within him. The war would continue, and he would press on, always with the hope that the tide would turn in favor of the Allies.

With each passing hour, John and his fellow paratroopers worked tirelessly to secure their objectives. They encountered fierce resistance, but their training, courage, and unwavering commitment pushed them forward. They fought for every inch gained, their efforts guided by the larger strategic plan that aimed to bring an end to the war.

Days turned into nights, and nights into days as the operation unfolded. John witnessed the cost of war, fallen comrades, wounded soldiers, and the indelible scars that etched themselves into the landscape. Yet, amidst the darkness, he also witnessed acts of bravery, compassion, and the resilience of the human spirit.

One evening, while nestled down in a bunker near the bridge by the river, a fellow soldier who went by the name "Guppy" started to talk about home. The distant sounds of gunfire and the occasional rumble of tanks provided the backdrop for their conversation. John looked over at Guppy, noticing the weariness etched on his face, and nodded in acknowledgement.

Guppy and John were good friends. They went through basic and jump training together and were assigned to the same platoon in Easy Company.

Guppy let out a deep sigh, his voice carrying a mix of longing and nostalgia. "You know, John, sometimes I can't help but think about home," he began, his eyes distant as if transported to another time and place. "I miss the little things—the smell of freshly cut grass in the summer, the laughter of my family around the dinner table. It feels like a lifetime ago."

John leaned against the bunker wall, his thoughts mirroring Guppy's. "I know what you mean, Guppy," he replied, his voice tinged with a hint of homesickness. "The war has a way of making everything seem so far away, doesn't it? It's like we're living in a different world, disconnected from the lives we used to know."

Guppy nodded, a bittersweet smile gracing his lips. "Exactly. I never thought I'd miss the simplicity of everyday life. The feeling of warmth from a crackling fireplace, the taste of my mother's homemade apple pie. It is the little things that keep us going, don't you think?"

John's gaze turned toward the river, its waters reflecting the moonlight, casting a silver sheen upon the wreckage of war. "Indeed, Guppy," he agreed. "It's the memories of home, the hope of returning to loved ones, which fuels our resilience. We fight not just for ourselves but for the chance to rebuild and cherish the things we hold dear."

A somber silence settled between them, punctuated only by the distant sounds of artillery. They both understood the gravity of their mission, the sacrifices made by countless soldiers like them. But in that moment, they allowed themselves to momentarily escape the harsh reality and find solace in reminiscing about the familiar comforts of home.

Guppy's voice broke the silence, filled with a newfound determination. "When this is all over, John, we'll go back. We will rebuild, we will create new memories, and we will honor the ones we left behind. Our struggles here will only make us appreciate home even more."

John met Guppy's gaze, a glimmer of hope in his eyes. "You're right, Guppy. We will carry those memories with us, and when we finally return, we'll ensure that the sacrifices we've made were not in vain. We'll rebuild a better world—one that embodies the values we fought for."

As they sat there, two soldiers in a bunker surrounded by the remnants of war, their conversation carried a shared determination. They found solace in each other's words, understanding that even in the darkest of times, the yearning for home and the dreams of a brighter future had the power to sustain them. And in that fleeting moment, amidst the chaos, they found strength to continue.

All of a sudden, John and Guppy's conversation was abruptly interrupted by the piercing whistle of incoming mortar fire. Their hearts raced as they exchanged alarmed glances, their eyes wide with fear.

John shouted over the deafening noise, "Guppy, we need to get out of here! It's not safe!"

Guppy nodded frantically; his voice strained with urgency. "I agree, John! Let's find some cover and get out of this kill zone!"

They scrambled to their feet, their movements fueled by a mix of adrenaline and sheer determination. The explosions seemed to grow louder and closer, urging them to move faster.

John spotted a nearby trench and pointed toward it. "Guppy, there! We need to reach that trench! It is our best chance!"

They sprinted toward the trench, their hearts pounding in their chests. The ground beneath their feet shook with each impact, sending shockwaves through their bodies.

As they reached the trench, they dove in, seeking whatever shelter they could find. Dirt and debris showered upon them, but they held on tightly to each other, finding solace in the shared struggle.

Between panting breaths, Guppy yelled, "John, we can't stay here for long! We have to keep moving!"

John nodded; his voice filled with determination. "You're right, Guppy! We can't let this mortar fire trap us here. Let's make a break for it when we get a chance!"

They waited, their bodies pressed against the cold, damp walls of the trench. The explosions seemed to be coming from all directions, the chaos intensifying with each passing moment.

Finally, they saw a momentary lull in the bombardment. Without hesitation, they sprang into action, their bodies propelled forward by sheer willpower. They ran as fast as their legs could carry them, desperate to escape the deadly rain of mortars.

Their breaths came in ragged gasps as they zigzagged through the treacherous terrain. The sound of explosions continued to echo in their ears, a constant reminder of the danger that pursued them.

"Keep going, Guppy!" John shouted; his voice strained with exhaustion. "We're almost there!"

Guppy pushed himself harder, his determination fueling his every step. "We can make it, John! We have to!"

They ran with every ounce of strength they had left, their bodies driven by an unwavering desire to survive. They could see a stand of trees up ahead, a potential haven from the mortar fire.

As they reached the cover of the trees, they collapsed to the ground, their bodies trembling with fatigue and relief. The distant sound of explosions slowly faded into the background, replaced by the thudding of their own hearts.

Breathing heavily, John turned to Guppy and mustered a weary smile. "We made it, Guppy. We're still alive."

Guppy nodded, his voice a mixture of exhaustion and gratitude. "We're fighters, John. We won't let this war consume us. We'll keep moving forward, no matter what."

They sat there for a moment, catching their breath, and allowing the gravity of their escape to sink in. Their bond had grown stronger amidst the chaos, and their shared experience had forged an unbreakable camaraderie. Once the shelling subsided, they picked up their gear and headed back to the front line to check in with their Sergeant.

"I wonder how angry Sarg is going to be since we ran out of the bunker," said Guppy. "He sure doesn't like to give up ground, that's for sure."

"I'm sure a lot of the boys ran for cover, without our own artillery to back us up, we have to make progress however we can," said John. "Let's hurry back down to the river and resume our post."

Sergeant Holmes, a former auto mechanic hailing from the heartland of Oklahoma, possessed courage that exceeded the boundaries of his prior occupation. Drafted into service during the war, Holmes swiftly proved himself as an exceptional soldier on the combat fields of North Africa. His unwavering bravery in the face of adversity and his innate ability to lead under pressure set him apart from his peers. Recognizing his exceptional qualities, Holmes was rightfully promoted to the rank of Sergeant, assuming a position of authority and responsibility. With each step he took, Holmes carried the resilience of his Oklahoma roots, displaying unwavering dedication to his fellow soldiers and an unwavering commitment to the cause they fought for.

The men under his command respected him, but never feared him because of his unwavering commitment to them as their leader and always had their best interest in mind. He was tough, but fair, perhaps that is why he commanded so much respect.

John and Guppy returned to their post, sweat glistening on their brows and determination etched on their faces. As they joined their platoon, their Sergeant's voice boomed, cutting through the tense air.

"Listen up, soldiers!" the Sergeant shouted, his voice commanding attention. "We've got a bridge to take, and we're not wasting any more time. Move your asses to the riverbank, double-time!"

John glanced at Guppy, exchanging a nod before turning his attention back to their Sergeant, who continued to bark out orders. The urgency in his voice conveyed the gravity of the situation.

"Alpha team, you're on point! Bravo team, provide cover fire! Charlie team, follow me and secure that damn bridge! Move, move, move!"

John tightened the grip on his weapon, adrenaline coursing through his veins. He exchanged a determined look with Guppy, both knowing the importance of their mission. They had trained for this, and now it was time to put their skills to the test.

With their Sergeant leading the charge, they moved forward, the sound of boots pounding against the ground. The weight of the task ahead hung in the air, but they were ready. They would do whatever it took to secure that bridge and fulfill their duty. Guppy and John stood at the edge of the river; their eyes fixed on the bridge that spanned the Wilhelmina Canal. It was a crucial objective for the 101st Airborne Division as part of the larger Operation Market Garden. The plan was clear in their minds: secure the bridge, hold their position, and pave the way for the advancing Allied forces.

As they prepared to make their move, memories of the intense battles and hardships they had faced in the past weeks flooded their minds. The weight of the operation's importance pressed upon them, but they were determined to conduct their mission with unwavering resolve.

Their division had been briefed on the objectives: the southernmost bridges at Son, the pair at St. Odenrode, the vital crossings near Veghel, and the town of Eindhoven. Their stretch of road, known as "Hell's Highway," had to remain open for the 101st Airborne's advance towards Arnhem.

Meanwhile, the 82nd Airborne Division was tasked with capturing bridges further north, including the massive bridge at Grave and the strategic positions near Nijmegen.

Guppy and John knew that their success relied on the element of surprise and the hope that German resistance would be minimal. Yet, doubts lingered in their minds. General Browning's optimism had painted the operation as a "party," but Gavin, their division commander, was more cautious. He understood the challenges Allied forces faced, especially with regards to the Nijmegen bridge and the control of high ground and supply routes.

The weight of responsibility settled on Guppy and John's shoulders as they prepared to move forward. They knew that the outcome of their actions would play a significant role in the success of Operation Market Garden. The time for hesitation was over; they had to seize the moment.

With a nod of determination, Guppy and John exchanged a glance, their silent communication conveying their shared determination and trust. They tightened their grip on their weapons and stepped forward, leading their fellow soldiers towards the bridge.

As they approached, the sound of gunfire and distant explosions echoed through the air. The intensity of the moment was palpable, adrenaline coursing through their veins. They moved swiftly, taking cover, and engaging enemy positions with precision and determination.

"Listen up, men!" Sergeant Holmes commanded, his voice echoing across the chaos of the battlefield. "We've got to secure this bridge and hold it at all costs. The enemy is advancing, and it's our duty to deny them passage. Reynolds, take your squad and set up a defensive position on the western end of the bridge. Keep an eye out for any incoming troops and be ready to engage."

John, known for his sharp instincts and quick thinking, nodded in acknowledgment. He turned to his squad, conveying the urgency of the situation. "Alright, boys, let's move! Take cover behind those sandbags and keep your eyes peeled. We need to hold this bridge until reinforcements arrive."

As they positioned themselves behind the sandbags, the sound of gunfire filled the air. Bullets whizzed past, hitting the metal structure of the bridge with a resounding clatter. The soldiers exchanged intense gazes, their eyes reflecting a mix of determination and apprehension.

Private Jenkins, his hands trembling slightly, glanced at John. "Corporal, what do we do if they start advancing? We can't let them cross."

John met Jenkins' gaze, his voice firm. "We hold our ground, Private. We've trained for this moment, and we will not let them get through. Stick to your positions and stay focused."

The battle raged on, with Sergeant Holmes and Corporal Reynolds coordinating the defense with precision. They relayed orders, strategized, and offered words of encouragement to their fellow soldiers, their voices cutting through the chaos of gunfire and explosions.

Private Thompson, his voice filled with determination, called out from his position. "Corporal, they're trying to flank us from the east! We need backup!"

John swiftly assessed the situation, his mind racing with solutions. "Hold tight, Private! I'm sending Jenkins and Anderson to reinforce your position. We cannot let them break through!"

Amid the chaos, Guppy and John exchanged quick words of encouragement, their camaraderie bolstering their resolve. They fought side by side, their training and experience guiding their every move.

Finally, after intense moments of back-and-forth, the tide began to turn. The enemy's resistance weakened; their forces pushed back. Guppy and John's division secured the bridge over the Wilhelmina Canal, a vital achievement in the grand scope of Operation Market Garden.

Exhausted but elated, Guppy and John stood atop the bridge, their hearts filled with a mix of relief and satisfaction. They knew that their success was not without sacrifice and that the road ahead would still be fraught with challenges. But in that moment, as they surveyed the scene around them, they felt a glimmer of hope.

They had played their part in a massive undertaking, a mission that aimed to change the course of the war. As they looked across the landscape, they knew that their actions had brought them one step closer to achieving their ultimate goal: a free and peaceful Europe.

Guppy and John shared a brief moment of silent acknowledgement, a mutual understanding passing between them. They had faced countless trials together, and this was just another chapter in their shared journey. With renewed determination, they prepared to face whatever lay ahead, united in their commitment to the cause and to each other.

"Reinforcements are here," said Guppy.

"Great," replied John. "Stay here and gather the men, I have to report back to the command post with Sergeant Holmes. They are looking at the map to determine what we should do next. The 82nd failed to take the bridge at Arnhem due to heavy German reinforcements and the operation has failed to secure a route into Germany. While we did capture a few bridges and move the line, we did not achieve the main objective."

The hope was that Operation Market Garden would end the war or shorten it. In time, the Allies would realize the weather conditions, bad intelligence, communications & logistics problems, the lack of boats to cross the river, and the resiliency of the German forces would ultimately contribute to its failure.

John headed off down the road behind Sergeant Holmes toward the battlefield command area. After turning over control of the bridge to Lt. Johnson of the 3rd army, Guppy gathered the surviving members of the company and headed away from the forward area.

GOING HOME

The train journey from Paris to Barcelona had been a whirlwind of emotions for Mary. As the train finally pulled into Barcelona's grand station, she stepped onto the platform with a mix of weariness and excitement. The memories of John flooded her mind, his warm smile and tender touch etched in her heart. Barcelona was a world away from the streets of Paris where they had wandered hand in hand, savoring the magic of their time together.

With a determined stride, Mary made her way through the bustling station, her eyes scanning the surroundings for the ticket counter. Finding it amidst the sea of travelers, she approached with a sense of purpose. The ticket agent greeted her with a warm smile, their conversation a mix of English and Spanish as she purchased a ticket for the ferry to Palma. The transaction brought back memories of the moments she and John had spent planning their journey, their voices intermingling with excitement and anticipation.

Ticket in hand, Mary stepped out into the vibrant streets of Barcelona. The city's architectural wonders and lively atmosphere embraced her, reminiscent of the moments she had shared with John as they explored the hidden gems of Paris. The bustling cafes and colorful marketplaces seemed to echo their laughter and whispered promises of a future together.

Navigating her way through the lively streets, Mary finally arrived at the bustling port. The sight of the ferry waiting at the dock filled her with a surge of anticipation. It stood proud and majestic, its decks inviting her to embark on the next leg of her journey. She felt John's presence beside her, his arm wrapped protectively around her as they had stood on the banks of the Seine, dreaming of the adventures that lay ahead.

As she stepped onto the ferry, Mary breathed in the salty sea air, savoring the tang of adventure. Finding a comfortable seat on the deck, she settled in, her eyes fixed on the horizon. The ferry's engines roared to life, vibrating beneath her feet as it began its voyage across the shimmering waters of the Mediterranean. She imagined John's voice in her ear, his words of encouragement and love intertwining with the sound of the waves.

As the ferry cut through the waves, Mary's mind wandered back to the memories she had created with John. The stolen kisses by the Seine, the shared laughter in cozy cafes, and the quiet moments of intimacy in her Parisian apartment. Each memory became a lifeline, a source of strength that propelled her forward on this journey towards the Island of Palma, where their dreams would find a new home.

With each passing moment, the ferry carried Mary closer to her destination. She watched as the azure waters sparkled under the golden rays of the sun, the gentle rhythm of the waves soothing her restless soul. The crossing became a time of reflection, a chance to hold onto the love she shared with John and to let it guide her towards a future that they had envisioned together.

As the ferry neared the shores of Palma, Mary's excitement reached its peak. The island emerged on the horizon like a beacon of hope, its lush green landscapes and picturesque villages promising a continuation of the love story she had started with John. She felt his spirit beside her, his hand intertwined with hers as they had walked along the sandy beaches, their footsteps leaving imprints on the shores of their memories.

As the ferry docked at the port of Palma, Mary disembarked, her feet touching the solid ground of her new home. The warm breeze kissed her cheeks, whispering tales of the adventures that awaited her. She took a deep breath, inhaling the scents of the island – the salty sea air, the sweet fragrance of blooming flowers, and the earthy aroma of olive groves. It felt as though John's presence enveloped her, assuring her that she had arrived at the place they had dreamed of together.

With a heart full of love and determination, Mary set forth into the embrace of Palma, her childhood home, hoping her parents had made their way back to the vineyards and groves of olive trees. The island welcomed her with open arms, its beauty serving as a constant reminder that love could transcend time and distance. And as Mary took her first steps on the soil of Palma, she knew deep in her soul that she had arrived at the place where her love story would continue to unfold.

After lunch, Mary walked up to the train station and asked, "How much for a ticket to Sóller?"

"5 pesetas." exclaimed the ticket agent behind the window.

"Fine, here you go, one ticket to Sóller." Said Mary. What time does the train leave today?

"The train to Sóller leaves at 5:00 pm. In about 45 minutes," said the ticket agent.

Mary stood at the train station in Mallorca, her heart pulsating with a mixture of excitement and impatience. The sun cast a warm glow upon the charming streets, while the scent of orange blossoms filled the air, intertwining with the aroma of freshly baked bread. She clutched her worn letter, its words etched upon her memory, and gazed at the tracks, anxiously awaiting the arrival of the train.

As minutes turned into what felt like hours, Mary's anticipation grew. She paced back and forth, stealing glances at her pocket watch, willing time to move faster. The minutes stretched into eternity, and she began to worry if something had gone awry. Just when her patience was wearing thin, an elderly couple caught her attention.

The woman, with her silver hair neatly tucked under a delicate hat, approached Mary with a kind smile. "My dear, I couldn't help but notice your restlessness. Waiting can be quite trying, especially when one is filled with anticipation," she said, her voice carrying the wisdom of years.

Mary's face lit up at the woman's words, grateful for the momentary distraction from her own thoughts. "Yes, I've been waiting for what feels like an eternity. I am heading to Sóller, you see, to for my love," she replied, her voice filled with a mix of hope and longing.

The elderly woman's eyes sparkled with understanding. "Ah, love can make even the briefest moments feel like an eternity. My husband and I have been married for over six decades, and let me tell you, waiting has been a constant companion in our journey," she shared, her voice laced with nostalgia.

The woman's husband, with a twinkle in his eye, chimed in, "Indeed, waiting has taught us patience and perseverance. But it has also rewarded us with countless beautiful memories and the joy of shared moments."

Mary's impatience softened as she listened to the couple's words. In their stories, she found solace and a reminder that love was worth every second of waiting. The elderly woman reached out and gently squeezed Mary's hand. "My dear, love has a way of finding its path, even through the longest of delays. Trust in your love, and soon you will be together again."

Just as the conversation reached its tender conclusion, a distant rumble reverberated through the air, announcing the approaching train. Mary's heart skipped a beat, and a smile spread across her face as she turned to bid farewell to the kind couple. "Thank you for your wisdom and words of encouragement. May your love continue to shine bright," she said, her gratitude evident in her voice.

The train came into view, its familiar form bringing a surge of anticipation. Mary boarded, finding a seat by the window, her eyes fixed on the passing scenery. As the train chugged along, it carried her through picturesque landscapes, vineyards stretching into the distance, and quaint villages nestled among the rolling hills. The rhythmic clatter of the wheels on the tracks echoed her heartbeat, each click bringing her closer to her destination.

Through the journey, Mary's thoughts drifted to the moments she had shared with her beloved John. The laughter, the whispered promises, and the stolen kisses flooded her mind, filling the compartments of her heart with warmth and love. She gazed out of the window, the passing vistas blending with her memories, intertwining the beauty of the present with the echoes of the past.

Finally, the train pulled into the station in Sóller, and Mary's heart leaped with joy. She stepped off the train, her eyes scanning the bustling platform until they locked onto a familiar figure. It was her mother and father, their faces etched with anticipation and love. Tears welled up in Mary's eyes as she rushed into their embrace, feeling the warmth and familiarity of home.

"Mary, my dear, you're finally here," her mother whispered, her voice filled with both relief and joy. Her father's arms encircled them both, creating a cocoon of love and safety.

With her parents by her side, Mary felt a profound sense of belonging and comfort. They guided her to a nearby horse and buggy, waiting patiently to take them back to the family home nestled among the vineyards. As the horse trotted along the winding road, the rhythmic clip-clop of its hooves created a soothing backdrop to their conversation.

Mary took a deep breath, her voice quivering with excitement, as she began recounting her time with John in Paris. She spoke of the romantic walks along the Seine, the charming cafes where they shared stolen moments, and the city's vibrant energy that seemed to dance in step with their blossoming love. Her parents listened intently, their eyes sparkling with curiosity and joy.

She described the nights they spent wandering the enchanting streets, hand in hand, discovering hidden corners and embracing the magic of the city of love. Mary's voice softened as she shared their dreams of a future together, of building a life filled with love and adventure.

Her parents smiled, their eyes brimming with pride and understanding. They saw that John held a special place in their daughter's heart, and they were grateful for the love that had grown between them. They listened attentively, cherishing every detail of Mary's tale.

As the horse and buggy approached the family home, Mary's heart swelled with a mix of nostalgia and anticipation. The sight of the familiar facade, draped in vibrant ivy and nestled among blooming flowers, felt like a balm to her soul. She stepped down from the carriage, her parents by her side, and together they crossed the threshold into a space filled with cherished memories.

Inside, the air was infused with the aroma of home-cooked meals and the comforting embrace of familiar furniture. The walls adorned with family paintings told stories of generations' past, weaving a tapestry of love and resilience. As evening descended, Mary and her parents gathered around the dining table, breaking bread, and sharing stories. Laughter filled the air, blending with the clinking of glasses and the soft murmurs of conversation. In that moment, surrounded by family, Mary felt an overwhelming sense of gratitude for the home that had nurtured her, the love that had sustained her, and the journey that had led her back to this place of warmth and belonging.

As they settled in for the night, Mary's heart overflowed with a renewed sense of hope. She knew that the path ahead would not be without its challenges, but she also knew that she had the support and love of her parents. And as she closed her eyes, her mind filled with dreams of the future, she whispered a silent prayer, grateful for the love that had brought her back home.

Maria and Miguel were born and raised in the picturesque town of Sóller, nestled among the rolling hills of Mallorca. They grew up in families that had been deeply rooted in the region for generations, their ancestors having cultivated the fertile land and nurtured the vineyards that defined the area.

Maria, with her captivating smile and gentle nature, was the daughter of a skilled winemaker. She had spent her childhood learning the art of winemaking from her father, immersing herself in the traditions and techniques that had been passed down through the years. Maria's passion for the vineyard and her unwavering dedication to the craft made her an invaluable asset to the family legacy.

Miguel, on the other hand, had been born into a family of farmers who tended to the vast orchards and groves that surrounded Sóller. From an early age, he had been captivated by the scent of the earth, the feel of the soil between his fingers. His strong work ethic and deep connection to the land made him a natural caretaker of the vineyards, which he eventually inherited from his own father.

When Maria and Miguel met as young adults, their shared love for the land and their mutual understanding of the sacrifices and hard work it entailed brought them together. Their courtship was filled with long walks through the vineyards, animated discussions about grape varietals, and dreams of a future intertwined with the rhythm of the seasons.

In time, their love blossomed, and they vowed to create a life together, building upon the foundations laid by their ancestors. They married in a humble ceremony, surrounded by the rolling vineyards that had been witness to generations of love stories.

As husband and wife, Maria and Miguel poured their hearts and souls into the vineyard. They faced challenges with resilience, weathering storms, and adapting to changing times. Their shared vision and unwavering commitment to preserving the family legacy forged a bond that only grew stronger with each passing year.

Their efforts bore fruit, quite literally. The wines they produced began to earn recognition beyond the local markets, captivating the palates of connoisseurs near and far. Through their tireless dedication, Maria and Miguel turned their vineyard into a thriving enterprise, earning the respect and admiration of their community.

But beyond the vineyard, they nurtured a loving home, where their children, including Mary, were raised with values of hard work, respect for the land, and an appreciation for the beauty that surrounded them. Maria and Miguel instilled in their children a deep connection to their heritage and the importance of preserving the traditions that had shaped their family for generations.

Their love for one another and their vineyard radiated through every aspect of their lives, creating a sanctuary of warmth, and belonging for their family. The story of Maria and Miguel was not just one of winemaking and agriculture but of resilience, determination, and a deep-rooted love that had the power to shape lives and transcend generations.

As Mary grew up, she witnessed the sacrifices and dedication of her parents firsthand, learning the art of winemaking from her mother and the value of hard work from her father. Their unwavering support and guidance would shape Mary's own journey, leading her back to Sóller, back to the vineyard that held her family's past, present, and future.

As the winds of war swept across Europe, the people of Palma, including Mary's parents, Maria, and Miguel Fuentes, couldn't escape the ever-present fear of the conflict reaching their shores. Palma, though distanced from the major battlefields, was not immune to the realities of war. Rumors and whispers of an impending Allied invasion fueled anxiety and uncertainty among the island's inhabitants.

Mary's parents, deeply concerned for their family's safety and the fate of their beloved vineyard, made the difficult decision to embark on a brief trip to southern France, seeking refuge from the growing tension. It was a journey fraught with apprehension and worry, leaving behind their cherished home and vineyard, unsure of what they would find upon their return.

Traveling by boat, Maria, Miguel, and Mary sailed across the Mediterranean, their hearts heavy with a mixture of hope and fear. France was at war, but the rolling hills of southern France had been spared the brunt of the war and the allure of the countryside provided a temporary respite from the looming threat that weighed heavily on their minds. They sought refuge in the town of Nîmes in southern France in the Zone Liberti, the unoccupied zone. They found solace in the company of other displaced families, sharing stories, and offering each other support during these uncertain times.

Days turned into weeks as Maria and Miguel waited anxiously for news from Palma, their thoughts consumed by the well-being of their family and the fate of their vineyard. Finally, as the tides of war shifted, news arrived that the feared invasion had passed, and Palma remained untouched by the conflict.

Relief washed over Maria and Miguel, their hearts filled with gratitude for the safety of their loved ones and the preservation of their home. It was with renewed hope that they made the journey back to Palma, eager to be reunited with their family and resume their responsibilities as caretakers of the vineyard. Mary, however, took a different path. In spite of her parents' stern objections, she wanted to remain in France to learn more about French winemaking and help out at the local hospital in Nîmes.

Upon their return, Maria and Miguel found the vineyard exactly as they had left it, the rows of vines reaching towards the sun, a testament to the resilience of the land they called home. The brief trip to Sicily had given them a renewed perspective, a reminder of the fragility of life and the importance of cherishing every moment.

As they stepped foot on Palma's shores once again, Maria and Miguel embraced the familiar scents and sights, their hearts filled with a renewed appreciation for their island and its people. The fear of war had left its mark, but it had also reinforced the importance of family, community, and the timeless beauty of their vineyard.

Early the next morning, as the first rays of morning light filtered through the window, Mary slowly opened her eyes, greeted by the familiar sight of her childhood bedroom. The soft rustling of leaves outside whispered a gentle reminder that she was back home in Sóller. Stretching her limbs, she sat up, a sense of purpose enveloping her.

Dressed in a simple cotton dress, Mary descended the creaking staircase, the scent of freshly brewed coffee mingling with the crisp morning air. In the kitchen, her mother, Maria, stood over the stove, tending to a pot of simmering stew. The warmth of her smile mirrored the love she poured into each dish.

"Good morning, my dear," Maria greeted, her voice filled with a mix of motherly affection and purpose. "I'm glad you're up. We have much to do today."

Mary embraced her mother, feeling a surge of gratitude for the strong woman who had shaped her upbringing. Together, they began their daily routine, preparing breakfast and setting the table with care.

After the meal, Mary's father, Miguel, joined them, his weathered hands still bearing the marks of toil. He had spent a lifetime nurturing the vineyard that had been in their family for generations, and now Mary longed to contribute to the legacy he had built.

She followed her father to the vineyard, her steps echoing the rhythm of her heart. The vineyard stretched out before her, its lush green vines swaying gently in the breeze. With every grape that ripened under the Mediterranean sun, Mary understood the labor of love that went into crafting each bottle of wine.

Under her father's guidance, Mary learned the intricacies of pruning, nurturing, and harvesting the grapes. Together, they worked side by side, their hands coated in the soil that had witnessed their family's triumphs and tribulations.

As the day progressed, Mary's hands grew calloused, but her spirit soared. With each vine tended to, she felt a deeper connection to the land, a kinship that transcended time. She understood that this vineyard was not just a means of sustenance; it was a testament to her family's resilience and determination.

In the late afternoon, as the sun began its descent, Mary and her father paused to catch their breath. They surveyed the vineyard, the fruit of their labor spreading out before them like a tapestry of life.

"You've done well, my daughter," Miguel said, pride glimmering in his eyes. "You have the touch of our ancestors, the same fire that has kept this land alive."

Mary's heart swelled with a mixture of gratitude and purpose. She knew that her journey had brought her back to Sóller for a reason. Her time with John in Paris had opened her eyes to a world beyond these vineyard hills, but it had also deepened her appreciation for the roots from which she sprang.

As the evening sky painted the horizon with hues of gold and orange, Mary stood in the midst of the vineyard, the legacy of her family embracing her. As the evening glow of the moon lit the vineyard, she closed her eyes, the scent of ripe grapes and the whisper of the wind through the vines, she whispered a silent vow to herself and her family. She would tend to this land with the same love and dedication that they had shown her, preserving its beauty, and passing it on to future generations.

THE SEINE

It was a Sunday afternoon. Mary gazed at John, her eyes filled with curiosity and compassion, as they continued their leisurely stroll along the banks of the Seine. The question that had been lingering in her mind finally found its voice. "John," she said softly, "since we met, I've been wanting to ask you... What was it truly like for you on the day you landed in France? We heard so many stories, read the accounts in the underground papers during the occupation. The sacrifices made on those beaches... it's hard to fathom."

John's expression turned somber as he recalled the details shared by his sergeant. "Mary," he began, his voice tinged with a mixture of gravity and determination, "the shoreline along those beaches was treacherous, heavily fortified by the Germans. Concrete structures held machine guns that seemed to rain an unending storm of bullets upon Allied forces. Many brave men lost their lives on that day, facing insurmountable odds. But, you see, it could have been even worse."

Intrigued, Mary leaned closer, her eyes fixed on John. "How so?" she inquired, her voice filled with a mix of anticipation and concern.

"Well, I didn't come up with the beach assault, my company was dropped in total darkness, a few miles inland from the beaches of Normandy," John explained. "Our mission was to disrupt German defenses, secure crucial positions, and create a path for the advancing Allied forces landing on the beaches. If we had failed in our tasks, German reinforcements would have pushed forward, potentially causing even greater loss of life and jeopardizing the success of the entire invasion."

A sense of awe filled Mary as she absorbed the weight of the responsibility carried by John and his fellow soldiers. She couldn't help but ask the question that lingered on her lips. "Were you scared, John? The thought of facing such overwhelming odds... it must have been terrifying."

A faint smile played on John's lips as he glanced at Mary, his eyes reflecting the courage and resilience of all those who had taken part in the D-Day operation. "Yes, Mary," he admitted, "fear was certainly present among us. From my platoon to the divisions that took off that night, we all knew the risks. We were prepared for the worst but hoped for the best."

As they continued their walk, John delved into the vivid account of his own experience. He recounted the landing in Saint-Germain-de-Varreville, northeast of Carentan, and the fierce fighting that ensued. The chaotic weather and navigation difficulties had scattered their forces far from their intended target zones. The element of surprise was compromised, and many soldiers fell victim to German patrols. Yet, against all odds, they managed to fulfill their objectives and contribute to the larger success of the invasion.

He told Mary the reason he was in Paris was that his Lieutenant approved a 14-day furlough for him after the conclusion of their last mission. He told her that he was awarded the Bronze Star from the U.S. Army and the Croix De Guerre from the French because of his bravery and heroic service in clearing machine gun nests outside of Caraten when his platoon and many French resistance fighters were pinned down by the gunfire.

John covered his eyes as if he were fighting again but fighting back tears.

"A lot more men were more worthy than me for this honor, but they gave their lives in that field," whispered John. "I would gladly burn them to see their faces again."

Mary put her hand in his, listening attentively, her admiration for John and his comrades growing with each word. The stories of heroism and sacrifice painted a vivid picture of the bravery displayed on that fateful day. As the sun set over the Seine, their conversation continued, and Mary's heart swelled with gratitude for the brave men who had risked or gave everything that day for freedom and the hope of a better future.

Mary grabbed John's arm and put her head of jet-black hair on his shoulder as they walked up the incline at the riverside to Promenade Maurice Carême, the boulevard that ran parallel to the river northeast of Notre Dame. This time a year the sun set late in the evening allowing just enough time for John and Mary to cross over the river to Le Reminet, a quaint café on the left bank of the Seine near Square René Viviani-Montebello adjacent to the church Saint-Julien-le-Pauvre.

Mary leaned over to John and said, "Let's get a tart and walk into the square."

John and Mary purchased a couple of strawberry tarts grown made from strawberries grown in the fields of southern France. They made their way over to the square.

"I was here a couple of months ago when the German soldiers were still patrolling the river," said Mary. "I met an older woman who told me about the history of this park."

As they strolled beneath the shade of the ancient locust tree, its branches reaching towards the sky, they marveled at its remarkable resilience and storied history.

"Can you believe," Mary said, her voice filled with wonder, "that this tree has been standing here for over four hundred years? It has witnessed so much history, including the trials and triumphs of the many wars."

John nodded; his eyes fixed on the gnarled trunk. "It's incredible," he replied. "This tree has seen the rise and fall of empires, the struggles and sacrifices of countless generations. It's a symbol of strength and endurance, just like the people of Paris."

They sat on a nearby bench, leaning against each other, taking in the serenity of the square. As they gazed at the tree, its branches gently swaying in the breeze, Mary couldn't help but draw parallels between its resilience and the indomitable spirit of the French people.

"In times of war," she said softly, "it must be reassuring to see this tree blooming every year, a symbol of life and hope amidst the destruction. It's a reminder that even in the darkest of times, there is always the potential for renewal and growth."

John looked at Mary, gazing into her beautiful brown eyes and quietly asked, "What about you? You and your family fled Sóller to come to the south of France, what was that trip like? Where did you go? Where are you parents now?"

With a touch of sadness in her voice, Mary recounted the journey her parents, Maria, and Miguel, undertook to find safety.

"Traveling by boat," Mary began, her eyes distant with the weight of the memories, "my parents, Maria and Miguel, along with me, sailed across the vast expanse of the Mediterranean. Our hearts were heavy with a mixture of hope and fear, unsure of what lay ahead."

She continued, painting a picture of their journey, "France was engulfed in the flames of war, but southern France had been saved from the brunt of the conflict. After landing in Marseille, we traveled northwest and sought refuge in a little village called Nîmes, nestled in the unoccupied zone."

"We stayed there with the people in the village, helping out with the local hospital where they were still caring for wounded soldiers who arrived from Morocco and Tunisia," said Mary. "But my parents were not happy. Once word got to the village that Allied forces did not invade Sóller, they longed to go home. I could not go with them. I felt a responsibility and a desire for adventure. I wanted to learn more about French winemaking and explore the country. I spent my entire life to that point in Sóller, I just wanted adventure. My parents and I argued and argued about it, but they eventually agreed. We parted ways as they left to return to Marseille to catch the boat back to Palma, and then the train to Sóller."

"How did you get to Paris?" inquired John.

"Once the soldiers left Nîmes, and word reached us that Paris had been liberated, I found myself longing to see the city," said Mary. "I traveled to Marseille with other people on the same journey and boarded the train to Paris. I really had been here only a week when we met at the café.

She explained that she was staying at a little hostel on the east side of the river in Paris and although she had a little money from her family vineyard, she was working in a café by the theater where Parisians still loved to go to the movies, even while recovering from German occupation.

As John and Mary rose from the bench in the Square René Viviani, a newfound closeness seemed to envelop them. The moonlight cast a gentle glow upon the city, illuminating their path as they strolled towards the river. The soft lapping of the Seine against the embankment provided a soothing backdrop to their footsteps, creating an atmosphere of intimacy and enchantment.

They paused at the edge of the river; their eyes drawn to the majestic Eiffel Tower standing tall against the night sky. Moonlight danced upon the iconic structure, transforming it into a beacon of romance. John's gaze shifted to Mary, his heart pulsating with a mix of anticipation and longing. In that moment, the world seemed to fade away, leaving only the two of them, entwined in a tapestry of emotions.

Unable to resist the magnetic pull, John gently took Mary's hand in his. Their fingers interlaced, their connection growing stronger with each passing moment. They turned to face each other, their eyes reflecting the moon's radiance and an unspoken understanding.

With hesitant yet determined steps, they closed the distance between them, their hearts beating in unison. In the stillness of the night, John's arms encircled Mary's waist, drawing her closer. They swayed gently, captivated by the ethereal beauty that surrounded them.

In that enchanting moment, time stood still. Their eyes locked, brimming with unspoken words. And then, with a mixture of trepidation and sheer longing, their lips met in a tender embrace. It was a kiss filled with the promise of dreams yet to be realized, of shared hopes and a future intertwined.

Under the moonlit sky and the watchful gaze of the Eiffel Tower, John and Mary surrendered to the magic of the moment. In that embrace, they discovered a love that would transcend the challenges and uncertainties that lay ahead. It was a promise, sealed with a kiss, that they would navigate the journey together, guided by their unwavering devotion and the boundless possibilities that Paris held.

John walked Mary back to the hostel on the east side of the river, a little place called L'auberge de Madam Boudreaux. It was nestled in the heart of a charming Paris street, exuding an air of warmth and history. The quaint hostel was a centuries-old building, its stone walls bearing witness to the passage of time. Claire Boudeaux, a kind-hearted and sprightly elderly woman, had been running the hostel for as long as anyone could remember.

As you stepped through the creaking wooden door, the inviting aroma of freshly baked bread and homemade soups greeted you. The common area was adorned with rustic furniture, and the walls adorned with vintage paintings and photographs, each telling a story of the hostel's rich past. A fireplace crackled in the corner, inviting guests to gather around and share stories of their travels.

The rooms were simple yet comfortable, each named after famous French landmarks and filled with antique furniture that Claire had collected over the years. The beds were adorned with soft, hand-stitched quilts, and the windows offered picturesque views of the surrounding countryside.

The residents of L'auberge de Madam Boudeaux were a diverse and lively bunch. There was Monsieur Dupont, a jovial retiree who spent his days sketching the picturesque landscapes that surrounded the village. Madame Dubois, a talented pianist, would often fill the hostel with the beautiful melodies of classic French music. And then there was Pierre, a young and ambitious chef, who had come to the village to learn the secrets of traditional French cuisine from Claire herself.

In the evenings, guests would gather around a large communal table in the dining area, where Claire would serve up hearty and delicious meals made from the freshest local ingredients. It was during these meals that friendships were forged, and stories exchanged, creating a sense of companionship that made L'auberge de Madam Boudeaux feel like a home away from home.

Outside, a charming garden bloomed with colorful flowers, and a cobblestone courtyard provided a peaceful spot for guests to relax and enjoy the French sunshine. Claire would often be found tending to her beloved garden, her wrinkled hands expertly nurturing each delicate bloom.

In the evenings, the hostel was known to come alive with laughter, music, and the clinking of glasses as guests raised a toast to new friendships and the beauty of life's simple pleasures. Many celebrated the liberation of Paris here drinking what champagne the Germans didn't take and enjoying a collection of cheeses and artisan breads.

As John and Mary walked up the old wooden staircase up to their room, Mrs. Boudeaux said, "Hello Mary, is this the young man you were telling me about at breakfast?"

"Yes, madame," she replied. "We have just spent the day together exploring the city."

"Well, if you're hungry, come back down and I will see what Pierre can find for you to eat."

"Thank you, Madame," said Mary.

Only a half hour later, John and Mary descended the old wooden staircase to the main floor, the tantalizing aroma of Pierre's cooking enveloped them. They found Mrs. Boudeaux and Pierre bustling in the kitchen, their faces beaming with warmth as they prepared a delicious feast for the young couple.

Pierre, a tall and lanky young man with a perpetual smile, greeted them with a flourish. "Ah, bonsoir! Mary, John, it is such a pleasure to see you both again. I've prepared a delightful dinner for you to enjoy. Please, have a seat."

They settled at a cozy table near the window, where the soft glow of candlelight danced upon the tablecloth. Pierre emerged from the kitchen, bearing plates of steaming coq au vin and ratatouille, classic French dishes that he had perfected under the watchful eye of Claire. The rich flavors and delicate textures tantalized their taste buds, leaving them in culinary bliss.

As they savored each bite, Mrs. Boudeaux joined them at the table, regaling them with tales of the hostel's history and the colorful characters who had graced its halls over the years. Her eyes sparkled with nostalgia as she spoke, and it was evident that L'auberge de Madam Boudeaux held a special place in her heart.

John and Mary listened attentively, captivated by the enchanting stories that seemed to weave the very fabric of the hostel's charm. They felt a deep connection to this place, as if they had become part of its living history, just like the generations of travelers who had passed through its doors before them.

After the delightful meal, Pierre surprised them with a delectable dessert, a velvety chocolate mousse topped with fresh strawberries. Each bite was a heavenly delight, and the couple couldn't help but compliment Pierre on his culinary skills.

As the evening stretched on, the three of them laughed and shared tales of their own adventures. John regaled them with stories of his platoon's journey and the camaraderie he had found amidst the chaos of war, while Mary spoke of her dreams and aspirations beyond the war's end.

In the warm embrace of L'auberge de Madam Boudeaux, the evening seemed to pass like a dream. The flickering candlelight, the laughter, and the heartwarming hospitality of Claire and Pierre created a sense of comfort and belonging that John and Mary had never experienced before.

As the evening waned, John gallantly escorted Mary to her room, their steps illuminated by the soft moonlight. As they reached her door, he leaned in and planted a gentle kiss on her cheek, bidding her a sweet goodnight. With a warm smile, Mary entered her room, and John lingered for a moment, watching her disappear from sight.

Leaving the hostel, John began his walk back to his own hotel, the Hotel Chopin. Nestled within the charming Passage Jouffroy shopping gallery, the hotel bore the name of the famed Polish composer and pianist, Frédéric François Chopin. This very neighborhood was said to have held a special place in Chopin's heart during his lifetime, just as it did for John now, who found solace in its historical charm amidst the chaos of wartime. The memories of the evening's enchanting moments lingered in his mind, and he felt a sense of tranquility in this picturesque setting, even amid the backdrop of war's turmoil.

Upon arriving back at the Hotel Chopin, John was greeted by the welcoming sight of its cozy interior. The warm glow of the elegant chandeliers cast a serene ambiance throughout the lobby as he made his way to his room. The sound of soft piano music playing in the background added to the comforting atmosphere, a fitting tribute to the hotel's namesake.

As he entered his room, John felt a sense of relief wash over him. The accommodations were modest but comfortable, providing a much-needed respite from the rigors of military life. He took a moment to unpack some items he purchased during the day and settled into the comfortable bed, his mind drifting back to the delightful moments spent with Mary.

Though the world outside was filled with chaos and uncertainty, John found solace in the sanctuary of his room. He decided to take a moment to write in his journal, documenting the events of the day, capturing every detail of his time with Mary, and expressing his hopes for the weekend ahead.

The rhythmic sound of the pen scratching against the paper served as a calming melody, much like the distant piano music downstairs. Writing was John's way of preserving memories, capturing fleeting moments of happiness amidst the backdrop of war's tragedies.

As he closed his journal and set it aside, a sense of contentment enveloped him. The events of the day had brought a glimmer of joy, reminding him that even amidst the darkness, there were still moments of light and happiness to be cherished.

With a weary but peaceful heart, John drifted off to sleep, feeling grateful for the rest provided by the Hotel Chopin and the enchanting company he had enjoyed earlier. As he closed his eyes, he couldn't help but wonder what the weekend had in store and hoped that it would continue to be filled with small hints of happiness, overshadowing the tragedies of war, even if just for a little while longer.

GEORGIA

"Hurry up," shouted Wilson. "We are gonna miss mess."

"I'm coming," exclaimed John. "I was reading a letter from home; seems my dog chased the coyote out of the horse pen yesterday and he didn't come back for three hours. Dang dog, I told my mother to watch him. His name is Roscoe, and he loves chasing the vermin out of our pasture."

"Well, Lieutenant Hobbs said we better be on time today because he has an announcement for the whole company."

John and Wilson hurried to the mess hall and arrived just in time to grab a tray and take a seat with their platoon. Already there at the table was Guppy, Jenkins, Parsons and Jackson, other members of John's platoon.

Wilson came from a small town in Tennessee. His father served in World War I, so he felt compelled to follow his father. He was a natural leader, never late, always listening, and following directions. He seemed to always keep the platoon on track. It was apparent one day he would be a leader.

Guppy, known for his infectious humor and unwavering loyalty, was a soldier who had joined the platoon with an unyielding spirit. With his quick wit and ability to find joy in even the toughest situations, Guppy had become an integral part of the group. His presence provided a sense of lightness and camaraderie during the darkest moments.

It was Guppy that introduced John to Jenkins in basic training. Jenkins was a young soldier who hailed from a farming family, possessed a quiet strength that belied his age. In fact, his age often came into question. He looked like he was sixteen. He was a diligent and disciplined soldier, always willing to lend a helping hand and carry out his duties with unwavering dedication. Jenkins had joined the platoon seeking a sense of purpose and a chance to make a difference as opposed to Parsons who was a seasoned soldier with a hardened exterior, carrying the weight of experience on his shoulders. He had seen the horrors of war firsthand in North Africa before requesting a transfer and had learned to navigate the battlefield with a steely resolve. Parsons' leadership and wisdom were invaluable to the platoon, guiding them through the challenges they faced and instilling a sense of confidence in their abilities.

Jackson, a soldier with a natural gift for marksmanship, had joined the platoon after demonstrating exceptional skills during training. His unwavering focus and sharpshooting abilities made him an invaluable asset, ensuring that their platoon could rely on his accuracy when it mattered most. Jackson's calm demeanor and steady aim were a source of inspiration for his platoon.

Together, they formed a tight-knit unit within the larger company with a set of strengths that complemented one another, creating a cohesive force that relied on trust, camaraderie, and unwavering determination. As John and Guppy sat down in the mess hall with the other members of the platoon, you could hear the rap of a gun barrel on the top of a metal table.

Lieutenant Hobbs, a seasoned officer with a commanding presence, rapped his rifle sharply on the mess hall table, its metallic sound reverberating through the room. The clatter of cutlery ceased, and conversations dwindled as every soldier turned their attention towards him. Lieutenant Hobbs was known for his no-nonsense demeanor and unwavering commitment to training his troops to the highest standards.

"Listen up, soldiers!" Lieutenant Hobbs' voice boomed, commanding attention. "Our time in basic training is over. We've laid a solid foundation, but now it's time to take things to the next level. We're moving on to jump training at Fort Moore!"

A murmur of excitement and anticipation rippled through the room. Jump training was a pivotal phase in their preparation for the challenges that lay ahead. It meant learning the art of airborne operations, mastering the techniques and skills necessary for parachute jumps into enemy territory.

Lieutenant Hobbs continued, his voice filled with authority and determination. "Jump training will test your mettle like never before. It will push you to your limits physically, mentally, and emotionally. But I have no doubt that each and every one of you has what it takes to excel. This is where we separate the boys from the men, where we forge an elite unit capable of facing any challenge on the battlefield."

The soldiers exchanged glances, their eyes reflecting a mixture of excitement and trepidation. They had heard stories of the grueling nature of jump training, but they were also aware of the immense pride that came with being part of an airborne unit. They understood that the training would be rigorous, but they were ready to embrace the challenge head-on.

Lieutenant Hobbs concluded, his voice resonating with conviction. "We will leave no soldier behind, and we will push each other to be the best that we can be. Jump training will prepare you for the battles that lie ahead, where your skills and courage will be put to the ultimate test. So, buckle up and get ready, soldiers. Jump school awaits, and we will come back stronger, more skilled, and ready to face whatever the enemy throws at us!"

With those words, Lieutenant Hobbs barked, "Pack up your trash and be prepared to leave at 0500 tomorrow morning......Dismissed."

As Lieutenant Hobbs finished his announcement and dismissed the soldiers, the mess hall buzzed with an excited energy. Platoon members gathered in small groups along their tables in the mess hall, their voices intertwining in lively conversation as they ate their last meal at Camp Toccoa. Laughter and banter filled the air as they discussed their upcoming jump training.

Guppy, his eyes gleaming with anticipation, turned to Jenkins with a mischievous grin. "Hey, Jenkins, you ready to fly through the sky like a bird? They better watch out for us airborne troopers!"

Jenkins chuckled, his eyes reflecting a mix of nerves and excitement. "You bet, Guppy! Can't wait to feel the rush of jumping out of that plane. We're going to make our mark, that's for sure."

At the end of the table, Parsons leaned back in his chair, a hint of a smile playing on his lips. He looked at Jackson, the sharpshooter of the platoon, and remarked, "You think all that target practice will come in handy during the jumps, Jackson?"

Jackson smirked, a glint of confidence in his eyes. "I've got a steady hand, Parsons. Those Germans won't know what hit them. But let's hope the winds are on our side."

John, known for his calm demeanor, approached Private Wilson. He placed a reassuring hand on his shoulder and said, "Don't worry, Wilson. We'll go through this training together. It'll be tough, but we've got each other's backs."

Wilson nodded, grateful for the support. "Thanks, John. I trust our training, and I trust you all. We'll make it through and come out stronger on the other side."

Amidst the conversations, there was an air of camaraderie and unity. The platoon members shared their hopes, concerns, and aspirations for the upcoming jump training. They offered words of encouragement, shared stories of past training experiences, and reassured one another of their collective strength.

As the mess hall buzzed with anticipation, the soldiers knew that they were about to embark on a challenging journey that would test their courage and forge an unbreakable bond. They would face the unknown together, relying on each other for support, and emerging as a tightly knit unit capable of overcoming any obstacle.

In that mess hall, amidst the clatter of dishes and the hum of conversation, the platoon members shared anticipation of what lay ahead. They were not just soldiers, but brothers, united by their commitment to serve and their unwavering dedication to each other.

0500 came early that day, shattering the stillness of the morning air. The soldiers of the platoon had risen before the sun, preparing themselves for the journey ahead. As the first rays of light peeked over the horizon, they gathered outside the barracks, their duffel bags slung over their shoulders and determination etched on their faces.

Lieutenant Hobbs, his voice steady and commanding, addressed the platoon. "Alright, soldiers, time to load up. Grab your gear, get on the trucks, and let's roll! Jump school is waiting for us."

The platoon members moved with purpose, loading their belongings onto the waiting trucks. Private Thompson, a strong and sturdy soldier, turned to John with a hint of excitement. "John, can you believe it? We're actually heading to jump school. This is what we've trained for."

John nodded; his gaze focused on the task at hand. "It's time to put our training into action, Thompson. We've got this. Stay focused and remember what we've learned."

Jenkins, his voice filled with enthusiasm, joined the conversation. "I can't wait to jump out of that plane, John. It's going to be one hell of an adrenaline rush."

John grinned, a glimmer of anticipation in his eyes. "Hold on tight, Jenkins. You'll get your chance soon enough. Just remember your training, and we'll all come out of this with flying colors."

As the trucks rumbled to life, the platoon members found their seats, their faces a mix of anticipation and nerves. The air was thick with a sense of purpose and the unknown. The journey to jump school had begun.

The rumble of the engines drowned out most of the conversation, but amidst the rolling wheels and the hum of the road, snippets of dialogue could be heard. Soldiers shared stories of their families, dreams for the future, and exchanged words of encouragement.

Guppy, always the joker, managed to bring a smile to their faces. "Hey, Thompson, I heard jump instructors are tougher than nails. But I know you've got the charm to win them over!"

Thompson chuckled; his nerves momentarily eased. "You think so, Guppy? Well, let's hope my charm works on them, or else I'll be doing a whole lot of extra push-ups."

"What's that?" said Guppy, pointing to the tattoo on Parsons upper arm.

"It's a rose, I got it in North Africa for my girlfriend," he replied.

"So, what's the writing inside?" asked Guppy.

"It's an A and an M, which stand for Anna Mae, that's her name," said Parsons. "There wasn't enough room to write it out and I was a little drunk in a Tunisian bar at the time they were doing tattoos."

"What happens if break up with her?" asked Jenkins. "You'll have to find another girl with the initials A and M. Ha Ha!"

Parsons, with a thoughtful look in his eyes, turned to Jenkins and asked, "Hey, Jenkins, you ever had a girl back home?"

Jenkins paused for a moment, his gaze drifting out the back of the truck. "Yeah, I did," he replied softly. "Back on the farm where I grew up, there was this girl, Emily. She lived on the neighboring farm, just a few acres away from ours. We practically grew up together, running through the fields, chasing after the chickens, and stealing sweet apples from the orchard."

A hint of nostalgia crept into Jenkins' voice as he continued, "We used to sit on the porch at night, watching the stars and dreaming about all the things we'd do one day. She had this sparkle in her eyes, you know? Like the whole world was waiting for her to conquer it."

Parsons listened intently, drawn into Jenkins' memories. "So, what happened between you two?" he asked gently.

Jenkins sighed, his expression growing pensive. "When the war came, I knew I had to do my part. I couldn't stay behind while the world was in turmoil. I enlisted, thinking it was the right thing to do. Emily was scared, and I was too, but I couldn't show it. We said our goodbyes, promising to write to each other whenever we could."

"But war changes everything," Jenkins continued. "The letters became less frequent as we got deeper into training.

I didn't want her to worry about me, so I kept my letters short and hopeful. But the truth was, I missed her every single day, and every step I take reminds me of the walks I took with the girl I left behind."

Parsons could feel the weight of Jenkins' words, understanding the pain and longing that came with being away from home and the ones you loved. "Do you think you'll ever see her again?" he asked quietly.

Jenkins looked up at Parsons with an uncertainty in his eyes. "I don't know, Parsons," he replied honestly. "I hope so, but it's hard to imagine what the future holds. All I know is that when this war is over, I'll head back to that farm, back to Emily, and try to rebuild the life we had before."

The platoon's convoy rolled to a halt as they arrived at the jump school, a sprawling complex nestled amidst a picturesque landscape. The soldiers stepped off the trucks, their eyes scanning the surroundings with a mix of curiosity and anticipation. The buildings stood tall and imposing, a reminder of the challenges that awaited them.

Lieutenant Hobbs gathered the platoon, his voice carrying with authority. "Alright, everyone, this is it. Welcome to jump school. Get your gear and follow me. We're going to get settled into our barracks."

The soldiers shuffled with excitement, grabbing their duffel bags, and marching in formation behind Lieutenant Hobbs. The barracks stood in neat rows, each one marked with a number. They entered their designated building, finding rows of bunks and lockers awaiting them.

Wilson, a spark of enthusiasm in his eyes, turned to Guppy. "This is our home for the next few weeks, Guppy. We're going to eat, sleep, and breathe jump training. Let's make the most of it."

Guppy nodded; his voice filled with determination. "You got it, Wilson. We've trained hard for this, and now it's time to show them what we're made of."

As the soldiers settled into their barracks, the sound of lockers opening, and gear being unpacked filled the air. Conversations buzzed throughout the barracks as the platoon members surveyed their surroundings.

Private Thompson, a natural leader, called out to the soldiers nearby. "Hey, anyone up for a game of cards later? Let's break the ice and have some fun."

The offer was met with enthusiasm, and soon a card game was in full swing, laughter echoing through the barracks. The soldiers shared stories of their previous experiences, their excitement for jump school.

John, always a calm and steady presence, approached Private Jenkins, who seemed a bit overwhelmed by the new surroundings. "Don't worry, Jenkins. We're all in this together. If you have any questions or need help, just ask. We've got your back."

Jenkins nodded, grateful for the support. "Thanks, John. It means a lot. I'm eager to learn, but I can't help feeling a bit nervous."

John patted him on the shoulder. "Nerves are normal, Wilson. Embrace the challenge and trust in your training. You'll do just fine."

The barracks slowly transformed into a home away from home, as personal touches were added to the bunks and friendship blossomed amongst the platoons. The soldiers exchanged advice, shared their excitement about the journey to embark upon.

Private Thompson, his eyes fixed on a poster in the jump school barracks, turned to Guppy with a grin. "Hey, Guppy, have you seen this? They say there's a tattoo parlor nearby that specializes in military ink. What do you say we get ourselves some screaming eagle tattoos?"

Guppy's eyes widened with excitement. "Are you serious, Thompson? That's badass! I've always wanted a tattoo, and what better way to show our pride as part of the 101st Airborne Division?"

Thompson nodded, the idea growing on him. "Exactly! It's like a permanent mark of our journey, our commitment to this brotherhood. Let's do it."

Word spread quickly through the rows of barracks, and soon the platoons were buzzing with chatter about tattoos. As the evening approached, Thompson, Guppy, and several other soldiers made their way to the tattoo parlor, their hearts pounding with a mix of nerves and excitement.

Inside the parlor, the smell of antiseptic and the sound of buzzing needles filled the air. The tattoo artist, a burly man with a shaved head and a gruff voice, greeted them. "So, you boys want the screaming eagle, huh?

Thompson took a seat in the chair, while Guppy sat nearby, his eyes wide with anticipation. As the needle touched Thompson's skin, he winced, feeling the sting, but also a surge of pride. Guppy, always the joker, couldn't resist a comment. "Hey, Thompson, they say getting a tattoo is more painful than jumping out of a plane. How are you holding up?"

Thompson chuckled through gritted teeth. "Just a little pain, Guppy. Nothing compared to what we've been through. It's worth it."

The artist worked diligently, etching the intricate design of the screaming eagle onto Thompson's arm. The platoon members looked on, some with admiration and others with a mix of excitement and nerves. They knew that getting a tattoo was more than just a mark on their skin—it symbolized their dedication, their shared experiences, and their unwavering bond.

As the tattoo took shape, Thompson's gaze shifted to Guppy. "Your turn next, Guppy. Ready for this?"

Guppy nodded; his voice filled with determination. "Absolutely, Thompson. Let's show the world that we're part of the Screaming Eagles, ready to soar."

One by one, the soldiers took their turns, each getting their own rendition of the screaming eagle inked onto their skin. The pain of the needle faded into the background as they shared stories, jokes, and encouragement. In that tattoo parlor, their brotherhood grew stronger, solidified by the permanent mark they carried with them.

As they left the parlor, their arms adorned with screaming eagle tattoos, the platoon members couldn't help but feel a surge of pride. They knew that their tattoos would serve as a constant reminder of their shared journey, the trials they had overcome, and the unbreakable bond they had forged.

With their new tattoos, they returned to the barracks, their spirits soaring high. They were no longer just soldiers; they were Screaming Eagles, ready to face whatever challenges awaited them.

As evening descended, the platoon settled into their beds, exhaustion mingling with anticipation. The barracks grew quiet, the only sound the gentle hum of conversation drifting through the air.

In those barracks, amidst the scent of polish and the shuffle of boots, the soldiers closed their eyes, knowing that the following days would test their limits. But they were ready.

PEGASUS

As the truck rumbled down the road, John found himself lost in thought. His eyes drifted towards his forearm, where the screaming eagle tattoo proudly adorned his skin. The image brought back a flood of memories, reminding him of the journey he had embarked upon since that day at jump school. A smile crossed his face as he looked out the back of the truck and then across at some of his platoon members.

"What?" said Guppy.

"Nothing," said John as he smiled. "I was just remembering jump school and the day we got these tattoos. What a bunch of nuts we were."

"Yea," said Guppy, "I'm up for another one. Perhaps when this is all over."

"Perhaps," replied John as his thoughts momentarily traveled back to Paris and Mary. When this is over, she will be his priority, his solace, and life.

It was October 1944, and the war had taken John and his platoon to the front lines with Easy Company, reinforcing the British troops at Nijmegen. The urgency of the situation was palpable, and the weight of their mission rested heavily on their shoulders. The British were in need of some sack time and re-supply after Operation Berlin.

The Battle of Arnhem had occurred in September 1944 as part of Operation Market Garden, a Western Allies' attempt to advance into Germany's industrial heartland. The operation required the First Allied Airborne Army to seize bridges in the Netherlands, with the 1st British Airborne Division dropping onto Arnhem. The division faced unexpected resistance, and only a small force reached the Arnhem Road bridge. The rest of the division was trapped in

Oosterbeek and withdrawn in Operation Berlin. Out of over 10,400 British and Polish paratroopers, around 2,400-2,500 safely withdrew, while approximately 7,900 were left behind, with many killed or captured by the Germans. After the battle, around 500 paratroopers remained in hiding in villages north of the Lower Rhine River.

What the platoon didn't know was that they would play a pivotal role in rescuing a great number of the stranded soldiers.

As John glanced out of the back of the truck, he saw the passing landscape, scarred by the ravages of war. Buildings stood in ruins, and the air was thick with the echoes of gunfire. Yet amidst the chaos, a sense of determination burned within him, fueled by the camaraderie he shared with his fellow soldiers.

His mind drifted back to the day they received their tattoos. It had been a symbol of pride, a testament to their commitment and bravery. But now, as they headed towards the battlefront, the tattoo carried an even deeper significance.

The rumble of the truck seemed to fade into the background as memories flooded John's mind. He remembered the adrenaline rush of jumping out of planes, the long nights of training, and the faces of his platoon, etched with determination and resilience.

A voice interrupted his thoughts, jolting him back to the present. It was Sergeant Holmes, barking orders and ensuring the platoon was ready for what awaited them. The urgency in his voice mirrored the seriousness of their mission.

John tightened his grip on his rifle, his fingers tracing the outline of his tattoo. It served as a reminder of the sacrifices they had already made and the ones that lay ahead.

As the truck rolled closer to our destination, John could see they were headed toward two larger river crossings south of Arnhem between Nijmegen and Ede. The British and Polish troops position on the northern bank of the Rhine had become weak. British and Canadian engineers helped to devise a plan to rescue the stranded airmen who were hiding in farmhouses using boats. While initially successful, many soldiers were capture or killed. Only 2,500 were rescued during Operation Berlin and many were still in hiding in the village.

"Sergeant Holmes," shouted John. "What's our objective here?"

"I'll brief you after we deploy at the riverbank," said Sergeant Holmes.

The truck tire screeched to a halt. The daylight had left, and a cool blanket of darkness smothered the countryside. The waxing moon was barely visible through the hazy clouds that hid the stars that night. In the distance, the thunder of German 88's could be heard, possibly trying to root out the remaining survivors hidden in the woods around the village of Renkum south of Ede.

"Alright men," shouted Sergeant Holmes. "Grab your stuff and meet up in front of the big farmhouse behind the hill."

John and his platoon joined the rest of Easy Company waiting for word back from Sgt. Holmes. The night air was palatable, an ominous orange glow on the horizon spoiled the moonlight and the sound of artillery drowned out the chorus of crickets hiding in the tall grasses.

"Attention, gather in," exclaimed Sgt. Holmes, "Dutch resistance has informed us that 2 days ago, the Germans ordered residents of villages near Arnhem to leave their homes by tonight. Joint operations command has decided to take advantage of the confusion of the residents leaving to evacuate the soldiers pinned down on the other side of the river. The Dutch Resistance will collect the stranded soldiers from their hiding places and take them to a location near the village of Renkum, 5 kilometers (3.1 mi) west of Arnhem on the German-controlled north side of the lower Rhine River. From our bank of the river, we will cross the river in rowboats and provide support for British, American, Russian and Dutch Resistance solders that will gather the escapees. "

"The Germans know we are here," he continued. "But they have no idea as to our numbers and are on the lookout for our patrols. So put some dirt on your face so you don't shine light a new penny in the light."

"Boat?" inquired Thompson. "I don't do boats Sarg, I can't swim."

"You will get in a boat if I have to strap you in myself," exclaimed Sgt. Holmes. "Guppy, you're responsible for Thompson while he is in the boat, make sure he doesn't drown. I don't want to write a letter home to his mother that says, Killed in Action: Drowned in River."

Guppy laughed, "Alright Sarg, I'll find him an innertube from an old tire near the farmhouse he can put around his waist."

"Wait, I got something better," said Jenkins. "Let's get him a set of those new inflatable water wings you get for children."

Laughter ensued around the group as Thompsons face flushed with embarrassment.

"Not funny guys," said Thompson. "I just never really learned."

"Alright, alright, alright," said Sgt. Holmes. "Enough of the jokes. Focus on the mission. Be ready to leave at 2100."

The night was dark and cold as the platoon gathered near the village of Renkum, close to Arnhem in the Netherlands. Operation Pegasus was about to commence. They needed to evacuate Allied soldiers who had been trapped behind German lines since the Battle of Arnhem. The bond among the soldiers was evident, even in the face of danger, as they exchanged banter and conversation while preparing for the operation.

"Oi, Jenkins, you ready for this one?" shouted Parsons over the sound of rustling gear.

Jenkins smirked, checking his weapon one last time. "Always ready, mate. Just like back in training."

Sergeant Holmes stepped forward to brief the soldiers. "Alright, lads, listen up. We're going to help these brave souls get back to our lines. Keep your wits about you, and stay quiet. We don't want any trouble with those Jerry patrols."

As they set off on their mission, the soldiers moved silently through the darkness, guided by the Dutch Resistance members who knew the area well. Despite the tension in the air, they kept their spirits high with light-hearted banter.

"I heard this Dutch Resistance is top-notch," said Harrison, a young private. "They've been helping these guys for months, like guardian angels."

"Guardian angels or not, I hope they know the way," remarked Jenkins with a grin. "Wouldn't want to end up in the German lap of luxury."

Amidst the jokes, the soldiers couldn't help but feel the weight of the mission they were undertaking. These men they were helping had been in hiding for weeks, facing the constant threat of capture or worse.

"Can you imagine what they've been through?" murmured Davis, another soldier. "Stuck behind enemy lines, never knowing if they'd make it out alive."

"Damn right," replied Parsons solemnly. "But tonight, we're going to change that. We'll get 'em out of here, safe and sound."

As they approached the crossing point on the Rhine, tension grew among the soldiers. The darkness hid the river from view, but they knew the treacherous waters that lay ahead.

"You see anything, Thompson?" asked Jenkins, peering into the night.

"Quiet for now," Thompson whispered back. "We've got to wait for the signal."

Suddenly, a series of torch flashes in the distance illuminated the sky. "There it is, lads. That's our signal," Thompson said, relief evident in his voice.

The soldiers boarded the rowboats, and as they began to paddle across the Rhine, the seriousness of the situation settled upon them. They were crossing into enemy territory, with the fate of these stranded soldiers in their hands.

"Steady, boys. We're almost there," Thompson urged, his eyes scanning the shoreline.

As they reached the north bank, they were met by the Dutch Resistance members, guiding the evaders to safety. The tension was broken by a shout of triumph from one of the men they were rescuing.

"We made it! We actually made it!" the soldier exclaimed.

The soldiers couldn't help but smile at the joy and relief in the man's voice. They knew they had made a difference, that their bravery and determination had brought hope to these weary souls.

Back on the south bank, the atmosphere was jubilant. Parsons and Jenkins shared a moment of quiet reflection, knowing that they had been a part of something bigger than themselves.

"We did it," Parsons said, clapping Jenkins on the back. "We helped them get home."

Jenkins nodded, his eyes shining with pride. "Yeah, we did. And I'll never forget this night as long as I live."

The British soldiers would eventually continue their mission, evacuating more stranded men over the coming weeks. A second operation would end up not being as successful. As John and his platoon looked back on Operation Pegasus, they knew that they had been a part of something truly extraordinary.

Over the next hour and a half, the combined forces all of the men were rescued, and the boats returned back to the farmhouse behind the hill where medics, food and water were waiting for the stranded soldiers. Pegasus was a success. Later, the men would eventually be flown by to England to rejoin the men who had escaped during Operation Berlin.

John and the rest of his platoon took to sleeping and eating in the barn south of the farmhouse. A dimly lit gas lamp their only light as to not attract enemy fire. While most of his platoon laid down to rest, John's thoughts reflected back to thinking about Mary. From his knapsack, he pulled out a pencil and a small writing tablet. He had hoped the address to the Sant Bartomeu, the Catholic cathedral would accept his letters and hold them for Mary.

As his fellow countrymen found much needed sleep in that barn, under the dim light of the gas lamp, John started writing a letter to Mary.

"Dear Mary,

I hope this letter finds you well and brings a smile to your face. It has been far too long since we last saw each other, and not a day goes by that you are not on my mind. The memories we shared in Paris, walking along the Seine, have remained etched in my heart, and I long for the day when we can create new memories together.

As I sit here, surrounded by the chaos of war, I find solace in our love and the dreams we shared. We are in Holland along the Rhine liberating the Dutch people and saving our comrades. I remember your question about D-Day, and it reminds me of the courage and sacrifice of the men who fought alongside me.

I vividly remember the fear and anticipation as we parachuted into France, the deafening sounds of gunfire and explosions, and the camaraderie that kept us moving forward. It was a day of both triumph and tragedy, as so many lives were lost on those shores. But through it all, I held onto the hope that we were part of something bigger, something that would change the course of history.

Mary, you are my strength during trying times. Your love and support fuels my determination to fight for a better future. I often thought of you as I navigate the challenges of war, drawing inspiration from the dreams we shared in Paris. You asked about my dreams after the war, and I can tell you that they revolve around a peaceful life with you, filled with love, laughter, and the simple joys of everyday moments.

I hope you and your family are safe amongst the grove of orange and olive trees. I would love to see them one day. I yearn for the day when I can hold you in my arms again, when the war is just a distant memory, and we can build a life together. Until then, know that I carry you with me, your presence guiding me through the darkest of days. Stay strong, my love, and keep faith in our future. We will endure these trials and emerge victorious, for our love is a force that can conquer anything.

With all my heart,
Love, John."

John folded the letter and put the name and address of the church on the front. He would ask the officer in charge of the post if there was a possibility it would reach Palma, that it would find its way to Sóller, to Mary. He lay his head down on his knapsack and fell asleep, the low, distant, thunderous sound of the war resonating in the background. He closed his eyes, trying to replace the images and thoughts of the war with those of Mary strolling through a vineyard in a sun dress, sunlight glistening off her skin, her long black braids of hair twirling in the wind as the waves of the Mediterranean kisses the cliffs and shores nearby with a thunderous noise. He imagined the war in the background as that noise and fell asleep.

John and his platoon would spend a few weeks assisting with the liberation of Holland, playing a pivotal role holding a 16-mile stretch of road through enemy territory from Eindhoven to Grave.

Their last morning came early. John awoke to Guppy and Jenkins shaking everyone awake.

"Wake up sleepy head!" said Guppy. "Sgt. Holmes says we need to be ready to assemble at 0900, a few hours are all you get for shuteye today."

Wilson rubbed his eyes and exclaimed, "Man, you woke me up in the middle of a great dream."

Guppy said, "She wasn't that pretty Wilson."

"It was a horse!" shouted Wilson.

"Your girlfriend is a horse?" asked Jenkins.

"No, you idiot," exclaimed Jenkins. "I was dreaming about riding my horse back in Tennessee. We have a number of thoroughbreds that my father is grooming for the Derby. I was riding Blazing Doll, offspring of Fiery Blaze and Baby Doll. A beautiful dark red horse with a black mane & tail with four white feet. She stood at almost 15 hands high. Strong-willed and muscular, she was the fastest horse I ever rode. When you saw her running in the pasture among the other horses on the farm, it was as if Poseidon himself was riding her. I miss her."

"Sorry," said Guppy. "We all miss something. John's been writing to his girl half the night. Wilson was playing solitaire and I was thinking about where I wanted to go when the war is over. I guess we all had a bit of trouble sleeping."

"Rise and shine, ladies," shouted Sgt. Holmes. "Prepare to load up, we are headed back to France to rest and get new orders. You will all get a 3-day pass in Paris."

Excited spread throughout Easy as word of leave made it from platoon to platoon. The sun, barely awake, was rising above the tree line to the east of camp and the hazy clouds that shrouded the night sky were all but gone. John and his platoon gathered their packs and supplies and headed toward the convoy of trucks that would carry them to Paris.

As they pulled out of the area, they left a part of the war that would stand in memory and after a failed second attempt to rescue soldiers, further ground across would not be gained until much later in the war. They felt a sense of anxiety over the soldiers still hiding in the German-occupied territory. The resistance would continue to aid them throughout the fall and winter until Allied forces pushed forward.

THE MARKET

It was a bustling morning in the center of Sóller as Mary and her mother, Maria, made their way to the market by horse and wagon. The air was filled with the fragrant aroma of fresh produce and the sounds of vendors calling out their offerings. They needed some vegetables and other supplies for bottling and storing wine. They got down from their carriage and started to stroll up and down the market. As they walked, they noticed a familiar figure, Catalina, sitting with her mother in front of the church, her mother's arms around her, and her face stained with tears.

Concerned, Mary and Maria approached Catalina and her mother Isabella, offering their support. Catalina's mother explained through her own tears that Catalina had received devastating news about her British soldier love, Alan Mason, who served in the 8th Army. He had been killed in the second battle of El Alamein months ago. The weight of the loss hung heavily in the air, and sorrow seemed to envelop them all.

As Catalina's mother tried to console her daughter, Mary reached out and held Catalina's hand gently, offering her own words of comfort. "Catalina, I can't imagine the pain you're going through right now. Losing someone we love is never easy, especially in these times of war. I am sure Alan was a brave soldier, and his sacrifice will never be forgotten."

Catalina looked up; her eyes filled with grief. "Mary, it's just so unfair. We were planning a future together, dreaming of a life filled with love and happiness. And now he's gone, and I'm left with this emptiness."

Mary nodded, her heart aching for her friend. "I understand how you feel, Catalina. I too have known the pain of separation and loss. But we must hold onto the memories we shared, the love that was so real. Alan lives on in your heart, and his spirit will guide you through these difficult times."

Catalina's tears continued to flow, but a glimmer of strength appeared in her eyes. She wiped her cheeks with the back of her hand and took a deep breath. "You're right, Mary. Alan wouldn't want me to dwell in sadness. He would want me to live my life fully and honor his memory. I will find the strength to carry on."

Mary's mother, Maria, wrapped her arms around Catalina, offering her motherly warmth and support. "You're not alone, Catalina. We are here for you, every step of the way. Lean on us, and together, we will find solace and strength."

Catalina had grown up in the beautiful town of Sóller, nestled among the scenic landscapes of Mallorca. She was known for her vibrant spirit, infectious laughter, and a curiosity that seemed to know no bounds. From an early age, Catalina had a thirst for knowledge and a desire to explore the world beyond the familiar streets of her hometown.

As she grew older, Catalina's love for learning led her to pursue higher education in London. She embraced the vibrant city, immersing herself in its rich culture and diverse communities. It was during her time in London that she crossed paths with Alan Mason, a British soldier stationed in the city. Their connection was instant, their hearts intertwined in a love that transcended borders and wartime uncertainties.

But as fate would have it, the outbreak of war abruptly disrupted their plans for a future together. Catalina made the difficult decision to return to her hometown of Sóller, a journey that was fraught with danger and uncertainty. Sailing through the perilous waters of the Strait of Gibraltar, she faced the harsh realities of wartime travel, clinging to hope amidst the chaos.

Months turned into agonizing waiting, as Catalina held onto the sliver of hope that Alan would return unscathed from the battles he fought. However, the devastating news of his demise in the second battle of El Alamein shattered her world. The weight of grief bore down upon her, threatening to consume her spirit.

Alan Mason was a young man with a spirit as vibrant as the city of Manchester where he was born and raised. Alan grew up surrounded by the hustle and bustle of his father's successful business and his mother's creative flair as a fashion designer. Despite his privileged upbringing, Alan possessed a down-to-earth nature and an insatiable thirst for adventure.

Growing up near the River Irwell, Alan developed a deep love for rowing. His passion and dedication led him to Oxford University, where he earned a place on the prestigious rowing team. With his natural leadership skills and unwavering determination, he eventually captained the team during his third year, fostering a spirit of camaraderie and pushing his teammates to achieve greatness.

However, the world around Alan was changing rapidly. As the dark clouds of war loomed over Europe, the promising trajectory of his university life took an unexpected turn. The outbreak of World War II interrupted his final year at Oxford, and without hesitation, Alan answered the call to duty. He enlisted in the British army, joining the Western Army and deploying to North Africa in Tunisia.

As a soldier in a foreign land, Alan faced the harsh realities of war head-on. The scorching desert sun and the ever-present dangers of battle became his new reality. Yet, amidst the chaos and uncertainty, his sense of duty and the bonds formed with his fellow soldiers sustained him. Alan's leadership skills and determination on the rowing team translated seamlessly into the battlefield, earning him the respect and admiration of his company.

Although Alan's journey in North Africa was cut short in the second battle of El Alamein when artillery fire from Italian and German forces struck near his position. His legacy will live on through the memories and stories shared by those who served alongside him. He was remembered not only for his prowess as a rower and leader but also for his unwavering bravery and the selflessness with which he faced adversity.

Mary helped Catalina to her feet and said, "Let's go, walk with us, take in the fresh air and fragrance of the market. It will make you feel better. We can go into the church tomorrow and light a candle for Alan."

"Okay," said Catalina as she wiped the tears from her face with her hand and stood up next to her mother. "Thanks for your kindness and support. I know that God has a plan for me and for Alan. He will be missed."

They walked down the row of vendors and Maria said, "Do you think the melons will be ripe? I haven't had a good melon yet this year."

"Sergio sells the best melons, his stand is on the end of the row," said Catalina.
"He grows them in the valley where they get plenty of sun. Let's walk down there and see what he has."

The women walked down the row to wear Sergio had set up his vegetable and fruit stand. Sergio was an older gentleman in his mid-50s who lived in the valley east of Sóller. Many years earlier his grandfather had left him a hundred acres of land in the valley that was passed down through his family. It had never been more than a simple farm and growing up around the turn of the century, Sergio has always told his grandfather he would make it a beautiful orchard. Sprawling across the valley, the southernly winds off the Mediterranean wafting through the valley and the right amount of rain and sunshine provided the perfect environment for practically anything he wanted to grow.

His wife, Serena, had passed twenty years earlier around the age of thirty-five after she contracted cholera during a time when it swept through the island of Palma. He named many of the fruits and vegetables after her in her honor such as Serena's Sweet Melons and Serena's Strawberries.

His stand was located in the back of a large wooden cart that he built himself from the hardwood trees that he cleared to plant his vegetables and fruit. Using bricks and wood shelving, he engineered a retractable staged display so that you can see all that he had to offer from his cart.

The women approaching, Sergio lifted his eyes and exclaimed, "Good morning, ladies. What a beautiful day it is today!"

"Awe," said Isabella, "you're always in such good spirits. I have a surprise for you today. Do you remember Maria's daughter, Mary?"

"Ah, of course," said Sergio. "I remember Mary! How could I forget the young lady who used to run through my orchard, picking strawberries with such enthusiasm? It's been a while, hasn't it, Mary?"

"It certainly has, Sergio!" said Mary blushing. "Your strawberries were always the best. I used to fill my little basket with them and bring them home for my mother to make jam."

"Yes, those were the days," he replied. "Your mother's jam was always a delight, Maria. Speaking of which, have you tried my Serena's Sweet Melons this year? They're the best I've ever grown, and I think you'll enjoy them."

"We haven't had a good melon yet this year, Sergio. We were just talking about that on our way here," said Mary.

"Sergio's melons are the juiciest and most flavorful, aren't they?" exclaimed Catalina. "I always make sure to get some whenever I'm at the market."

"Indeed, they are I," said Isabella. "I remember when we used to visit your orchard as children, Sergio. Your fruits were like a taste of paradise."

"Those were cherished times, indeed. I'm glad my farm and produce have brought joy to so many over the years," said Sergio.

"Your farm is truly remarkable, Sergio., said Mary. "I've always admired the care and dedication you put into growing these fruits and vegetables year after year. It seems God has blessed your hands and land with his bountiful harvest."

"Thank you, Mary. It's a labor of love, just like the memory of my dear Serena. Naming some of the produce after her was a way to keep her spirit alive, you know," said Sergio.

"It's a beautiful tribute," said Catalina. "I can see how much love and passion you pour into your work."

"Well, enough about me. How can I help you lovely ladies today?" asked Sergio. "Would you like some of Serena's Sweet Melons or perhaps some of her strawberries?"

"Oh, I'd love some of the strawberries," exclaimed Isabella. "They remind me of our childhood days."

"Count me in for some melons too, please. They're perfect for this warm weather," said Catalina.

"I'll take a bit of both," said Mary. "Your fruits always bring back wonderful memories."

Beaming ear-to-ear Sergio replied, "It's my pleasure to bring joy to you all. Here, let me get some for each of you."

As Sergio skillfully picked the ripest strawberries and the juiciest melons, the women continued chatting, reminiscing about their past visits to Sergio's orchard and sharing stories of their families. The warm sun and the vibrant colors of the fruits and vegetables created a cheerful atmosphere, and in that moment, they felt a deep sense of community and connection.

After purchasing their fruits, they bid farewell to Sergio, their hearts filled with gratitude for the memories and the flavors he had brought into their lives. As they strolled away from his stand, the friendship between the women grew stronger, and they looked forward to returning to the market and sharing more moments of joy in the days to come.

With their baskets of strawberries and melons in hand, Mary and Maria bid Catalina and Isabella a warm goodbye and continued their stroll through the market. They stopped by the stalls selling fresh herbs and spices, carefully selecting the ones they needed for their winemaking back home. The scent of basil, thyme, and lavender filled the air, and the vibrant colors of the spices added to the market's lively atmosphere.

Next, they made their way to the cheese vendor, where they picked up a few rounds of their favorite artisanal cheese to enjoy with their evening meals. The vendor, Franco, an old friend of Maria's, greeted them warmly and shared stories of his recent travels to the neighboring towns, where he had sourced the finest cheeses.

One last stop was the mercantile across from the church where they placed an order for wine bottles and corks to arrive in a few weeks when it was time to bottle the wine.

With their shopping complete, Mary and Maria made their way back to the horse and buggy waiting for them near the market entrance. The horse, a gentle creature named Bella, always seemed to recognize them and nuzzled Mary's hand as she climbed aboard. Maria took the reins, guiding Bella along the familiar path back home.

As they rode through the charming streets of Sóller, they exchanged greetings with familiar faces, and Mary's heart swelled with a sense of belonging. The town's colorful buildings, adorned with blooming flowerpots, stood as a testament to the resilience of its people, who had weathered the storms of war and continued to thrive.

Arriving at their family home nestled among the vineyards, Mary and Maria unloaded their baskets and supplies. They exchanged a knowing smile as they saw the vines, heavy with grapes, waiting to be harvested. Their yearly tradition of winemaking was about to begin, a labor of love that brought them closer together as a family.

In the coming weeks, as the cool temperatures of the fall and the migration of the birds had begun, Mary and Maria would spend hours tending to the vines, carefully picking the ripest grapes, and transforming them into the rich and aromatic wine that was a symbol of their heritage. It was a time of hard work and celebration, and they would share laughter, stories, and meals together as they continued the tradition passed down through generations.

As they worked in the vineyards, the sun would dip below the horizon, casting a golden glow on the rolling hills of Sóller. The air would be filled with the sweet scent of grapes and the sound of laughter and chatter as neighboring families joined in the harvest. The harvest season was not just a time of toil; it was a time of unity, as the entire community came together to celebrate the bounty of the land.

During the long days, Mary would often steal a moment to look at her mother, her hands weathered from years of labor, her eyes reflecting the wisdom of age. In those moments, Mary felt a deep sense of gratitude for the values her mother had instilled in her—the importance of hard work, the love for the land, and the beauty of preserving their heritage.

In the evenings, after the hard day's work was done, they would gather around the kitchen table, their faces flushed from the sun and their hands stained with the purple hue of the grapes. The air would be filled with the aroma of hearty stews and freshly baked bread, and they would toast to another successful day of winemaking.

As the weeks passed, the vineyard would slowly transform, its vibrant green leaves turning into hues of red and gold. The grapes, once plump and green, would become clusters of deep purple, ready to be harvested. Each step of the winemaking process was a dance of precision and tradition, with Maria passing down her knowledge to Mary, just as it had been done for generations before them.

While working side by side, Mary and Maria would share stories of their ancestors, the trials they had faced, and the triumphs they had celebrated. They would talk about their dreams for the future and the legacy they hoped to leave behind. In those moments, the vineyard became not just a place of labor but a sacred space where memories and aspirations intertwined.

Mary often talked about John, telling her mother where he was born, where he went to school and all manners of questions. She especially liked to recall their days in Paris and the adventures they had during his stay.

"I am so happy for you," said Maria. "I hope he stays safe and journeys here to our home. We will welcome him with open arms. He will be part of our family."

At the end of their work, when the last barrel was filled and the last grape picked, they would sit under the starlit sky, sipping last year's vintage. Their faces would be illuminated by the soft glow of the moon, and in that moment, they would feel the deep connection to their roots, to their family, and to the land they called home. And as they raised their glasses in a toast, they would know that the true essence of their winemaking tradition was not just in the drink they held but, in the love, and bond they shared as mother and daughter, carrying forward the legacy of their family's journey through time.

HARRY'S

The sun was setting over the horizon as John and his platoon trudged back to camp outside Caraten after weeks of intense battle in the rugged terrain of Holland. Fatigue weighed heavy on their shoulders, but their spirits were lifted knowing they had survived their mission. As they approached their camp, the familiar faces of their fellow soldiers greeted them, offering nods of recognition and camaraderie. They had formed a tight bond through the trials of war, and each step brought them closer to much-needed rest and respite.

Although they had no new orders, the three days of leave that Sergeant Holmes told them they received, was welcomed by the weary soldiers, and they couldn't have been more excited. Paris, the city of lights, awaited them with its promise of adventure, beauty, and a break from the harsh realities of the battlefield. Conversation buzzed among the platoon as they discussed their plans for the short but precious time they would spend in the enchanting city.

"I heard there's a fantastic jazz club on Rue Daunou called Harry's New York Bar," said Wilson, a fellow soldier in John's platoon. "They say it's a taste of home, and they serve the best cocktails in town."

John's eyes lit up with excitement. The thought of sipping a well-crafted drink in the heart of Paris brought a smile to his weary face. "That sounds like the perfect place to unwind," he replied. "And you never know, maybe you will meet some pretty girls there."

The idea of meeting local Parisian women filled the group with playful banter and laughter.

As the platoon members gathered in the courtyard, the memories of their time in London at Garret's pub came rushing back. Jenkins, with a mischievous grin, nudged Guppy and said, "Remember that French lady who threw her drink in your face, Guppy? That was a classic!"

Guppy rolled his eyes and chuckled. "Yeah, thanks to your brilliant pickup line, Jenkins. You said it was foolproof!"

Jenkins laughed heartily. "Well, it worked for me, but I guess not everyone has my charm!"

Wilson joined in the banter. "I still can't believe you tried that line, Guppy. 'Do you have a map? Because I keep getting lost in your eyes.' Really?"

Guppy shrugged, a sheepish grin on his face. "Hey, it seemed like a good idea at the time! Besides, the look on her face was worth it."

John chimed in, adding to the laughter. "I can't believe you're still using pickup lines, Jenkins. Haven't you learned by now that genuine conversation and a good sense of humor work better?"

Jenkins playfully nudged John back. "Hey, I've had my fair share of success too, you know!"

Parsons, who had been listening to the stories with amusement, interjected. "Well, it's a good thing you guys had each other for entertainment. Just remember, we're in France now, so you might want to brush up on some French phrases if you want to impress the ladies here."

Guppy grinned. "Don't worry, Parsons. I've got a few better lines up my sleeve this time. I'm not making that mistake again!"

As they continued to exchange stories and laughter, the bond between the platoon members grew stronger. They knew that in the midst of war, moments like these were precious, and they were grateful for the camaraderie that helped carry them through the challenges ahead. "Unlike London, maybe this time you will find one Guppy that won't throw a drink in your face," said Wilson.

"Hey," yelled Guppy. "Next time I won't trust Jenkins to give me pickup lines in French. I have no idea what I said to her, but she did not like it."

Each soldier shared his hopes and dreams for the upcoming adventure, and for a moment, the weight of the war was lifted as they looked forward to the prospect of a carefree evening in the city of romance.

As they settled into their camp for the night, the anticipation of their Parisian escapade mingled with gratitude for their safety and the hope for a brighter tomorrow. The stars above seemed to twinkle with approval, as if the universe itself was conspiring to grant them a few days of reprieve from the chaos of war. With the memories of their recent battles still fresh in their minds, they allowed themselves to be carried away by the enchanting allure of Paris, where dreams and possibilities awaited them around every corner.

The morning sun cast a golden glow over the camp outside Caraten as Sergeant Holmes called the platoon to order. The soldiers gathered around, their eyes attentive and eager for their well-deserved 3-day leave in Paris. The sergeant's voice was firm, yet tinged with warmth as he addressed his men.

"Alright, boys, listen up," he began. "You've done us proud out there on the field, and you've earned yourselves a few days of rest and recreation. But remember, we're still in a war zone, so stay sharp and stick together. Paris may be a beautiful city, but it's not without its dangers."

The platoon shouted in agreement. They knew the importance of looking out for one another, especially in a place where the war's impact was still visible in the villages around Paris in the form of rubble-strewn streets and buildings bearing scars of conflict.

With a nod from Sergeant Holmes, the soldiers were dismissed, and a wave of excitement rippled through the ranks. They hastily made their way to the waiting trucks and jeeps that would take them on their journey to the City of Light.

As they boarded the vehicles, the platoon exchanged animated conversations about their plans for the upcoming days. Some spoke of visiting famous landmarks like the Eiffel Tower and Notre-Dame Cathedral, while others were eager to explore the charming streets and cafés of Montmartre. Sergeant Holmes, seated in the front of one of the trucks, listened to his men's chatter with a faint smile, proud of their resilience and camaraderie.

"Alright, lads, settle down," he called out, his voice cutting through the excitement. "Remember, we've got to keep our wits about us. Paris might be a beauty, but it's still a city in recovering from German occupation."

The platoon nodded in agreement, reassured by their sergeant's watchful eye. With a final check to ensure everyone was accounted for, the convoy set off, rolling through the war-torn countryside towards their much-anticipated destination.

As the trucks rattled along the uneven roads, the sights of destruction were a stark reminder of the war's toll. Yet, amidst the devastation, the soldiers held onto the hope that in Paris they would find a brief respite from the harsh realities of battle.

Conversation among the platoon continued during the journey, filled with anticipation and eagerness to explore the city's wonders. They shared stories and exchanged tips on the best places to visit. John, leaning against the truck's metal frame, couldn't help but feel a sense of excitement and gratitude for the chance to experience Paris again, this time with his fellow soldiers, a bond forged not only on the battlefield but also amidst the magic of a city that had endured so much. His thoughts traveled back to the days of exploring the city with Mary. He wondered what she was doing, was she okay, and how much he missed her tender touch and soft kisses.

As they neared the outskirts of Paris, the Eiffel Tower came into view, its majestic silhouette rising against the sky. John's heart swelled with pride and wonder, knowing that he and his platoon were about to embark on an unforgettable adventure in the City of Light.

As the trucks and jeeps dropped off the platoon near Avenue de l'Opéra and Rue de la Paix, the soldiers stepped onto the Parisian streets with a sense of awe and wonder. The bustling city greeted them with its charm, and they couldn't wait to explore. With John and his platoon leading the way, they began their stroll up Rue Daunou, their eyes taking in the lively atmosphere and the vibrant energy of the city.

"Look at this place," said Jenkins, his eyes wide with excitement. "I never thought I'd see Paris, and here we are!"

"Isn't it something?" replied Guppy, a smile spreading across his face. "This city has got it all—history, culture, and the best damn food you'll ever taste."

As they continued their walk, they arrived at the famous New York Bar, now renamed Harry's New York Bar, known for its legendary status as a spot where expatriates and tourists felt at home. John couldn't help but recall the bar's fascinating history, which he had heard while in Paris with Mary.

"Hey, did you guys know the story behind Harry's New York Bar?" he asked, eager to share the intriguing tale.

"I think I've heard bits and pieces," Parsons replied, curious. "Tell us!"

"Alright, here's the deal," John began. "It was originally owned by a former American jockey named Tod Sloan in 1911. He brought over a bar from Manhattan, dismantled it, and shipped it all the way to Paris. He hired a barman from Scotland named Harry MacElhone to run it."

"Wow, talk about dedication," Wilson chimed in, impressed.

"Yeah, but they say his lavish lifestyle eventually got the better of him, and he had to sell the bar," John continued. "That's when MacElhone took it over, added his name and made it into the legendary spot we know today."

The platoon stood outside the iconic bar, admiring its rich history and its connection to the thriving expatriate community in Paris.

"Sounds like the perfect spot for us to enjoy some downtime," Guppy said with a grin.

"Definitely," John agreed.

With laughter and camaraderie, the soldiers walked through the famed doors of Harry's, smiling, and talking among themselves.

As the platoon stepped into Harry's New York Bar, they were immediately enveloped in an atmosphere that felt both lively and comforting. The dimly lit interior was adorned with vintage decor, giving it a timeless and classic charm. Mahogany-paneled walls exuded warmth, while the soft glow of Tiffany lamps cast a warm hue across the space. The bar itself, a beautiful mahogany structure, stretched along one side of the room, lined with gleaming bottles of liquor. Above it, a collection of faded photographs and memorabilia told tales of the bar's rich history and the characters who had passed through its doors over the years.

The chatter of fellow patrons mingled with the smooth jazz music playing softly in the background, creating a soothing ambiance. The air was filled with the delightful aroma of well-mixed cocktails and the occasional whiff of a Cuban cigar. The platoon found themselves amidst a diverse crowd of expatriates, artists, writers, and locals, all engaged in lively conversations and laughter.

As they settled in at a corner table, the soldiers felt a sense of ease and comfort wash over them. The bartenders, clad in crisp white shirts and bowties, greeted them warmly and recommended some of the bar's signature cocktails. With drinks in hand, they raised their glasses in a toast to newfound adventures in the heart of Paris.

The cozy, intimate setting of Harry's New York Bar welcomed them with open arms, an in that moment, the war and its hardships seemed distant, and for a brief time, they were simply young men in a legendary bar, ready to make memories that would forever be etched in their hearts.

Amidst the charming ambiance of Harry's New York Bar, they toasted to their long-awaited three-day leave in Paris. John, with a mischievous grin, raised his glass and exclaimed, "Gentlemen, here's to leaving our rifles behind for a while and enjoying the City of Light!"

Laughter erupted among the soldiers as they shared their plans for the next few days. Wilson, always the adventurous one, exclaimed, "I've heard of this famous cabaret called the Moulin Rouge! Who's in for some can-can dancing and a night of revelry?"

"Count me in!" said Guppy, his eyes gleaming with excitement. "And don't forget Montmartre! I've heard it's the perfect spot to meet some pretty French girls."

John, who was nicknamed "Rebel" for his Southern roots, playfully added, "Well, while you all dance the night away, I'm thinking of visiting some art galleries and museums. I want to soak in more of the culture and history this city has to offer."

"You'd rather look at paintings than beautiful women, Rebel?" Jackson teased with a wink. "Don't worry; we'll make sure you have plenty of eye candy during our time here."

"Take it easy on him," said Guppy. "He's beholden to his Spanish flame, Mary who traveled back to Palma."

Sgt. Holmes said, "I'm with Corporal Reynolds, not sure my wife would want me gallivanting around Paris with strange women. I'll accompany you on your sight-seeing."

"Reynolds," Sergeant Holmes exclaimed interrupting the conversation. "Tell me about Mary."

Corporal Reynolds smiled, feeling a warmth in sharing his thoughts about Mary with his platoon leader. "Well, Sergeant, Mary is like a breath of fresh air. She's got this vibrant spirit that can light up a room. She's passionate about art and the beauty of her hometown, Sóller. She's smart, funny, and incredibly caring. She's been a constant source of strength for me during these tough times, and I can't wait to see her again."

Sergeant Holmes nodded approvingly, "Sounds like you've found something special, Reynolds. I'm glad you have someone waiting for you. It gives you something to hold on to during the rough moments."

The platoon members smiled, happy to see their friend so taken with someone special. Jenkins chimed in, "Are you going to bring her a souvenir from Paris, like a little Eiffel Tower?"

John chuckled, "She lived here for a short time, I would be more inclined to bring her a nice bottle of wine. You know, she lives on a vineyard and is skilled in making wine."

Wilson grinned, "You better make sure to get her a good bottle. You don't want to disappoint the girl."

"Don't worry, Wilson," John replied with a playful glint in his eye. "I won't let her down."

As the conversation continued, the platoon shared their own stories of loved ones back home and dreams of what the future might hold. They spoke of plans for after the war, the places they wanted to visit, and the people they longed to see again.

Sergeant Holmes listened intently, knowing that these conversations were essential for maintaining morale within the platoon. In the midst of war, talking about loved ones and future aspirations reminded them all of the life they were fighting to protect and the hope that kept them going.

As the afternoon progressed, they continued to share their aspirations for their Parisian adventure. Jenkins, the platoon's resident foodie, couldn't wait to sample the finest French cuisine. "I've heard the croissants here are to die for," he said with a mouth-watering grin. "And let's not forget about the cheese! I plan on trying every variety I can get my hands on."

Sergeant Holmes, leaning back in his chair, listened to the banter with a smile. "Alright, boys, let's make sure you stick together and keep an eye on each other," he said in a more serious tone. " We've got three days to make the most of it, so let's enjoy ourselves responsibly."

The platoon's conversations and light-hearted banter continued well into the afternoon. They shared stories of their families back home and the dreams they had for the future. Amidst the jokes and laughter, all thoughts of the battlefield seemed to settle in the distance, at least for a while.

As the soldiers finished their drinks, they stepped out onto the bustling streets of Paris, eager to explore the city and make memories that would last a lifetime. With the Eiffel Tower standing erect in the distance, in defiance of the occupation it had seen, they felt a renewed sense of hope and a reminder that, even in the midst of war, life still offered moments of joy and wonder. And so, arm in arm, they set off into the afternoon, ready to embrace the magic of Paris and all the adventures it held in store for them.

As the afternoon sunbathed the cobbled streets of Paris with a warm glow, the platoon eventually decided to venture out into the city to explore and enjoy the sights.

Sergeant Holmes, a seasoned and charismatic leader, suggested a site-seeing adventure for some of the platoon members. John and Parsons, two young soldiers eager to experience Parisian culture, eagerly joined him. With John leading the way, they embarked on their adventure through the picturesque streets.

Their first stop was the Eiffel Tower, an iconic symbol of Paris. As they marveled at the grand structure and took in breathtaking views from the top, John regaled them with fascinating historical anecdotes about the tower and the city that he discovered during his time with Mary. His thoughts traveling back to those days holding her hand and dreaming of days gone by and their future.

Next, they strolled along the Seine River, where the beauty of the city's architecture, reflected in the water, left them in awe. John pointed out various landmarks and shared captivating stories about the rich history of Paris.

Meanwhile, the rest of the platoon, led by Corporal Davis, had a different plan in mind. They made their way to the famous Ritz hotel bar, hoping to find some local girls to charm or perhaps catch a glimpse of the legendary Ernest Hemingway, who had earned a reputation for his love of martinis and his time spent at the bar. Shortly after the Germans had pulled out of Paris, it was recorded that Ernest Hemingway showed up to liberate the bar.

Serving as a war correspondent, On August 25th, he arrived at the hotel on the picturesque Place Vendome in Paris, leading a group of Resistance fighters in a Jeep equipped with a mounted machine gun. Upon entering the hotel, he declared his personal mission to liberate it and its bar, known to have been frequented by high-ranking Nazi officials like Hermann Goering and Joseph Goebbels.

The hotel's manager, Claude Auzello, approached him, and he demanded to know the whereabouts of the Germans, stating that he had come to free the Ritz. Auzello informed him that the Germans had long since departed and insisted that he couldn't allow him to enter with a weapon.

Hemingway agreed to stow the gun in the Jeep and returned to the bar, where he is said to have ordered and enjoyed 51 dry martinis. He carried himself with such authority in his uniform that many mistook him for a general, as recalled by the Ritz's head barman, Colin Field.

Hemingway, accompanied by his men, conducted a thorough search of the hotel, finding two prisoners and a fine stock of brandy in the cellar. As they inspected the roof and upper floors, they discovered only sheets drying in the wind, but they still fired bullets at them as a precaution in case any Germans were hiding behind them.

Later, Hemingway expressed his revulsion at the idea that the Germans had defiled the room he shared with his lover, Mary Welsh, whom he would marry in 1946.

As the soldiers entered the Ritz, the opulence and elegance of the surroundings immediately struck them. The bar was a hub of activity, with people laughing, chatting, and savoring the moment. The platoon members tried their best to blend in with the sophisticated crowd, hoping to catch the attention of some Parisian ladies.

The atmosphere buzzed with excitement and anticipation, and everyone kept an eye out for Hemingway, who was known for his larger-than-life presence. Though they didn't spot the writer that day, they felt his spirit linger in the air, as if his legacy had become intertwined with the very essence of the bar.

Back on the streets of Paris, Sergeant Holmes, John, and Parsons continued their sightseeing journey. They passed by quaint cafes, art galleries, and charming boutiques, soaking in every aspect of the enchanting city. John, with his deep knowledge of the history and culture of Paris, made the experience all the more special for his companions.

As the day drew to a close, both groups of the platoon reconvened, each having had their share of adventure and excitement. They exchanged stories and laughs, relishing the unique experiences they had enjoyed in the heart of Paris.

Little did they know that these moments of respite would become cherished memories, reminding them of the beauty of life amidst the chaos of war. In that fleeting afternoon, Paris had worked its magic on the platoon, leaving an indelible mark on their hearts and souls.

As the evening progressed, the men found a small café to have a late dinner. After four years of occupation, Paris was still short on food, many families sticking to the rations given to them or acquiring more delectable items on the black market.

Cafés and restaurants depended on local farms and markets for ingredients and supplies. The city was slowly recovering however, things were still in short supply.

American and British soldiers celebrating a few days of respite in the City of Lights had deep pockets and jump started the economy. They frequented the bars and pubs, burlesque shows, theater, and hotels.

After dinner, Sergeant Holmes and the platoon bid their goodnights, and proceeded back to their hotel. They had made arrangements to stay at the Hotel Meurice on rue de Rivoli. The hotel was the German occupation headquarters for Greater Paris. In fact, it was the location where General von Choltitz was asked by a foreign diplomat if he wanted to be remembered as the man that destroyed or saved the City of Lights. Hitler had ordered explosives to be placed under Paris monuments such as the bridges of the Seine, the Louvre, the Eiffel Tower, and the Senate.

The Hotel Meurice was an elegant and grand hotel, adorned with beautiful columns and tapestries in the lobby and salons on the second floor. The rooms were spacious compared to the hostels and other hotels in the city.

The soldiers leisurely strolled under the gentle glow of the moonlight, making their way to the hotel on the street. After exchanging a few words and nods of acknowledgement, they retired to their respective rooms for the evening. It was a well-deserved break, and they had savored every moment of their first day of leave. The beginning of this weekend held the promise of overshadowing the tragedies of war, if only for a brief respite, providing them with a glimmer of hope and a much-needed reminder of life's joys amidst the turmoil.

ANDREA'S STORY

As the first rays of sunlight gently filtered through the curtains of John's room at the Hotel Chopin, he began to stir from his peaceful slumber. However, his awakening was soon accompanied by a sound that caught his attention—the distant rumble of trucks rolling through the streets of Paris. The noise grew steadily louder, and John realized that the city was coming alive with activity.

Curiosity piqued, he got out of bed and approached the window. As he drew back the curtains, he was met with a remarkable sight—a convoy of trucks filled with supplies and foodstuff making their way through the city. The trucks seemed to stretch on endlessly, a symbol of hope and renewal for a city that had endured so much hardship during the war.

The liberation of Paris had brought not only freedom but also the pressing need to address the city's dire food situation. John had heard stories of how scarce food had become for the Parisians in recent days, and he knew that the city had suffered greatly under German occupation.

The allied forces had recognized the urgency of the situation and had swiftly organized food convoys to deliver much-needed supplies to the capital. The destruction of the French rail network had posed a challenge, but the determination to assist the people of Paris prevailed. Surrounding towns and villages had also answered the call, contributing their resources to support the city's revival.

John felt a surge of pride knowing that allied soldiers had even shared their own meager rations to help the desperate Parisians. It was a testament to the solidarity and compassion that had formed between the liberators and the liberated.

As he watched the convoy passing below, labeled 'Vivres Pour Paris,' he couldn't help but admire the spirit of cooperation that was now driving the city's revival. British and American supplies were flown in, and at least 500 tons of food were being delivered daily by each nation, helping to overcome the food crisis within a mere ten days.

Witnessing this incredible effort to rebuild and nourish the city, John felt a renewed sense of purpose. The war had been fraught with hardship and loss, but seeing the allied forces actively supporting the people of Paris reminded him why they fought—to restore freedom, hope, and dignity to those who had suffered under occupation.

As the sound of the convoy slowly faded into the distance, John closed the curtains and took a moment to reflect. The trucks rolling through the city were not just delivering food; they were carrying the promise of a new beginning for Paris and its resilient inhabitants. And for John, it was a powerful reminder of the importance of their mission and the profound impact they were making on the lives of those they had come to liberate. With a sense of gratitude and determination, he readied himself for the day ahead, eager to contribute to the city's resurgence in any way he could.

As the morning sun embraced the streets of Paris with a warm hug, John left his hotel with a sense of purpose. He was eager to meet up with Mary, who had informed him of a friend in need of assistance. Her name was Andrea, an older French woman and a talented seamstress known for creating beautiful dresses. But in these trying times, her dress shop had suffered, and she needed help to reopen.

John's heart went out to Andrea, especially when he heard the circumstances surrounding her current predicament. Her son and daughter, Gisele, and Albert, had been dedicated members of the resistance, bravely fighting against the occupation. However, they had been captured by the enemy and taken to a prisoner camp. The uncertainty of their fate weighed heavily on Andrea's heart, and she lived with the constant fear that they might be subjected to torture in an attempt to extract information about the whereabouts of others in the resistance.

He found himself contemplating the resilience of the people of Paris. Despite the challenges they faced, their spirits remained unbroken, and their determination to rebuild their lives and stand against oppression was unwavering.

John's thoughts were interrupted as he arrived at the designated meeting spot. There was Mary, waiting patiently. Her eyes carried a mixture of empathy and determination as she spoke about Andrea's situation. John nodded, understanding the urgency and importance of helping her in any way they could.

Together, they made their way to Andrea's dress shop. The once lively boutique now bore the scars of the war—shattered windows, damaged shelves, and debris strewn about. John could see the pain in Andrea's eyes as she opened the door to her once-beloved establishment.

Andrea was born and raised in the vibrant city of Paris, France. She grew up with a passion for fashion and an innate talent for sewing and design. As a young girl, she would watch her mother, who was also a skilled seamstress, create elegant dresses for the high-society women of Paris. Her mother's artistry and attention to detail inspired Andrea, igniting a lifelong passion for fashion and craftsmanship.

In her late teens, Andrea began working at a renowned dress shop in the heart of Paris. There, she honed her skills, and her talent quickly caught the eye of the shop's owner, Madame Renée. Under Madame Renée's guidance, Andrea's talent flourished, and she soon became one of the most sought-after dressmakers in the city.

As the years passed, Andrea met and fell in love with a young man named Henri. They shared a deep connection and a shared dream of starting a family together. Henri was a kind-hearted and ambitious individual, and together, they brought joy and love into each other's lives. The couple married, and not long after, Gisele, their first child, was born.

Gisele grew up in a household filled with creativity and love. Andrea's passion for sewing and design had become contagious, and Gisele often spent her free time at her mother's side, observing and learning the art of dressmaking. As she grew older, Gisele became an apprentice at her mother's shop, eager to contribute her own ideas and style to the dresses they created.

A few years later, Andrea and Henri were blessed with another child, a son named Albert. From an early age, Albert showed a natural aptitude for craftsmanship and engineering. He had a keen mind and a fascination with machines and how things worked. While Gisele followed in her mother's footsteps, Albert found his calling in working with his hands and understanding the intricacies of mechanics.

The family's happiness, however, was threatened when the dark clouds of World War II descended upon Europe. As the German occupation of France began, and Paris transformed into a city under siege. The once-thriving fashion district suffered as resources became scarce and fear gripped the city.

Despite the hardships, Andrea's dress shop remained open, providing a glimmer of hope and a refuge for Parisians looking for beauty and normalcy amidst the chaos of war. But the family's courage extended beyond the dress shop. Gisele and Albert, inspired by their parents' unwavering resilience, joined the resistance, using their talents to support the fight for freedom.

Gisele became an integral part of the resistance network, using her dressmaking skills to conceal messages and documents within the seams of dresses, passing vital information to other resistance members. Albert, on the other hand, used his mechanical expertise to create hidden compartments in various objects, allowing the resistance to transport sensitive materials discreetly.

Their involvement in the resistance was both a source of pride and worry for Andrea and Henri. They knew the risks their children were taking, but they also understood the importance of the fight against tyranny. Each day, Andrea prayed for their safety, hoping that they would return home, unharmed.

But fate took a cruel turn when Gisele and Albert were captured by the occupying forces. The news shattered Andrea's heart, and she lived in a constant state of fear and uncertainty. The thought of her children suffering at the hands of the enemy haunted her, and she did everything she could to find information about their whereabouts and well-being.

During the past few years, the treatment of the French Resistance by the German occupying forces in Paris was harsh and brutal. The Resistance, although loosely organized, still engaged in acts of sabotage, intelligence gathering, and resistance against the Nazi occupation. The Germans viewed the Resistance as a significant threat to their control over France and responded with ruthless measures to suppress and eliminate the resistance fighters.

One of the most notorious tactics employed by the Germans was the practice of collective punishment. If any act of resistance occurred in a particular area, the German forces would often retaliate by carrying out reprisals against the local population. This could include mass arrests, executions, and even the burning of entire villages as a warning to others. This was how Andrea's dress shop was destroyed. After Gisele and Albert's capture, the Germans ransacked the stores, stealing everything, breaking windows, and doors and in some cases, burning the establishments to the ground.

The Germans also used various forms of torture and intimidation to extract information from captured resistance members. Many resistors were subjected to harsh interrogations, physical abuse, and even torture to reveal the identities of their fellow fighters and the locations of resistance networks.

The occupation forces were relentless in their pursuit of resistance members, conducting frequent raids and searches to root out any signs of resistance activity. They also targeted civilians suspected of supporting the Resistance, leading to the arrest and imprisonment of many innocent people.

In an attempt to stifle communication and disrupt resistance networks, the Germans imposed strict censorship and controlled all forms of media, including newspapers, radio, and public announcements. They suppressed any anti-German sentiment and attempted to maintain an atmosphere of fear and control.

Despite the extreme risks and dangers, they faced, Gisele and Albert showed incredible bravery and determination. They continued their fight against the occupation, often operating in secret and carrying out acts of resistance in the shadows.

Andrea drew strength from her memories of Gisele and Albert growing up in a loving and creative home. She clung to the hope that they would one day return, bringing with them the joy and spirit that had once filled their lives. In the face of adversity, Andrea's determination to protect her family and her passion for her craft became her guiding light, inspiring those around her to never give up hope in the darkest of times. "I remember when Gisele and Albert used to help me every day," Andrea said with a heavy heart, tears welling up in her eyes. "They were so passionate about the resistance, and now they're gone. I fear for their safety every moment."

Mary placed a comforting hand on Andrea's shoulder, expressing her sympathy and support. "We're here to help you, Andrea. We'll clean up the shop together, and once it's ready, we'll find a way for you to make beautiful dresses again. Your talent deserves to shine, and we won't let the darkness of war overshadow it."

With renewed determination, they set to work, sweeping away debris, and organizing the shop. John and Mary were inspired by Andrea's strength, as she refused to let fear and despair consume her. She was a symbol of resilience, like so many others in the city, who had endured and fought for their freedom.

As they worked, John couldn't help but think of Gisele and Albert, the brave resistance fighters who sacrificed so much for their beliefs. He silently prayed for their safety and hoped that they would return to their mother soon. It was resistance members like them that helped them in Holland and provided valuable intelligence during war operations.

Throughout the morning, the trio labored tirelessly, transforming the dress shop back into a haven of creativity and beauty. As afternoon approached, they stood back to admire their work—a small victory amidst the chaos of war.

Andrea gazed around her rejuvenated shop, a glimmer of hope returning to her eyes. "Thank you both," she said with gratitude, "You've given me strength and hope to carry on, even in these dark times."

"It's the least I could do," said Mary. "You remind me so much of my mother back home in Sóller. "She has your strength and dedication to your craft. I am sure she is tending the grape vines and olive trees anticipating a bountiful harvest this season. I hope to return home soon. I miss her."

"I am sure you do," replied Andrea. "Where are your family, John?"

"My family owns a ranch outside of Austin. It's been in our family for generations, just like your dress shop," replied John.

Andrea looked up from the fabric she was carefully measuring, her eyes curious. "A ranch? How fascinating! Tell me more about it."

"It's a beautiful place," John replied, his voice tinged with pride. "Wide open fields, rolling hills, and the sweet scent of wildflowers in the air. It's always been a haven for our family—a place of hard work, but also a place to find peace and connection with nature."

"And who runs the ranch?" Andrea inquired, genuinely interested.

"My father is the rancher," John answered. "He's a strong and wise man, someone who knows the land like the back of his hand. He's taught me so much about the importance of respecting nature and the value of hard work."

"And your mother?" Andrea probed gently.

John's eyes softened with affection as he spoke of his mother. "My mother is the backbone of the ranch. She's a remarkable woman, strong-willed and compassionate. She's the one who runs the business side of things, making sure everything runs smoothly. Her love for the ranch and our family is unwavering."

Andrea nodded in understanding. "It sounds like a wonderful partnership. Your parents seem to complement each other perfectly."

"They do," John agreed with a smile. "They're a team, always supporting each other and making the ranch thrive. I've always admired their bond and the way they face challenges together."

"And have you always wanted to follow in your father's footsteps?" Andrea asked, her eyes gleaming with curiosity.

"As much as I love the cattle ranch, I am not sure. I have two other older brothers, Mark, and Samuel, who do most of the wrangling on the ranch now. I left college to join the army when the war started. I am not sure about my future; the legacy of the ranch is safe in their hands as don't want to do anything else but run the ranch."

"Mark got married to Emily, his high school sweetheart right after graduation and moved into the abandoned house on the southern tip of the ranch. He is well positioned to inherit the ranch. Myself, I have a great interest in engineering, and the focus of my learning at college.

When this is all over, I am sure the world will have a place for me somewhere. For now, I have a responsibility to my company and platoon."

"I understand," said Andrea. "Some friends of mine are planning to help me search for Gisele and Albert. They also have family that were captured by the Germans."

With a warm smile, Andrea excused herself for a moment and disappeared into the back of the dress shop. John and Mary could hear the soft clinking of cups and the gentle hum of a kettle as Andrea prepared something special. A few minutes later, she returned with a tray adorned with steaming cups of coffee and delicate pastries.

"Please, have a seat outside and enjoy the coffee," Andrea invited, gesturing towards a cozy table and chairs set up on the quaint terrace just outside the shop. "It's my special blend, a little taste of home."

John and Mary gladly accepted the offer and settled into the comfortable seats. The aroma of freshly brewed coffee filled the air, wrapping them in a sense of comfort and familiarity. As they sipped the warm beverages, Andrea leaned in with a sparkle in her eyes.

"I must say, you two seem like you've known each other for a long time. How did you meet?" Andrea inquired, genuinely curious about their story.

Mary chuckled softly, her gaze fondly resting on John. "We met at a small café on the other side of the river."

John chimed in, a smile tugging at the corners of his lips. "Yes, it was during the afternoon, our paths crossed in the midst of everything, and we instantly felt a connection."

Mary reached out to gently squeeze John's hand, her voice soft with gratitude. "And Andrea, your courage and strength in the face of uncertainty are truly inspiring. We see it in the way you handle your shop and the love you have for your children."

Andrea's smile softened, touched by their words. "Thank you, my dears. Life has not been easy but knowing that there are good people like you out there gives me hope."

They continued to share stories and laughter as they sipped their coffee, finding solace in each other's company.

The sun began to set, casting a warm golden glow over the city, and in that moment, they felt a sense of kinship, brought together by the extraordinary circumstances of war.

As the afternoon drew to a close, Andrea thanked them for their help and for being such wonderful company. John and Mary promised to return and continued to visit Andrea's dress shop whenever they could, knowing that amidst the uncertainties of war, they had found a friend who shared their resilience and belief in the power of love and hope.

The late afternoon sun was warm on their faces as John and Mary bid farewell to Andrea's dress shop. Their hearts were filled with gratitude for the woman's resilience and kindness, and they promised to return soon to help her further in any way they could.

Hand in hand, the couple strolled through the picturesque city, taking in the sights and sounds of post-liberation Paris. The lively energy of the streets was infectious, and the city seemed to come alive with a newfound spirit of hope and freedom.

As they made their way towards the Montmartre area, they could see the Seine River shimmering in the fading sunlight. The sound of distant laughter and chatter from nearby cafes added to the ambiance, making the evening feel like a dream.

In Montmartre, they found themselves amidst a bustling artists' quarter. The air was filled with the scent of freshly baked bread and the sight of colorful paintings adorning the streets. Talented artists displayed their work, hoping to capture the essence of Paris on their canvases.

As they meandered through the cobbled streets, a painter named Jacques caught their eye. He had a small setup by the riverside, his easel displaying a vibrant and picturesque scene of the Seine and the setting sun.

"Bonjour, madame et monsieur," Jacques greeted them with a warm smile, his eyes twinkling with the spark of creativity. "Would you allow me the pleasure of painting your portrait? There's something quite enchanting about your presence."

Flattered by the request, Mary exchanged a knowing look with John, and they agreed to pose for Jacques. The artist seemed to capture the essence of their love and connection with every brushstroke, and as he worked diligently on the canvas, they engaged in light-hearted banter and laughter.

As the sun dipped below the horizon, the painting began to take shape, each stroke reflecting the harmony and affection they shared. The Seine flowed serenely in the background, mirroring the tranquility of the moment.

As the masterpiece neared completion, Jacques stepped back, a look of satisfaction on his face. "Voilà! It is finished," he proclaimed with a flourish. "A tribute to love in the City of Love."

John and Mary were in awe of the painting, touched by the artist's ability to capture the essence of their bond. They thanked Jacques profusely and purchased the artwork as a cherished memento of their time in Paris.

The trio spent the evening together, sharing stories and anecdotes over a delightful meal at a nearby bistro. Jacques regaled them with tales of his artistic journey and the beauty he found in capturing the human spirit on canvas.

"Many years ago, I was just a young boy living in a small village on the outskirts of Paris," Jacques started. "My father was a struggling artist, and my mother worked tirelessly to support our family. Despite the hardships, they instilled in me a deep love for art and the beauty that surrounds us."

"As I grew older, I knew that I wanted to pursue my passion for painting," Jacques continued. "But the path of an artist is not always easy, and I faced countless challenges and setbacks along the way. Yet, I refused to give up, for my heart was set on expressing the emotions and stories of this city through my art."

His eyes sparkled with determination as he recalled his journey. "I remember the first time I set foot in Montmartre. It was as if the streets were alive with creativity, and I felt an instant connection to this place. Inspired by the countless artists who had come before me, I knew that this was where I belonged."

"I spent years honing my craft, sometimes struggling to make ends meet, but always driven by the desire to create something meaningful," Jacques said. "My paintings became a reflection of the city's soul, capturing its essence and the spirit of its people. I knew that through art, I could connect with others on a level that transcends language and time."

"The past four years have been hard, taking work where I could to survive. Having to paint German officers for virtually no money. I could not refuse. I once refused to paint a portrait of three SS officers, and they beat me. It was weeks before I could find the strength in my fingers to paint again.

His passion for his work was evident in every word he spoke. "And now, here I am, Paris is free, surrounded by its very essence, painting the stories of those who cross my path," Jacques said with a smile. "It brings me immense joy to immortalize love, friendship, and the beauty of life on my canvas. Each stroke is a tribute to the human spirit and the resilience that resides within us all."

John and Mary were captivated by Jacques' story, moved by his dedication to his art and the way he saw the world. They thanked him for sharing such a personal journey, realizing that beyond the beautiful paintings he created, there was a heart and soul poured into every brushstroke.

As the night wore on, the streets of Montmartre came alive with the soft blush of streetlights, and the city seemed to sparkle with a magic all its own. John and Mary knew they would forever cherish this serendipitous encounter with Jacques, a painter who had immortalized their love in the heart of Paris.

With heartfelt farewells, they bid Jacques adieu, knowing that they had made a friend whose art had touched their souls. Hand in hand, they continued their evening stroll along the Seine, the painting safely tucked under John's arm.

Under the moonlit sky, they embraced and John gently kissed Mary and said, "Thank you for a wonderful day. I could not imagine being anywhere else in the world than here in your arms on such a charming night. I love you."

There, he said it thought Mary. Finally, love had found her. She responded, "I love you too. You have brought such joy to my life."

As she looked into her eyes, they kissed once more and then holding hands began walking back and as their feet touched the ground, every cobblestone seemed to whisper stories of love, resilience, and hope. And as they reveled in each other's company, they knew that this extraordinary day in Paris would forever be etched in their hearts.

MOURMELON

Late November 1944 found Easy Company, part of the 506th Parachute Infantry Regiment of the 101st Airborne Division, stationed in Mourmelon-le-Grand, a town in northeastern France. Fall had settled in, and the landscape was dominated by vast fields and dense forests. The men of Easy Company were resolute and ready for whatever challenges lay ahead.

Easy Company found themselves stationed at the historic military camp de Châlons, also known as camp de Mourmelon, near the town of Mourmelon-le-Grand in northeastern France. The vast camp, covering approximately 10,000 hectares, was steeped in military history, having been established by Napoleon III during the Second French Empire on August 30, 1857.

As the soldiers of Easy Company settled into their surroundings, they couldn't help but be in awe of the camp's long and storied past. The camp had witnessed the presence of various military forces over the years, including the Russian Expeditionary Force in France during September 1916. Its primary purpose was for military maneuvers and training, particularly for cavalry units. Adjacent to it lay the expansive Camp de Moronvilliers, adding to the vastness of the training grounds.

For the men of Easy Company, this historic camp now became their home, a place where they could rest, refit, and recover from the intense fighting they had experienced in Holland during Operation Market Garden. As part of the 501st Infantry Regiment of the renowned 101st Airborne Division, they were given rest while awaiting replacements for their fallen friends.

The camp's landscape was a mix of open fields, dense woodlands, and training facilities. Tents and makeshift barracks dotted the area, serving as the soldiers' temporary quarters. The chilly late November air made the camp's vastness feel even more imposing, and the soldiers did their best to keep warm with the limited resources available to them.

Throughout the day, the camp was a hive of activity. Training exercises were conducted to keep the men sharp and ready for whatever the war would throw at them next. Their leaders, including Captain Richard Winters, knew the importance of maintaining their combat skills and tactical expertise even during periods of rest.

In between drills and training sessions, the soldiers found moments of solace. They sought refuge in the memories of home and loved ones, their thoughts drifting back to the familiar sights and sounds of their families and friends. Letters from home provided a glimpse of normalcy amidst the chaos of war, a reminder that there was still a world beyond the battlefield.

As Thanksgiving approached, the soldiers came together despite the challenging circumstances. A sense of solidarity prevailed as they gathered for a makeshift feast, sharing stories and laughter, finding comfort in the company of their fellow soldiers.

As the evening settled in and the platoon gathered around a small campfire, the crackling flames provided both warmth and a comforting ambiance. They sat on makeshift logs and crates, their tired but eager faces illuminated by the flickering glow. The talk shifted from battle stories to the simple luxuries they had come to appreciate during their stay at the camp de Châlons in Mourmelon.

"Did you guys see the new showers they set up near the barracks? It's like a piece of heaven after weeks of field training," said Private Evans, a fresh-faced replacement soldier who had recently joined Easy Company.

"Yeah, no more freezing cold water from a canteen cup. Showers are a small luxury that can make a big difference," added Guppy, his voice filled with gratitude.

"Yeah," said John. "You were getting a little ripe back in Holland.

"As were we all," said Guppy, laughing along with the rest of the group. "I could even smell myself, barely keep my rations down."

"Hey," said Jenkins. "I was the one in the back of the platoon. I was downwind from all of you. Imagine how I felt. I'm surprised the Germans didn't smell us coming across the river in those little boats."

"And let's not forget about the mail. Getting letters from home is like a lifeline, a reminder that there's still something worth fighting for," chimed in Sergeant Holmes.

The conversation then shifted to the town of Mourmelon-le-Grand, where the soldiers often sought solace from the rigors of military life.

"Anyone planning on hitting the town tonight? There's a good chance I'll head to that little pub near the square," said Private Jenkins, looking around at his platoon.

"I might join you, Davis. It's been a while since I had a cold beer," replied John, a smile spreading across his face.

"Remember that time we all played baseball against another unit? Those guys didn't know what hit 'em!" chuckled Jackson, reminiscing about a friendly sports match that brought the platoon together.

"And the poker games! I've never seen so many men so eager to part with their paychecks," laughed Guppy, who occasionally joined in the friendly gambling sessions.

As they shared stories and laughter, the conversation took a more serious turn.

"I heard Lassiter and Johnson from 2nd platoon are trying to get an early discharge from the hospital to rejoin Easy. Can't say I blame them; Easy Company feels like home," said Sergeant Holmes, a sense of pride evident in his voice.

"Absolutely. We've been through hell together, and I wouldn't want to fight alongside anyone else," added Corporal Jenkins, nodding in agreement.

"Hey, did you guys hear? The higher-ups are talking about promotions. With all the changes, Easy Company is evolving," remarked Parsons, excitement building in his eyes.

"Yeah, it's bittersweet, though. We lost some good men, but it's also a testament to how far we've come," Sergeant Holmes acknowledged, his tone tinged with a mix of emotions.

"How long do you think we will be encamped here?" asked John.

"Well," answered Sergeant Holmes. "I know that we will be here until reinforcements arrive and get through jump school. With winter on the way, I suspect it may be early Spring before our forces start pushing into Germany."

"Looks like Christmas here by a fire!" exclaimed Parsons.

As the soldiers of Easy Company huddled closer to the crackling fire in the camp de Châlons, the anticipation of Christmas in Mourmelon filled the air.

Private Evans, eager to break the ice, spoke up first. "You know, last Christmas, I was supposed to be home with my family, exchanging gifts and enjoying my mom's cooking. Instead, I found myself in the middle of nowhere, trudging through the mud and snow. Last Christmas was quite an adventure," Private Evans began, his eyes glinting with excitement as he recalled the memories. "You see, back home in Texas, my family owns a big piece of land, and we go hunting every year during the holidays. It's a tradition, you know?"

The rest of the platoon leaned in, eager to hear Evans' story.

"So, there I was, knee-deep in snow, with my uncles leading the way. We were tracking a deer, hoping to have a nice venison feast for Christmas dinner," he continued. "The snow made it tough to walk quietly, but my uncles were expert hunters. They taught me everything I know about tracking game and staying patient."

"Sounds like a real bonding experience," said Sergeant Holmes with a nod.

"It sure was, Sergeant," Evans replied. "We spent hours out there, waiting and watching. The forest was so serene, covered in a blanket of snow. It was like being in a winter wonderland."

"I can almost picture it," Corporal Jenkins remarked.

"Yeah, and then finally, after what felt like forever, we spotted the deer," Evans continued. "My heart was pounding, and I had to steady my aim. It was a test of patience and skill, but in the end, I managed to take the shot and got my first deer ever."

The platoon let out a cheer, impressed by Evans' hunting prowess.

"That's not all, though," Evans continued with a grin. "Once we had the deer, we had to drag it all the way back to the cabin through the snow. It was heavy, and the going was tough, but we did it together."

"I can imagine the feast that followed," said Lieutenant Anderson, who walked up in the middle of the story, intrigued by the tale.

"You bet! We cooked up some of the venison over an open fire, and my grandma made her famous cornbread. We shared stories, laughed, and enjoyed each other's company," Evans said, his voice tinged with fondness.

"Sounds like a Christmas to remember," said Private Rodriguez.

"It truly was," Evans agreed. "And while I miss being with my family, I'm glad to be here with all of you. We may not be hunting in the snow, but the bond we share is just as strong."

Lieutenant Anderson, a veteran of several Christmases spent in unexpected places, joined in. "One year, I was stationed in the mountains, and we had to get creative. We fashioned a tree out of pine branches and decorated it with whatever we could find—canteen cups, socks, even bits of tinsel we scrounged up."

"And did you sing carols around the fire, sir?" asked Private Reynolds with a chuckle.

"You bet we did. Our voices weren't the best, but it felt like home for a little while," the lieutenant replied, his eyes glinting with fond memories.

Corporal Martinez chimed in, "Last year, I was on leave, and I didn't think I'd make it back in time for Christmas. But a group of local folks in the town I was visiting invited me to their celebration. They treated me like family, even though I was a complete stranger."

"That's the beauty of the season, isn't it? It brings people together, no matter where they're from," Sergeant Holmes remarked, a hint of nostalgia in his voice.

Private Davis, feeling inspired, shared his own story. "When I was in basic training, we couldn't go home for Christmas. But our drill sergeant surprised us with a feast and let us call our families. It made us feel like we weren't so far away after all."

As the stories flowed, the platoon members exchanged laughter, empathy, and understanding. They discovered that they all shared a similar sense of longing for the comforts of home during the holiday season.

John, who had been listening quietly, finally spoke up. "You know, in a strange way, being here together feels like a family reunion. We may not be with our blood relatives, but we're bound by something even stronger—a brotherhood forged through hardships and shared experiences."

"And what better way to celebrate that bond than with a Christmas here in Mourmelon?" added Corporal Jenkins.

With the fire crackling and the stars twinkling above, the platoon of Easy Company felt a sense of peace and belonging amidst the chaos of war. As they continued to share stories of Christmases past and dreams of Christmases future, they knew that even in the most unexpected circumstances, the spirit of the season would always find a way to light up their hearts and keep them united as one.

"Alright," said John. "Who's ready to go into town and get a beer?"

"Or a shot of whiskey," exclaimed Jenkins. "It's cold out here. I need a warm-up."

"You boys going into town tonight?" asked Lieutenant Anderson.

"Do you mind if I tag along? Inquired Anderson. "I've been typing reports all day and need to blow off a little steam."

Lieutenant Anderson had always felt a strong sense of duty and honor instilled in him from an early age. Born into a military family, his father had served in the Army, and his grandfather before him, creating a long line of soldiers. Growing up, Anderson was surrounded by stories of bravery, sacrifice, and service, which fueled his own desire to follow them.

As a boy, Anderson would spend hours listening to his father's war stories, captivated by tales of bravery and resilience on the battlefield. He admired the way his father spoke of the men he had served with, emphasizing the bonds formed in the crucible of combat. These stories not only fascinated Anderson but also instilled in him a deep respect for the sacrifices made by those who served their country.

When he came of age, Anderson enlisted in the military and was accepted into West Point Academy, carrying on the family tradition. He excelled in his studies, showing exceptional leadership skills and a keen strategic mind. During his time at West Point, Anderson formed close friendships with his fellow cadets, further solidifying his belief in the importance of camaraderie in the military.

Upon graduating from West Point, Anderson was commissioned as a Second Lieutenant and began his service in various units, gaining experience and honing his leadership abilities. His dedication and unwavering commitment to his men did not go unnoticed, and he steadily rose through the ranks, earning the respect of his superiors and peers alike.

As the war raged on, Anderson found himself assigned to the 101st Airborne Division, joining Easy

Company during their deployment to Europe. He embraced the responsibility of leading the platoon, knowing that the lives of his men depended on his decisions. Anderson took pride in fostering a strong sense of unity within Easy Company, drawing from the lessons of brotherhood and sacrifice he had learned from his family and experiences at West Point.

Through the challenges and trials of war, Anderson never lost sight of the values instilled in him since childhood. He remained steadfast in his duty to protect and lead his men, often drawing on the stories of his father and grandfather for inspiration during the darkest moments.

"Sure," said John. "The more the merrier. Do you think we could use your jeep? I'd rather not walk that distance in the cold."

"Yes," said Anderson. "I'll have Corporal Smith bring it over in a bit. I need to turn in my reports and let Captain Winters know I will be going into town."

As the haze cleared and a canopy of stars appeared, obscured by a crescent moon, Anderson returned with his jeep. Lieutenant Anderson, John, Guppy, Sergeant Holmes, and Jenkins piled into the rugged jeep. Their faces were a mix of excitement and camaraderie, looking forward to some respite from the rigors of war. With Lt. Anderson at the wheel, they embarked on a much-needed journey into the town of Reims, where they heard of a quaint pub named George's that offered a brief escape from the realities of combat.

The jeep rumbled along the narrow streets of Reims, passing by charming old buildings that bore the scars of war but stood proud as a testament to the town's resilience. The air was filled with the remnants of the scents of the day and cool night breeze, a welcome change from the acrid smell of gunpowder that had become all too familiar.

Finally, they arrived on the bustling street where George's was located. The pub's warm light spilled out onto the sidewalk, drawing them in like moths to a flame. Its cozy, brick exterior exuded a sense of comfort, and the lively chatter of patrons could be heard from inside.

Stepping through the door, they were greeted by the lively ambiance of George's. The interior was adorned with vintage posters and photographs, reminiscent of happier times before the war had cast its shadow over the land. The bar was lined with an impressive array of liquors, and the clinking of glasses added a musical undertone to the cheerful chatter. This was Champagne country, and Reims was known for being the center of champagne bars.

The men made their way to a round booth table tucked away in the corner of the pub. Its dimly lit alcove offered a degree of privacy, a welcome diversion from the prying eyes of the outside world. The worn leather seats cradled them, providing a sense of comfort that had become a rarity in their lives. Far from sitting on rotten logs around a campfire or on the side of a bunker.

They ordered pints of ale from a friendly barmaid, whose smile seemed to light up the entire room. As the amber liquid was poured into their glasses, they raised them in a toast to friendship and survival, their clinks of glasses joining the symphony of the evening.

As they sat there relaxing, the men began to share stories from their time in the military. Lieutenant Anderson spoke of his days at West Point and the dream of serving his country with honor. John recounted memories of his family's ranch outside of Austin, describing the vast expanse of land where he had spent his carefree days before the war.

Guppy, always the joker, interjected with tales of their misadventures during training, causing laughter to erupt from the group. Sergeant Holmes, with his quiet demeanor, listened intently to the stories, occasionally adding a thoughtful reflection.

As the night wore on, the pub became a sanctuary, where the weight of war seemed to momentarily lift from their shoulders. Other groups of soldiers from the 101st and other units piled into every corner of the pub.

"Hey," said Jenkins. "I got a letter from home. My mother writes to me once a week, while the letters pile up, she does provide some news. Would you like to hear?"

"Absolutely!" exclaimed Lt. Anderson. "I've had virtually no news in the past two weeks."

Jenkins pulled out a letter from his pocket. It was a worn and creased piece of paper, bearing the familiar handwriting of his mother. The anticipation in the air was palpable as his comrades leaned in, eager to hear the news from home.

"Alright, fellas, here's the latest from back in the States," Jenkins announced with a smile. "Let's see what Mama's got to say this time."

He unfolded the letter and began to read aloud, his voice carrying a mix of pride and nostalgia.

"November 1st, 1944: Well, dearest Jenkins, it's been quite a month here at home. We finally got our hands on those new ration books they've been talking about. And goodness gracious, the grocery lines have gotten longer than a Texas summer day!"

The group chuckled, knowing all too well the challenges their families faced on the home front.

"November 6th, 1944: The presidential election took place, and it looks like FDR will be staying in the White House. We've been following the news closely, hoping for the best for our country."

A sense of patriotism filled the air, and the men exchanged knowing nods.

Jenkins continued to read, recounting news of significant events happening inside the United States, from the opening of a new hospital in New York to a celebration of Native American heritage in Oklahoma. It was a glimpse into a world far from the battlefields of Europe, a world that seemed so distant yet so familiar.

But as he turned the page, Jenkins noticed a snippet of the letter that made him pause. His cheeks flushed slightly, and he grinned mischievously. "Ah, well, seems like my dear mama's got a bit of gossip in here," he teased, holding the letter slightly away from the others.

Sergeant Holmes leaned forward with a playful glint in his eye. "Oh, come on, Jenkins, don't keep us in suspense. What's the juicy news?"

John, always the joker, chimed in with a grin. "Yeah, don't leave us hanging' now, buddy!"

Jenkins chuckled and shook his head. "Sorry, boys, but this part's classified information. Mama's got her ways of keeping me on my toes, you know."

The others laughed, understanding that some things were meant to be kept private. Jenkins folded that page of the letter and tucked it back into his pocket, his heart warmed by the love and support from home.

"Alright, enough of that," he said, returning to the news. "Now where were we? Ah, yes..."

He continued reading, sharing news from home, the release of the movie Thirty Seconds Over Tokyo, the Detroit Tigers, his father's favorite baseball team in second place, and other news of the war in the Pacific.

"I sure hope we get to see that movie," said Guppy.

"Me too," replied Sgt. Holmes. "The ones they show at the canteen at night, they keep replaying the same movie. Not sure how many times I can watch Casablanca."

Jenkins nodded in agreement. "Yeah, variety would be nice. I'm getting pretty tired of watching Bogart and Bergman mumble those lines over and over again."

John smirked. "Well, I wouldn't mind seeing some real action, not just on the silver screen. How about we wrap up this war quickly, and then we can all go catch that movie together back in the States?"

Guppy chimed in eagerly, "Sounds like a plan! I can almost taste the buttered popcorn now."

Sergeant Holmes chuckled and raised his glass. "To the end of this war and watching movies without hearing the sound of artillery in the distance."

The clinking of glasses resonated through the corner booth, and for a moment, they were transported away from the realities of war. The lively atmosphere of George's and the warmth of companionship helped to momentarily drown out the constant reminders of conflict and danger that awaited them.

As the conversation continued, Jenkins mentioned more news about hometown heroes and community events that brought fond memories to the forefront of his mind. He told them about the local baseball team's victory in the state championship, and his father's jubilant celebration.

"My dad used to take me to those games," Jenkins recalled with a hint of nostalgia. "He'd cheer so loud you could hear him from the bleachers. Those were some good times."

After finishing the letter, Jenkins looked around the table at his comrades. "I don't know about you fellas, but moments like this, when we can just relax and be ourselves, make me feel like we're more than just soldiers. We're brothers, and we'll have stories to tell for the rest of our lives."

The sentiment resonated deeply with everyone present. They were a band of brothers who had experienced loss, fear, and triumph together. They had become each other's support, finding strength in one another as they navigated through the uncertainties of war.

As the evening drew to a close, Lieutenant Anderson checked his watch. "Alright, boys, time to head back to camp."

They all rose from the round booth table, the lingering echoes of laughter still filling the air. They stepped out of George's and into the cool night air of Reims.

The jeep ride back to their camp in Mourmelon was eerily quiet, perhaps it was the solace of normalcy that each man felt, even for a brief moment that night, that for the moment, they felt at peace.

As the jeep rolled into camp, the soldiers exchanged words of thanks and headed back to their quarters. Thanksgiving was a few days away; they would have more time to exchange stories and take their mind off the horrors of war and the struggle of a continent. They could be thankful, thankful they are alive, thankful that God had placed them in his service to fight against evil.

PALMA

The soft rays of the morning sun filtered through the curtains; gently coaxing Mary awake. She stirred in her bed, amongst the soft linens, blinking sleep from her eyes, and was about to drift back into slumber when she heard her mother's voice calling her from the kitchen.

"Mary, mi amor, are you awake?" her mother's tender voice rang through the hallway.

Mary sat up, rubbing her eyes, and replied, "Yes, Mama, I'm up now."

Her mother's footsteps approached her bedroom door, and she pushed it open with a warm smile. "Buenos días, mi niña," she greeted, her eyes filled with motherly affection.

"Buenos días, Mama," Mary replied, mirroring her mother's smile. Never had a morning passed when Maria was in a bad mood. Perhaps it was her nature, she always seemed to be in good spirits, even under the worst circumstances.

As Mary's mother entered the room, she carried with her the scent of freshly brewed coffee. She always had a way of making the mornings feel cozy and inviting. Mary's mother sat on the edge of the bed, her eyes filled with concern and love.

"Mary, I was thinking," her mother began, "how about we go visit your friend Margerite in Palma today?"

Surprised by the suggestion, Mary's eyes widened, "Really, Mama? You want to go to Palma today?"

Her mother nodded, "Yes, mi amor. I heard from Margerite's mother that she has been feeling unwell lately, and I thought it would be nice for us to pay her a visit. It's been a while since you've seen each other."

Mary's heart warmed at the thought of seeing her dear friend again. She and Margerite had been inseparable since childhood, and the distance that had grown between them due to the war had been difficult. A visit to Palma to see Margerite felt like a balm for her soul, a chance to reconnect and bring some joy to her friend's life.

"I would love to go, Mama," Mary said with gratitude in her voice. "Thank you for suggesting it."

Her mother smiled and gently brushed a strand of hair away from Mary's face. "It's my pleasure, mi niña. Now, get ready, and I'll make us a nice breakfast before we set off on our little adventure."

As Mary and her mother, Maria, sat down for breakfast, the aroma of orange marmalade and steaming coffee filled the air. They exchanged warm smiles, grateful for the opportunity to spend the day together.

"So, mama," Mary began, "besides visiting Margerite, what else would you like to do in Palma today?"

Maria took a sip of her coffee, savoring the rich flavor, and replied, "Well, I was thinking, since we're in the city, maybe we could do some shopping. There's this new dress I saw in one of the shop windows last time I was in Palma. I think it would be perfect for the upcoming winter festival."

Mary's eyes lit up with excitement, "That sounds wonderful! I'd love to help you pick out a new dress. It'll be a nice surprise papa, too. He always loves to see you in new clothes. He just gushes with compliments."

Maria nodded, knowing her husband's appreciation for the little things in life. "And speaking of Papa," she continued, "remember how he accidentally broke his watch while clearing rocks from the vineyard last month?"

Mary chuckled softly, "Yes, I remember. Rocks can be quite a nuisance in the fields, they are everywhere, but they're a reminder of the island's volcanic history."

"That's true," Maria agreed, "but I think it's about time we get Papa's watch fixed. It's been sitting on his bedside table, and he's been using the sun to guess the time."

Mary chuckled again, "He does have a way of making do with what he has. We can take it to the watchmaker's shop in Palma. I'm sure they can repair it for him. I'd also like to look and see if I might be able to find him a gift. You know his birthday is rolling around in a couple of weeks."

"Great," replied Maria. "After you finish your breakfast, go and get dressed for town, and hitch up Bella to the wagon."

"Okay, Mama," said Mary.

With their errands in mind, Mary quickly got dressed in a simple yet lovely dress, perfect for a day in town. She tied a scarf around her hair to protect it from the wind, and together with Maria, they made their way to the barn to hitch up Bella to the wagon.

"Alright, Mama, let me help you up," Mary said, extending her hand to assist her mother onto the wagon seat.

Maria smiled warmly and climbed up with ease into the wagon seat. "Thank you, my dear," she said, patting Mary's hand affectionately. "Now, scoot over and let me take the reins."

Mary chuckled, knowing how much her mother loved driving Bella. She moved over, allowing Maria to take control. With a gentle flick of the reins, they set off, Bella's hooves clopping softly on the dirt path.

The one-hour ride to Sóller was a delightful journey through the picturesque landscape of Mallorca. Orange groves and olive trees stretched out in every direction; their branches heavy with unpicked fruit. Many people had not returned to their homes or were unable to find laborers to help with their harvest. They passed by other farms and vineyards, each with its unique story.

As they rode along, Maria pointed out the farms and vineyards they passed, recounting tales of their owners and their histories. "You see that vineyard over there?" she said, gesturing toward a sprawling field of grapevines. "That one belongs to the Ramirez family. They left the island during the Spanish Civil War but returned after the war ended. They never left when the Italians came. They've been working hard to rebuild their lives here and vowed to never leave again."

"And what about that farm with the beautiful garden?" Mary inquired. "Isn't that the one owned by Mr. Pedro?"

"Oh, you remembered. Yes, you are correct, that one is owned by the Fernandez family," Maria explained. "They left the island during the outbreak of World War II, seeking safety in mainland Spain. It must have been hard for them to leave their home behind, but they too returned about a month before we did."

They continued their conversation, learning about the stories of each family they passed. Some had left to escape political unrest, while others sought opportunities in different countries. Each return to the island was a testament to the enduring connection they felt to their homeland.

As they approached Sóller, the vibrant town came into view, its charm evident in the colorful buildings and lively streets. Mary and Maria smiled at each other, grateful for the peaceful ride and the opportunity to explore their beloved town.

As Bella trotted into Sóller, they made their way through the bustling streets, navigating the wagon with ease.

The clip-clop of the horse's hooves echoed through the narrow streets as they headed toward the east side of town, where the livery stable was situated a few blocks away from the train station.

"Isn't it wonderful to be back in Sóller, Mama?" Mary remarked, her eyes bright with excitement. "There's always such a vibrant energy here."

Maria nodded, a contented smile gracing her lips. "Indeed, my dear. Sóller holds a special place in my heart, and I'm glad we get to visit so often."

As they approached the livery stable, they saw the familiar sign hanging above the entrance. Maria expertly guided Bella into the stable yard, where a friendly stable hand greeted them.

"Good morning, Maria! And hello, Mary!" the stable hand said cheerfully. "It's been a while since you've been here. How have you both been?"

"Good morning, Diego," said Maria. "We've been well, thank you, we're here to park Bella for the day as we are taking the train into Palma to do some shopping.

"Of course, no problem at all," said Diego, as he began helping them unhitch Bella from the wagon. "We'll take good care of her. You ladies go ahead and enjoy your day in Palma."

"Thank you," Mary said gratefully. "We'll be back in the late afternoon to pick her up."

Diego was born and raised in Sóller, Mallorca, just like Mary. He grew up in a modest house on the outskirts of town, where his parents worked as farmers, tending to their small orchards and vineyards. Diego was always drawn to animals and the natural world. He spent hours exploring the countryside, learning about the local flora and fauna, and developing a deep affinity for horses.

As he grew older, Diego's fascination with horses only intensified. He would often spend his free time at the local livery stable, offering to help out in any way he could. The stable owner, a kind-hearted man named Miguel, recognized Diego's passion, and willingness to work hard. He took the young boy under his wing and taught him the art of horse care and handling.

Diego's knowledge and skill with horses grew rapidly, and it wasn't long before he became an indispensable part of the stable. He could sense the needs and moods of the horses, calming even the most skittish of them with his gentle touch and soothing voice. People in Sóller began to notice Diego's natural gift with animals, and he became well-known for his expertise in handling horses.

As Diego entered his teenage years, he faced a difficult decision. While he loved Sóller dearly, he yearned to explore the world beyond the island's shores. A sense of wanderlust tugged at his heart, urging him to seek new experiences and challenges. However, leaving his family and the town he loved dearly was no easy feat.

Ultimately, Diego made the decision to embark on a journey beyond Mallorca. With tears in his eyes, he bid farewell to his parents, promising to return someday. Armed with determination and a sense of adventure, he set off to explore different places, eager to learn more about horses and the world at large.

Diego's travels took him to various regions, where he worked with horses in different settings, from vast ranches to busy cities. He honed his skills and learned valuable lessons along the way. Despite his experiences in far-off lands, his heart remained tied to Sóller, and thoughts of his hometown often filled his mind.

After a few years of exploring, Diego decided it was time to return to Sóller. He missed the familiar sights, the sound of the waves crashing on the shores, and most of all, the gentle neighs of the horses he grew up with. As he arrived back in town, he was warmly welcomed by his family and friends, and word quickly spread about his return.

Diego's reputation as a skilled horseman and his genuine love for animals earned him the respect and admiration of the locals. When Miguel, the stable owner, retired, Diego took over the reins of the livery stable. Under his care and expertise, the stable flourished, attracting visitors from near and far who sought the best horse care and riding experience.

As Diego grew older, he became an integral part of the Sóller community, known not only for his equestrian skills but also for his kind heart and unwavering loyalty to his hometown. And so, Diego's story intertwined with the fabric of Sóller, a young man whose love for horses brought him back home, where he found his true calling and his place in the world.

As Mary and Maria settled into their seats on the train to Palma, the rhythmic chugging of the locomotive filled the air. The train car was bustling with passengers, but the mother and daughter found a moment of privacy to share their thoughts.

"Isn't Diego such a kind young man, Mama?" Mary asked, her eyes filled with admiration. "He's always been so good with the horses, and the way he takes care of them is incredible."

Maria nodded, her expression thoughtful. "Yes, he truly is a good man, Mary. He's been a part of this town for as long as I can remember, and he's always been dedicated to his work at the livery stable. And you know, I can't help but notice how he looks at you, dear."

Mary blushed slightly, her heart beating a little faster. "Oh, Mama, you think so? I've always felt comfortable around him, and he's been such a good friend."

Maria smiled warmly. "Exactly, my dear. Diego has known you since you were a little girl, and it's clear that he cares for you deeply. I see the way he pays attention to you, the way he smiles when you're around. It's evident that he has eyes for you."

Mary's face lit up at her mother's words. "But Mama, what if he's just being friendly? I don't want to misinterpret his kindness or lead him on, I have John."

Maria shook her head gently. "Trust me, Mary, I know a thing or two about love. And it's not just his kindness; it's the way he looks at you – with such tenderness and admiration. I believe there might be something more there."

"But what about John, Mama?" Mary asked, her voice tinged with uncertainty. "I care about him so much, and he's so brave and wonderful. I can't stop thinking about him."

"I understand, my dear," Maria said softly. "John seems to be an incredible young man, and I can see how much he means to you. But we can't ignore what's right in front of us. Diego is here, in Sóller, and he has feelings for you. You owe it to yourself to explore that possibility too. What if the war takes him? What if he decides to go home to Texas? You know he has family there, what does he do? Abandon them?"

As the train continued its journey to Palma, Mary pondered her mother's words. She couldn't deny the special bond she had with Diego, and the idea of exploring a deeper connection with him felt both exciting and comforting. At the same time, her heart ached for John, who was fighting far away on the front lines.

Mary knew she had to follow her heart, just as her mother had advised. She realized that love could be complex and unpredictable, and she might have to navigate through difficult choices. Yet, as she looked out of the train window, she felt a sense of hope and gratitude for having two caring and wonderful men in her life. Whether her path led her to Diego or John, she knew that love would guide her, and she would cherish every moment of her journey.

The train pulled into the bustling station in Palma, its brakes hissing as it came to a stop. Mary and her mother gathered their belongings and disembarked, stepping onto the platform amid the hubbub of travelers and locals. The city was a stark contrast to the quiet charm of Sóller, with its grand buildings and bustling streets.

As they walked through the streets of Palma, the sun was bright above the city, the lively chatter of people going about their day surrounded them.

Their steps led them to the heart of the city, where the streets were lined with shops, boutiques, and open-air markets. The vibrant colors of fruits and vegetables on display added to the lively atmosphere. Maria couldn't help but smile as she looked around, her eyes taking in the sights and sounds of the bustling city.

Finally, they reached Margerite's home – a charming little house tucked away on a quiet street. The white-washed walls and colorful flowers in the front garden gave it a welcoming feel. Mary knocked on the wooden door, and it was quickly opened by Margerite herself, her face lighting up with joy at the sight of her dear friends.

"Mary, Maria, you've come!" Margerite exclaimed, her voice filled with genuine happiness. She embraced them both warmly, her hug conveying the warmth of their friendship.

"It's so wonderful to see you, Margerite," Mary said, returning the embrace.

Maria added with a smile, "Yes, we heard you weren't feeling well, and we wanted to come and see you."

Margerite ushered them inside, and they were greeted by the comforting aroma of home-cooked food. The interior was cozy and inviting, adorned with photographs and memories that told the story of Margerite and Carmela's life together.

Margerite's early years were marked by the tragedy of losing her father, Rodrigo, to a devastating outbreak of cholera when she was just five years old. Left without a father's guiding presence, her mother, Carmela, faced the daunting challenge of raising Margerite on her own. The loss of Rodrigo was a deep blow to their family, and Carmela found herself having to navigate a world suddenly without him.

Despite the difficulties, Carmela's determination and resilience shone through. With a heart full of love and a fierce dedication to her daughter's well-being, Carmela took on the role of both mother and father. She worked tirelessly, taking up jobs as a maid in various households to provide for their needs. Every day, she rose early and returned home late, juggling her responsibilities while ensuring that Margerite was cared for and nurtured.

Carmela's sacrifices were not in vain. Margerite grew up surrounded by her mother's unwavering love and strong example. She witnessed firsthand the power of resilience and determination, as Carmela worked hard to provide them with a stable life despite the challenges they faced. Carmela's sacrifices and the lessons she imparted helped shape Margerite into a woman of strength, compassion, and gratitude.

Carmela entered the room with a warm smile. "Welcome, my dears," she said in her gentle voice. "It's lovely to have you here."

"We brought you some fresh oranges from our orchard in Sóller," Mary said, presenting a small basket to Margerite.

Margerite's eyes sparkled with gratitude. "Oh, you shouldn't have. Thank you so much."

As the four women settled into chairs, Mary's mother inquired, "How have you been feeling, Margerite? Mary was quite worried about you."

Margerite's eyes sparkled with gratitude. "I'm much better, thank you. My fever broke a few days ago, and I'm regaining my strength. It's a relief to finally be on the mend."

Carmela, Margerite's mother, joined the conversation with a kind smile. "Yes, she's been a trooper, enduring those long days of fever with such grace."

Mary couldn't help but admire the close bond between mother and daughter. "You've taken such good care of each other," she remarked.

Margerite nodded, her gaze turning fondly toward Carmela. "My mother has been my rock, always by my side through thick and thin."

Carmela's eyes twinkled with pride. "We've weathered our share of storms, haven't we, Margerite?"

"Speaking of storms," Margerite began, a hint of worry in her voice, "there was a fierce one that swept through Palma earlier this week."

Mary's interest was piqued, and she leaned forward, eager to hear the details. "A storm? What happened?"

Carmela, Margerite's mother, nodded solemnly. "Yes, my dear. It was quite a tempest. The kind that rattles windows and shakes the very ground you stand on."

Margerite's expression grew more serious as she continued, "Many homes along the coast suffered damage. Roofs torn off; windows shattered. It was a sight of devastation."

Mary's mother's brow furrowed in concern. "And the fishermen?"

Carmela let out a sigh, her gaze distant. "Ah, the fishermen had a tough time. The sea was wild and unforgiving. Boats were tossed about like mere toys, struggling to stay afloat against the furious waves."

Mary shook her head, a mixture of sympathy and disbelief in her expression. "That sounds truly terrifying. Did anyone get hurt?"

Margerite nodded, her voice tinged with sadness. "Unfortunately, yes. A few people were injured, but thankfully, no one lost their lives."

Carmela's eyes reflected a mixture of gratitude and empathy. "Yes, we must count our blessings in these times. It's a reminder of the power of nature and our need to come together in its aftermath."

Mary's mother nodded in agreement. "Community support is crucial during such moments. I heard that the people of Palma have been rallying together to help those who were affected."

Margerite's gaze softened as she looked at her mother. "Yes, it's heartening to see how everyone comes together in times of need."

As the conversation continued, Mary and Margerite exchanged a knowing look, silently agreeing that there were matters they wished to discuss in private. With a subtle nod, Margerite rose from her seat, and Mary followed suit. Their mothers, engrossed in their own conversation, didn't seem to notice as the two young women slipped out of the living room and made their way toward the back garden atrium.

The garden was a peaceful oasis, tucked away from the bustling streets of Palma. A small pond adorned with water lilies glistened in the sunlight, and colorful flowers lined the paths that wound through the greenery. Mary took a deep breath, relishing the tranquility of the space.

Margerite turned to Mary, her expression one of curiosity mixed with concern. "Mary, there's something I wanted to ask you about. Something I overheard my mother mention to a neighbor."

Mary's brow furrowed slightly. "Oh? What did she mention?"

Margerite hesitated for a moment, as if gauging how to phrase her words. "She mentioned John. Your soldier."

Mary's heart skipped a beat, and she met Margerite's gaze with a mix of surprise and anticipation. "John? What did she say?"

Margerite's gaze was compassionate. "She told the neighbor that you were waiting for him, even though the war is still ongoing."

A faint blush colored Mary's cheeks, and she looked down at her hands for a moment before meeting Margerite's gaze again. "Yes, that's true. John and I... well, we've connected in a way that's hard to explain. He's a part of me, Margerite."

Margerite's expression softened, her understanding evident. "I can see that. There's a depth to your feelings for him."

Mary nodded; her voice tinged with emotion. "But it's not just about my feelings for him. I believe in the cause he's fighting for, the hope for a better world. And I want to be a part of that hope, of his journey."

Margerite placed a reassuring hand on Mary's arm. "I admire your dedication, Mary. Your strength to wait, to believe. But I also sense a shadow of doubt."

Mary sighed softly, her gaze distant. "Yes, I'll admit it. Waiting is not easy. And sometimes, I wonder if it's wise to hold on to something that feels uncertain."

Margerite's gaze held a gentle understanding. "Mary, have you ever thought about the possibility of finding happiness here, right now?"

Mary's eyes met Margerite's, and she let out a quiet breath. "You mean... with Diego?"

Margerite's smile was warm, her voice kind. "Yes. Diego is a good man, Mary. He cares for you deeply. And he's been patient, waiting for the right time to express his feelings."

Mary looked down; her thoughts conflicted. "Diego is wonderful, and I care for him too. But my heart is with John. I know it might sound foolish, but I believe that he'll come back to me."

Margerite placed a hand on Mary's cheek, her touch gentle. "Mary, follow your heart, but also consider where you can find happiness and support. Sometimes, the path we least expect can lead us to the most beautiful destinations."

As Mary gazed into Margerite's eyes, she felt a sense of comfort and reassurance. In the quiet garden, their conversation had opened up new perspectives, stirring thoughts and emotions that Mary would carry with her as she faced the uncertain future.

Meanwhile, inside the house, Carmela and Maria had been engaged in a conversation of their own. The topic had shifted to the men in their lives, as it often did when they had a chance to catch up.

Carmela sipped her tea, her expression thoughtful. "Maria, mi querida, I can see the way Diego's eyes light up when he talks about Mary. He was in town last week to buy some new harnesses for the stable and came by to see me."

Maria's gaze dropped to her cup. "Carmela, it's not that simple. Yes, Diego is a wonderful man, and he's been a dear friend. But there's something about Mary's connection with John, something that has captured her heart. I can't ignore that."

Carmela's eyes softened with understanding. "I know. Mary's bond with that soldier is strong. But you've always been practical, my dear. Diego cares for her deeply. He's dependable, and he's been there for you and her."

Maria sighed, her fingers tracing the rim of her cup. "I won't deny that Diego has always been supportive, and I've grown fond of him. But it's just... when Mary talks about John, I can see the way her eyes light up. She's found something special in him."

Carmela reached out and touched Maria's hand, offering a reassuring squeeze. "It's not wrong to hope for Mary's happiness. There's no harm in exploring what might blossom between her and him."

Carmela's voice was gentle, laced with maternal wisdom. "Life is full of surprises, my friend. Sometimes, the unexpected path leads to the most beautiful destination. You may find that a relationship with Diego brings its own joys and fulfillment to Mary."

Maria nodded slowly, her thoughts still a whirlwind of uncertainty. "I'll think about what you've said, Carmela. I know you're right in wanting what's best for Mary, but I feel I don't have the right to intervene in her journey."

Carmela smiled; her eyes filled with hope. Mary should follow her heart, but also consider the path that can bring you the most happiness. And remember, I will always be here to support you."

As their conversation continued, the bonds of friendship and love were being strengthened, both in the garden between Mary and Margerite and in the house between Carmela and Maria.

After their private conversation in the garden, Mary and Margerite rejoined their mothers in the cozy sitting room. The air was filled with the fragrant aroma of tea, and the soft chatter of the women created a warm atmosphere that wrapped around them like a comforting embrace.

Carmela poured tea into delicate cups, her gaze shifting between the two young women. "So, my dears, have you had a chance to catch up on everything?"

Margerite shared a smile with Mary before turning to her mother. "Yes, Mama, we've had a good talk. It's wonderful to have Mary and Maria back in Palma."

Maria nodded in agreement. "Indeed, it feels like we've been away for ages."

Carmela leaned forward; her eyes curious. "And what have you two been discussing?"

Mary exchanged a quick glance with Margerite before taking a sip of tea. "We were talking about the storm that came through Palma earlier this week. It must have been quite an ordeal."

Margerite nodded, her expression solemn. "Yes, it was a fierce storm. But we were fortunate that our home didn't sustain much damage. Others in the neighborhood weren't as lucky."

Carmela sighed; her gaze distant. "Times have been difficult for everyone, especially since the Italian soldiers left a few months ago. We really didn't want them here, but they spent a lot of money in the markets."

Mary's brows furrowed in curiosity. "Did you witness their departure, Mama?"

Carmela nodded, a touch of happiness in her eyes. "Yes, we watched them leave the city. It was a welcome sight, as we knew that the British soldiers would no longer look at Mallorca as a threat."

Maria chimed in; her tone thoughtful. "I hope that someday soon we can truly celebrate the return of peace."

Carmela's expression brightened as she looked at her daughter. "Yes, Maria, let's hold onto that hope. The news from Europe has been mixed, but we can only pray for a swift end to the war."

Margerite's gaze shifted to Mary. "Have you heard anything about the war, Mary? You've been in Paris, after all."

Mary sighed, her gaze dropping. "I've heard bits and pieces from the people I met, but it's hard to know what's true and what's just rumor. I am waiting on a letter from John, but in our parting, we were not sure if the post would make its way to Sóller."

Carmela patted Mary's hand comfortingly. "It's the same for all of us, my dear. I would love to get a letter from my sister in Rome, but the post is slow. We must stay strong and hopeful, regardless of the uncertainty that surrounds us."

"Well, we need to be heading back so we can make the last train back to Sóller," Maria said, breaking the somber tone that had settled over the room.

Carmela nodded, her expression softening. "Of course, my dear. Thank you both for coming to visit us. It warms my heart to see you."

Margerite stood up, her smile warm and genuine. "Yes, thank you for brightening our day, Mary. It's been too long."

Mary returned the smile and stood as well. "Thank you for having us, Margerite. I'm glad to see you're feeling better."

As they exchanged farewells and promises to visit again soon, Mary and Maria made their way back to the front door. The afternoon sun casting shadows over the quaint streets of Palma, and a sense of contentment settled over Mary's heart.

Carmela followed them to the door, her eyes sparkling with affection. "Take care, both of you. And remember, you are always welcome here."

Mary nodded, her heart touched by the genuine warmth of the invitation. "Thank you, Carmela. We'll come back to visit again soon."

Margerite added with a playful wink, "Yes, and next time we'll have a tea party that will rival any in the city."

Maria chuckled, her eyes dancing. "Count us in for that."

As they stepped out into the sunlight, Mary and Maria felt the embrace of friendship and family love. The echoes of their conversations and the shared moments of the day lingered in their hearts, reminding them of the strength they drew from each other.

With one last wave, they made their way back through the streets of Palma, their steps light and their spirits lifted. As they headed to the train station, Mary couldn't help but imagine what John might be doing. And as they boarded the train that would carry them back to Sóller, she carried with her the warmth of the day, the strength of their bonds, and the hope that she would see John again, soon.

Mary and Maria made their way from the train after their arrival in Sóller over to the livery where Diego had hitched up Bella, readying her for the ride back to their home.

"All good ladies?" he asked.

"Yes," said Maria. "It was a lovely trip into Palma and a very nice midday with Carmela and Margerite. You should get by to visit again next time you head into Palma. They would very much like to see you again."

"I'll take your advice," said Diego. "Bella is all hitched up and ready. We had a nice nap this afternoon in the stable."

"Thank you, Diego." Said Mary. "We just bottled a new vintage of wine in the past couple of weeks. Come by sometime soon before winter sets in and help us toast to the coming new year."

"Accepted," exclaimed Diego. "You ladies have a nice ride home."

Bella set off in the direction of Maria and Mary's home as the afternoon sun dwindled below the mountain, hiding the valley of orange trees. The smell of winter was on the horizon. Soon the upper elevations of the mountain ranges would have snow while the valley enjoyed brisk temperatures that make cuddling by a fire with a glass a wine a tradition.

Reaching home, Mary put Bella up in the barn and bid her mother and father goodnight. She went to her closet and put on a nightgown that John had bought her in Paris to remind her of him, their time together and the promises made to young love.

As she closed her eyes, she said a prayer, a prayer that John would be safe. That he would endure and persevere through the trials of war and one day, one day show up on the shores of Mallorca and walk off the steps of the train into her arms.

WACHT AM RHEIN

Within the dense embrace of Jack's Forest, an ancient realm hidden amidst the Ardennes Mountains, history was poised to etch an indelible chapter of courage and resilience. The stage was set against the backdrop of the Ardennes Offensive, a pivotal German thrust aimed at reshaping the final chapters of World War II.

On December 16, 1944, a pivotal event unfolded that would come to be known as the Battle of the Bulge. In a daring move, German forces launched a surprise offensive across a 75-mile front in the Ardennes region of Belgium during the later stages of World War II. This audacious maneuver aimed to disrupt the Allied lines and create a pronounced "bulge" in the American front, thus the battle's name. Catching the Allies off-guard, the initial success of this surprise attack would set the stage for a series of intense battles and shifting fortunes over the coming weeks.

The heart of this offensive lay in the area of the Ardennes where vital crossroads existed in the town of Bastogne and held the key to unlocking victory or defeat. A network of highways converged in this crucial town, making it a linchpin in the unfolding drama.

It was December 17th, a bright Sunday afternoon in Mourmelon. The thwack of a baseball bat meeting the ball echoed against the backdrop of army tents, as the platoon members engaged in a spirited game of baseball. Their uniforms swapped for more relaxed attire, they reveled in the opportunity to momentarily escape the weight of their responsibilities and savor a sense of normalcy.

"Man, that swing of yours, Guppy," John chuckled, watching as the ball sailed far from its intended path.

Sergeant Holmes, ever quick on his feet, darted across the field to snatch the ball from the air. "Well, Guppy, maybe you should have a talk with that ball, make sure you're on the same page."

Guppy grinned; his frustration momentarily forgotten. "You're just jealous, Holmes. My wild swings keep everyone guessing."

Holmes laughed, his tall frame stretching as he returned to the makeshift field. "Maybe, Guppy, but I think we'd all prefer some predictability in our swings."

Parsons, stationed on the sidelines with a pad of paper and a pencil, chuckled at the banter. "You guys sure know how to put on a show."

John shot a playful look at Parsons. "And what about you, Parsons? No desire to join the entertainment?"

Parsons grinned back. "Oh, I'm capturing the real action here, you know. Someone's got to document these epic swings."

Guppy raised an eyebrow. "Epic swings? You sure you're watching the same game, Parsons?"

Parsons leaned back, scribbling a few lines in his letter. "Epic or not, it's all going down in history." He was actually penning a letter to his parents but didn't want to put a damper on the fun in the activity.

Sergeant Holmes nodded toward the field. "Speaking of history, let's see if Guppy can finally make some."

Guppy huffed with mock offense. "Hey, I'll have you know, these wild swings are my signature move."

John laughed, grabbing his bat, and stepping up to the plate. "Alright, Guppy, show us how the signature move is done."

The game continued, a mix of skillful plays and comical mishaps, the players soaking in the fun and lightheartedness that temporarily pushed aside the weight of their duties. Guppy's wild swings earned their fair share of chuckles, Holmes's agility drew admiration, and John's graceful moves sparked friendly banter.

As the sun began its descent, casting long shadows across the field, the game eventually wound down. "Alright, folks," John called, wiping sweat from his brow, "looks like we're wrapping it up for now."

Guppy feigned disappointment. "Aw, and I was just getting warmed up."

Sergeant Holmes patted Guppy on the back. "Maybe next time, Guppy. And by next time, I mean after you've had a little batting practice."

Laughter echoed across the field as they gathered their equipment. Parsons, having finished his letter, joined them with a grin. "So, are we ready to discuss the important stuff?"

John raised an eyebrow. "Important stuff? What's that?"

Parsons smirked. "Well, gentlemen, rumor has it there might be another batch of those precious three-day passes to Paris coming our way."

Guppy's eyes lit up. "Paris? Seriously?"

Holmes chuckled. "Ah, Can't say no to that."

John nodded in agreement. "You're right, Parsons. It's about time we got another shot at exploring Paris."

Parsons folded his arms with a satisfied grin. "Thought you might say that. Word is, we'll get the details later in the evening."

With the promise of a three-day pass, the platoon's spirits lifted even higher. The banter continued as they made their way back to camp, their minds already wandering to the adventures that awaited them in the vibrant streets of Paris. As the sun dipped below the horizon, the platoon carried with them the memory of the game and their anticipation of the upcoming pass to go unwind in Paris.

As evening descended over the camp, the men of the platoon gathered in their bunk area, their bunks illuminated by the glow of lanterns and the occasional bursts of laughter. Stories from the day's baseball game were exchanged, each one growing more embellished with every retelling. Guppy's wild swings became legendary feats of athleticism, and Holmes's agile catches took on an almost mythical quality.

Just as the joviality reached its peak, the door swung open, and Sergeant Holmes strode in with a mischievous grin tugging at the corner of his lips. "Hey, ladies," he announced, his voice dripping with playfulness, "guess what I got."

A collective murmur of excitement rippled through the room as the men leaned in, eager for the news. "Well?" John prompted, a grin spreading across his face.

Holmes reached into his pocket and produced a small stack of papers, and the room erupted into cheers and whoops of delight. "A handful of three-day passes, my friends!" he declared, handing them out with theatrical flair.

As the passes were distributed, Holmes offered sage advice with a wink. "Now, gentlemen, remember moderation in all things. Paris is a grand city, but don't go causing any international incidents, alright?"

Laughter and banter filled the air as the men began discussing their plans for the upcoming pass. Some were already making lists of must-see places, while others were speculating about the best places to find good food and entertainment. The room buzzed with excitement, the promise of a break from the routine injecting new energy into their weary bodies.

Just as Holmes was about to share a particularly humorous anecdote about his own adventures in Paris, the door swung open once again. This time, it was Lieutenant Anderson, his expression grave and businesslike. The room fell silent as the lieutenant's commanding presence drew everyone's attention.

"Gentlemen," he began, his tone serious, "I regret to inform you that all three-day passes have been revoked."

A collective groan filled the air, followed by mutters of disappointment. Holmes's expression fell, and he exchanged a somber look with John and the others. The lieutenant continued; his voice steady. "There's been a change in the situation. We've received new orders, and a briefing is being held at the canteen in ten minutes. I suggest you all head there immediately."

The room grew tense as the reality of the situation sank in. Plans for leisurely strolls through the streets of Paris and leisurely meals at charming cafes were abruptly dashed. The men exchanged glances, a mix of disappointment and determination in their eyes.

With a final nod, Lieutenant Anderson left the room, leaving behind a heavy silence. As they prepared to leave, the excitement that had filled the air just moments ago was replaced by a solemn resolve. The three-day pass may have been taken away, but their duty remained, and they would face whatever new challenges awaited them with the same courage and unity that had carried them this far.

The platoon members filed into the canteen, their footsteps creating a soft cadence that echoed in the room. As they entered, they found themselves surrounded by the rest of Easy Company, and the canteen hummed with the subdued murmur of conversation. The tension in the air was palpable, a mixture of curiosity and apprehension as soldiers gathered and took their seats.

Sergeant Holmes exchanged nods with a few familiar faces as they found a place to sit, John and Guppy on one side and Jenkins on the other. The room seemed to hold its collective breath, awaiting the commencement of the briefing. Rumors circulated, voices speculating on what had prompted the sudden change in plans.

The commanding general and many senior officers had taken leave, the expectation being that Christmas would be celebrated in France without major interruptions. It was widely believed that any potential German offensive would not occur until after the new year or possibly even early spring. As such, the soldiers hadn't anticipated any immediate action, making the need for this briefing all the more perplexing.

Lieutenant Anderson stood at the front of the room, his posture composed and his gaze steady as he surveyed the assembled soldiers. He could sense the curiosity and confusion that rippled through the ranks, the weight of responsibility heavy on his shoulders. With the commanding officers away, it was up to Lieutenant Anderson and other officers to brief the division.

Clearing his throat, Lieutenant Anderson began to speak, his voice carrying across the room, the murmur of conversation gradually subsiding. "Gentlemen," he started, his tone measured, "I understand that this change in plans has caught many of us off guard. The situation has evolved, and it falls on us to adapt accordingly."

He paused, his eyes sweeping over the faces before him, taking in the mixture of anticipation and uncertainty. "Recent intelligence reports indicate that the Germans have launched a significant offensive in the Ardennes region. Contrary to our expectations, the enemy has chosen this time to strike, catching us off guard."

A murmur of disbelief and concern rippled through the room, soldiers exchanging incredulous glances. The Ardennes Offensive was met with both surprise and unease. The realization that the war's uncertainties could intrude on even the most anticipated moments was a harsh reminder of their reality.

Lieutenant Anderson's gaze never wavered as he continued to address the platoon. "Our division has been called upon to reinforce the defensive lines. Our position may be altered, and our responsibilities may shift. It's essential that we remain vigilant and adaptable in the face of these unexpected developments."

With a commanding presence, Lieutenant Anderson pressed on, his voice unwavering. "Gentlemen, we have little time to spare. I need each one of you to be ready to move out at dawn. Collect your gear, ammunition, and supplies. Our division's deployment will be swift, and we must be prepared for whatever challenges may arise."

The gravity of the situation was clear in every soldier's eyes as they absorbed the lieutenant's orders. The carefree atmosphere of earlier that day was replaced by a sense of urgency. Their anticipated three-day pass had been snatched away, replaced by the immediacy of duty.

As Lt. Anderson's voice fell silent, the soldiers dispersed, the canteen slowly emptying as they made their way back to their respective quarters. The platoon members, including John, Guppy, and Jenkins, moved with purpose, their brotherhood evident in the way they supported each other.

The night was short as the hands of the clock crept toward 0400. In the pre-dawn darkness, the camp was alive with activity. Flashlights flickered, casting erratic beams of light as soldiers gathered their belongings. The muted shuffle of boots against the ground and the clatter of gear being assembled echoed through the quiet morning.

John and his comrades moved with a mix of determination and practiced efficiency. Conversations were brief but laced with camaraderie and shared resolve. "Make sure you've got enough ammo, Guppy," John called over his shoulder as he checked the straps on his pack.

Guppy's response was a confident grin. "Don't worry, I've got more rounds than I've got sense."

Jenkins, situated nearby, chimed in with a chuckle. "You might want to save some for the enemy, though."

Amidst the exchange of words and preparations, the platoon members felt the weight of responsibility settle on their shoulders. Each man knew that this was their moment to contribute to the larger effort.

As the first light of dawn crept over the horizon, the soldiers moved with a sense of purpose. They gathered their gear, slung packs over their shoulders, and adjusted helmets snugly in place. The sound of shuffling feet and hushed conversations filled the air.

Soon, the trucks awaited, engines idling as they formed a convoy, their headlights piercing through the dimness. A column of tanks off in the distance as part the armed force heading to Belgium. There, they were to meet up with other armored divisions and artillery. The platoon members climbed aboard; faces illuminated by the vehicle's glow. Lieutenant Anderson's voice carried over the stillness as he offered final instructions, the weight of leadership evident in his demeanor.

And then, with the loud hum of engines and a procession of headlights, the convoy set in motion. Sitting across from each other in the convoy of trucks, the reality of the moment etched on their faces. Looking out the back of the truck, the camp lights of Mourmelon fading in the early morning fog that moved in from the east.

As the convoy rolled on, the platoon's collective focus sharpened. The urgency of their situation was palpable as they journeyed toward the heart of uncertainty. The landscape morphed around them, transitioning from familiar to increasingly foreign terrain.

On the night of December 18th, as the platoon and the 101st Airborne Division made their way into Bastogne, the German offensive was proving relentless. The enemy advance had been swift, closing in on the town's outskirts. Just kilometers separated the German forces from the town's defense, and the paratroopers knew they had won a race against time.

The German forces' rapid approach had set the stage for an imminent confrontation. As the platoon and the division moved into Bastogne, the defense of the town fell squarely on their shoulders. With VIII Corps retreating from the area, the responsibility was now thrust upon the paratroopers.

Even as they entered Bastogne, the situation remained fluid, ever-changing, and unpredictable. The town was a contested prize, a vital crossroads that both sides recognized as pivotal. The platoon's arrival had narrowly forestalled the enemy's encroachment, and now they faced the daunting challenge of holding the line.

JACK'S FOREST

The arrival of the advance force Combat Command B of the 10th Armored Division signaled to the Germans that Bastogne would not be surrendered. Easy Company followed shortly and had made it through to Bastogne.

With a sense of urgency and determination, the soldiers of the 101st Airborne Division dispersed into the streets of Bastogne. The town, once a tranquil and ordinary place, had now transformed into an arena of conflict. Orders were clear – defend the city at all costs. The platoon members moved with purpose, their training kicking in as they took up their positions.

The streets of Bastogne were alive with the movement of troops. Soldiers hustled through the cobblestone pathways, their eyes scanning the surroundings for any sign of the approaching German forces. The sound of boots hitting the ground echoed through the chilly air, a steady rhythm of commitment to the task at hand.

As they reached their designated perimeter, the platoon split into teams, working together to establish their defenses. Bunkers were hastily constructed, foxholes dug with a fierce sense of purpose. Jack's Forest, the very terrain that had initially seemed so serene, now became a fortress of determination. The soldiers transformed the landscape, digging in with a shared resolve to withstand the German offensive.

The platoon's movements were synchronized, a testament to their training and cohesion. Northwest to southeast, they formed a defensive line that would stand as a bulwark against the enemy's advance. Bunkers and foxholes dotted the forest, interconnected by a network of purposeful strategy.

As they worked, conversations were brief, and orders were executed with precision. The forest echoed with the sounds of digging, the rustling of gear, and the occasional commands exchanged between platoon members. Despite the gravity of the situation, an unspoken bond of unity and camaraderie threaded through their actions, reinforcing their commitment to one another and their mission.

The platoon's efforts mirrored those of their comrades throughout the division. The defenders of Bastogne were a symbol of resilience, brought together by a shared purpose. Every bunker, every foxhole, was a testament to their dedication and the determination to hold the line against the impending German onslaught.

While the 101st Airborne Division sprang into action, forming a protective perimeter around the town of Bastogne. Other divisions were arranged and meticulously positioned strategically to halt the German advance. The 502nd PIR stood steadfast on the northwest flank, effectively blocking the 26th Volksgrenadier. To prevent entry from Noville, the 506th PIR took a resolute stance, while the 501st PIR guarded the eastern approach. Meanwhile, the 327th Glider Infantry Regiment spread its forces from Marvie in the southeast to Champs in the west along the southern perimeter.

The soldiers of the 101st Airborne, along with engineer and artillery units, fortified the gaps in the line. Their ranks were bolstered by those who, initially assigned to support services, now joined the thin ranks on the front lines. CCB of the 10th Armored Division, despite suffering significant losses, formed a mobile "fire brigade" with a fleet of tanks, acting as a rapid response force in case of emergency.

Amid the relentless German advance, the American artillery units united, forming a temporary artillery group. Equipped with twelve 155 mm howitzers each, they transformed into heavy firepower hubs capable of repelling threats from all directions. Even the antiaircraft batteries were repositioned to augment the defense against enemy armor, while the antitank batteries, working alongside tank destroyer battalions, created an unyielding defense network.

Facing the formidable American presence to their north and east, the German commanders devised a plan to encircle Bastogne. Their approach aimed to strike from the south and southwest, pushing against the American forces. The Winter Solstice marked the commencement of this pivotal engagement, setting the stage for a desperate clash.

As the German Panzer reconnaissance units gained an initial foothold, they nearly overran American artillery positions. However, the ingenuity of a makeshift defense quelled their advance. Despite the resourcefulness of the American forces, all seven highways leading to Bastogne were severed by the Germans, signaling the encirclement of the allied troops and Easy Company.

The situation within Bastogne was dire. Outnumbered by approximately five to one, lacking in essential supplies, and confronted with treacherous weather, the American soldiers found themselves facing a formidable challenge. The absence of key senior leaders, compounded by adverse weather conditions, further compounded their predicament. As a result, tactical air support was unattainable due to the cloud-covered skies, leaving the surrounded U.S. forces cut off from both resupply and crucial reinforcements.

Sergeant Holmes moved with purpose through the snow-covered forest, his boots sinking into the icy ground with every step. Around him, the sounds of distant artillery reverberated through the air, a constant reminder of the precarious situation they found themselves in. He knew that his platoon's survival depended on their ability to hold this line, to withstand the German onslaught that was sure to come.

As he hopped from one foxhole to another, he checked on the supplies and ammunition, making sure each man was equipped for the challenging days ahead. The bitter cold was unforgiving, seeping through layers of clothing and chilling to the bone. The men of Easy Company did not have winter gear and there was no time to secure any prior to their muster. He couldn't help but marvel at the toughness of his men, their determination to protect their position despite the harsh conditions.

"Everything all right in here?" he asked, peering into a foxhole where John and Guppy were stationed.

John nodded, his breath visible in the frosty air. "Yeah, we're good, Sarge. Just trying to stay warm."

Guppy shivered, clutching his rifle. "I've never felt cold like this before. Makes those training exercises back home seem like a walk in the park."

Sergeant Holmes patted Guppy's shoulder. "You'll get used to it, kid. Just gotta keep moving and keep your mind off the chill."

He moved on to the next foxhole, where Parsons and Jenkins were huddled together. Parsons was busy writing in his letter, the pencil shaking slightly in his gloved hand.

"Hey there, Parsons," Holmes said, crouching down. "Writing home again?"

Parsons looked up and grinned. "Yeah, trying to let my folks know I'm still kicking. Just wish I had more exciting news to tell them."

Holmes chuckled. "Well, surviving this is pretty exciting, if you ask me."

Jenkins adjusted his helmet, his eyes scanning the forest. "You think they'll break through?"

Sergeant Holmes looked out into the woods. "We'll do everything we can to stop them, Jenkins. Just gotta hold tight and trust in the men around us."

As he continued his rounds, he couldn't help but be impressed by the resiliency of his platoon. Despite the uncertainty and the biting cold, their spirits remained high. He knew that their determination would be their greatest weapon in the days to come.

Hours passed, the sun sinking below the horizon as the temperature dropped even further. The men in their foxholes chatted in hushed tones, sharing stories and jokes to keep their spirits up. The distant rumble of artillery continued, a constant reminder of the battle that raged beyond the forest.

Sergeant Holmes made his way back to his own foxhole, where Lieutenant Anderson was stationed. The two exchanged a nod, their eyes reflecting a shared understanding of the weight of their responsibilities.

"Everything secure, Sergeant?" Lieutenant Anderson asked.

Holmes nodded. "Supplies are holding up, morale's as good as it can be in these conditions. We are going to need more ammunition and supplies. We were already running short in Mourmelon, so there wasn't much to load prior to leaving."

Anderson glanced out at the snow-covered landscape. "We're in for a tough fight. Command tells me that they will try and airdrop supplies just west outside of town when they can."

Sergeant Holmes gripped his rifle, his determination unwavering. "We'll give them hell, sir. No matter how cold it gets out here."

Evans shifted in the cramped foxhole, his teeth chattering from the biting cold. He cast a glance at Jackson, who was huddled beside him.

"Hey, Jackson," Evans whispered, "you got a smoke?"

Jackson fumbled in his pocket and pulled out a crumpled pack of cigarettes, offering one to Evans. "Yeah, sure thing. It's freezing out here."

Evans gratefully took the cigarette and cupped his hands around it, trying to keep the wind from extinguishing the flame. He took a drag and exhaled a plume of smoke that quickly dissipated in the frigid air.

Jackson nodded, his breath visible in the cold. "Tell me about it. Never thought I'd miss the Texas heat so much."

Evans chuckled softly. "You and me both. This cold is something else."

As they huddled together for warmth, Evans couldn't help but reminisce about his hometown in northwest Texas. "You know, back home, we used to hunt and camp in the snow sometimes. Thought I knew cold until now."

Jackson raised an eyebrow, intrigued. "Hunting in the snow? That sounds wild."

Evans nodded, a hint of nostalgia in his eyes. "Yeah, me and my buddies would head out to the woods, set up camp, and stay out there for days. Sometimes it'd snow so much, we'd wake up with a blanket of white covering everything."

Jackson shivered at the thought. "I can't even imagine sleeping outside in this."

Evans took another drag from the cigarette, the warmth briefly soothing his chilled fingers. "It's a different kind of cold, that's for sure. But you get used to it after a while. Makes you appreciate a warm bed when you finally get back to it."

Jackson looked out into the dark forest, the snow crunching under their boots. "I can't wait for that warm bed."

Evans chuckled. "Hang in there, buddy. We'll get through this. And someday, we'll be telling stories about this to our grandkids."

Jackson smiled, a small glimmer of hope in his eyes. "Yeah, you're right. And they'll probably think we're exaggerating."

Evans grinned. "Well, let's hope they never have to find out for themselves."

As the wind howled around them and the temperature dropped even further, Evans and Jackson huddled closer in the foxhole, sharing warmth as the night enveloped them in a cold vice.

Lt. Anderson adjusted his collar against the biting cold and turned to Sgt. Holmes. "Sergeant, I need to head back to command for a quick status meeting. Keep an eye on things here, will you?"

Sgt. Holmes saluted crisply. "Of course, sir. I'll make sure everything's running smoothly."

Lt. Anderson nodded; his expression serious. "Good. And remember, let's keep everything as low-key as possible. We don't want to give the Germans any unnecessary hints about our positions."

Sgt. Holmes' brow furrowed slightly. "Understood, sir. You think they're close?"

Lt. Anderson's gaze swept the forested landscape, his tone measured. "It's hard to say, but we can't afford to take any chances. Keep the men vigilant, but also remind them to be cautious in their movements. No unnecessary noise or actions that might attract attention."

Sgt. Holmes nodded, his eyes reflecting his commitment. "I'll make sure they're aware, sir."

"Good, Holmes," Lt. Anderson said with a firm nod. "I'll be back as soon as I can. If anything comes up, use your judgment, but remember our priority is maintaining this defensive line."

Sgt. Holmes saluted again. "You can count on me, sir."

Lt. Anderson returned the salute and turned to head back toward the command center. As he walked away, Sgt. Holmes watched his commanding officer's retreating figure, the weight of their responsibilities resting heavily on both of their shoulders. In the midst of the winter chill and the tension of battle, their trust in each other was a vital lifeline.

Not long after Lt. Anderson walked out of Jack's Forest to talk to command, a sudden eruption of sound shattered the night's silence. Artillery shells screamed through the air, crashing into the trees and earth with an explosive force that sent shockwaves rippling through the ground. Trees splintered and shattered; their once-solid trunks reduced to twisted debris. The deafening noise echoed through the forest, drowning out any other sound.

Men scattered in all directions, their training kicking in as they huddled in their fox holes. Shouts and commands mingled with the roar of the artillery, the forest now a chaotic labyrinth of destruction and chaos. The sky lit up in fiery bursts as the impact of the artillery illuminated the night, casting eerie shadows that danced across the snow-covered ground.

The frigid wind and light snow blowing in a cauldron of flames and debris. The sky, heavy with gray clouds, mixed with the smoke of the explosions. Sgt. Holmes needed to act.

He shouted to his men, his voice cutting through the chaos as he directed them to stay in their fox holes. Private Evans and Jackson huddled behind a fallen tree, which fell across their fox hole, their faces streaked with dirt and sweat. "This is insane!" Evans shouted over the cacophony, his eyes wide with both fear and adrenaline.

Jackson gripped his rifle tightly, his voice strained. "Keep your head down and stay focused! We trained for this!"

The men around them sought refuge wherever they could, diving into foxholes and behind trees as explosions continued to shake the ground. The forest seemed to quake with the intensity of the barrage, the air thick with the acrid smell of smoke and burning wood.

As the initial shock of the attack subsided, the platoon's resilience began to shine through. Voices grew steadier, and orders were shouted back and forth, a chorus of determination rising above the chaos. Sgt. Holmes moved among his men, jumping from one foxhole to another, his presence a reassuring anchor in the storm.

"Medic!" he called out, his voice cutting through the tumult as he discovered two of his men had taken a direct hit from an artillery shell, and another who was still alive lay bleeding from arterial wounds on his leg. "Hold on," he told the soldier, Corporal Smith is on his way.

Through the mayhem, Smith had been attending to the wounded and arrived at the two soldiers' side just in time to pronounce them dead. Their wounds were too severe, and they died instantly.

"I'm sorry Sarg," exclaimed Smith. "It's Moore and Johnson, their dead. Looks like they took a mortar shell directly into their foxhole. I will have a detail get the wounded and dead as soon as I can.

As the shelling subsided, a tense calm settled over the forest. John's heart pounded in his chest, his senses on high alert. He climbed out of his bunker to check on Evans and Jackson. Amid the smoke and debris, he thought he caught a flicker of movement, a glimmer of light cutting through the darkness. He strained his eyes, trying to pierce the shadows, his grip tightening around his rifle.

Suddenly, the air was split by the high-pitched whine of machine gun fire. Bullets whizzed overhead, their deadly trajectory a stark reminder of the danger that lurked just beyond the trees. John's instincts kicked in, and he dove into a nearby bunker, landing alongside his fellow soldiers. The earthy walls provided a crude but necessary shield from the hail of bullets that sliced through the air.

His heart raced as the machine gun fire intensified, the relentless rattle of gunfire ringing in his ears. The forest erupted with flashes of light as the tracer rounds streaked through the night, casting an eerie glow that illuminated the battlefield. The soldiers hunkered down in the bunker, exchanging urgent glances as they sought to assess the situation.

"Keep your heads down!" someone shouted, their voice barely audible above the cacophony.

The soldiers knew what they had to do. Gritting their teeth, they raised their rifles and returned fire, muzzle flashes punctuating the darkness as their bullets found their mark. The forest erupted with a chorus of gunfire, the crackling symphony of battle echoing through the trees.

Sgt. Holmes's voice rose above the chaos, his orders firm and unwavering. "Hold your positions, men! Return fire and suppress their advance!"

The forest transformed into a war zone, where the boundary between friend and foe blurred in the shadows.

The soldiers fired with a determined fury, their training binding them together in the face of the enemy onslaught. Bullets tore through the undergrowth, the thud of impacts and the pained cries of wounded men blending into the night's symphony.

As the firefight raged on, the soldiers clung to their bunkers and foxholes, their fingers gripping their weapons with unyielding resolve. The forest became a deadly arena, where the darkness concealed both danger and opportunity. In the midst of the chaos, the platoon fought back against the German infantry's audacious attempt to breach their defenses.

The relentless exchange of gunfire continued as John, Evans, and Jackson huddled in their foxhole. Their breaths came in ragged gasps, their hearts pounding in rhythm with the chaos around them. Suddenly, a sharp ping echoed in the air, followed by the unmistakable sound of metal striking metal. The bullet had struck Evans's helmet, sending a jarring shockwave through the trio.

Evans's wide eyes met John's, his expression a mix of disbelief and incredulity. "That did not just happen," he muttered, his voice laced with a blend of shock and dark humor.

John managed a faint, wry smile, his grip on his rifle tightening. "Guess someone's taking potshots at your fashion sense, Evans."

Jackson, a sense of urgency in his eyes, interrupted their banter. "We've got movement to the right, near that fallen tree!" he shouted, his voice cutting through the chaos.

Without hesitation, Jackson retrieved a grenade from his pouch and swiftly pulled the pin. He launched it with practiced precision, the explosive hurtling through the air like a harbinger of impending destruction. The seconds stretched out; each heartbeat punctuated by the knowledge of the explosion to come.

Then, with a deafening roar, the grenade detonated in a burst of fire and shrapnel. The forest was consumed by a blinding flash, the explosion's shockwave reverberating through the air. The ground trembled beneath them, and the once-still night was shattered into chaos.

The forest fell momentarily silent, the echoes of battle momentarily quelled. The soldiers held their breaths, ears ringing and senses on high alert, waiting to see the results of Jackson's daring move.

As the smoke began to clear, the soldiers exchanged glances, their faces illuminated by the eerie glow of flames. The fallen tree that had concealed the enemy muzzle flash was now splintered and smoldering, a testament to the lethal effectiveness of Jackson's grenade.

"Nice throw, Jackson!" John shouted over the ringing in his ears, his voice tinged with both admiration and relief.

Jackson's grin was visible even in the dim light. "Just trying to level the playing field a bit," he replied, his gaze still fixed on the smoldering aftermath.

Evans let out a shaky laugh, the tension momentarily broken. "Well, I'd say mission accomplished."

But their respite was short-lived. The forest soon reverberated with renewed gunfire, the battle's rhythm resuming its relentless beat. The soldiers braced themselves, their determination unshaken, as they continued to hold their ground against the unrelenting tide of the German offensive.

As the night wore on, the intensity of the siege began to subside, the sporadic gunfire gradually giving way to an uneasy quiet. The forest, once a battleground of deafening chaos, now echoed with an eerie hush. It was as if even the very trees held their breath, waiting for what the next day might bring.

Smith, the platoon medic, his face smudged with dirt and exhaustion, moved from foxhole to foxhole, offering what solace he could to the wounded and the weary. His presence was a reassurance in the midst of uncertainty, a reminder that even in the darkest of hours, they were not alone.

Sgt. Holmes, his voice a mixture of weariness and authority, made his rounds among the platoon. He leaned into each foxhole, his words carrying the weight of experience. "Alright, lads, listen up. It's been a hell of a night, but the worst seems to be over for now. We're not out of the woods yet, but we've weathered the storm. Try to get some rest. We'll do two-hour shifts—one on watch, one catching some shut-eye."

The soldiers nodded, their faces etched with exhaustion but also a steely determination. As the night wore on, their vigilance never wavered. One would sit with rifle in hand, eyes trained on the forest's edge, while their companion found brief respite from the cold and the tension.

In one of the foxholes, John carefully opened a can of peaches he had stashed away, the metal lid yielding with a satisfying hiss. He looked over to Guppy, his expression a mix of weariness and fright. "Hey, Guppy, you want to share these with me?"

Guppy's tired eyes brightened at the offer. "You're a lifesaver, John. I could use something to take the edge off. My stomach has been growling all evening."

As they savored the sweetness of the peaches, John couldn't help but chuckle. "You know, Guppy, earlier tonight, when I was in Evans and Jacksons foxhole, a bullet bounced off Evan's helmet, it was like something out of a movie."

Guppy grinned; his fatigue momentarily forgotten. "Oh, that is classic. I bet Evan's face was priceless."

John's laughter mingled with the stillness of the night. "I thought he was going to keel over right there. 'That did not just happen,' he said."

Guppy shook his head, a smile playing on his lips. "Well, we've certainly got some stories to tell when we make it out of this mess."

John's gaze turned somber for a moment, his thoughts briefly drifting to the uncertainty of their situation. "Yeah, we will. And we will make it out of this. Just gotta keep our wits about us and watch each other's backs."

Guppy nodded, his determination echoing John's. "Damn right, John. We're in this together."

The night wore on, the soldiers fighting to stay warm in the turmoil. As the sky began to lighten with the approaching dawn, they clung to the hope that the new day would bring not only the sun's warmth but also a renewed sense of resilience and strength.

They were wrong; the weather was not about to relent. Instead, it seemed to grow fiercer with each passing hour. The forest, once a serene backdrop, was now engulfed in a swirling tempest of snow and wind. The cold pierced through every layer of clothing, seeping into the very bones of the soldiers. The promise of resupply seemed like a distant dream, as the storm grounded any efforts to fly in much-needed supplies.

In the midst of this icy turmoil, the platoon huddled together for what warmth they could muster. They shared what little food they had left, passing around cans of rations and taking turns sipping from canteens. The act of sharing sustenance was more than a matter of nourishment; it was a reminder of their unity and the bonds forged through shared hardship.

John lit a cigarette and offered one to Guppy. The small flame of the lighter danced against the waning darkness, casting fleeting shadows on their faces. As they inhaled the smoke, the acrid scent mingled with the biting cold air. It was a moment of simple comfort, a brief break from the turmoil that surrounded them.

"Never thought I'd say this," Guppy mused between drags, "but I miss the days of getting yelled at in training."

John chuckled, his breath forming misty clouds in the frigid air. "Yeah, at least then we knew what we were in for. This... this is something else."

Their conversation was punctuated by the distant rumble of artillery, a grim reminder that the enemy was still out there, lurking beyond the reach of their vision. They exchanged a glance, their eyes filled with determination.

"We'll get through this," John said, his voice unwavering.

Guppy nodded; his gaze fixed on the forest beyond.

As if in response to their resolve, the morning erupted, once again spoiling a moment of rest. The forest came alive with the thunderous roar of gunfire and the shriek of incoming shells. The soldiers sprang into action, seeking cover within the confines of their foxholes.

Machine gun fire whizzed through the air, cutting through the snow and wind like a deadly symphony. The soldiers returned fire, their own shots echoing against the chaos. The forest was a maze of shadows and danger, each muzzle noise revealing the direction of enemy fire.

In the midst of the firefight, the platoon's unity shone through. They shouted warnings to each other, shared ammunition, and fought side by side against the relentless onslaught. Jackson's voice rang out, calling for a grenade, and a moment later, the explosion reverberated through the air, followed by a triumphant shout.

Lt. Anderson emerged from the woods behind Sgt. Holmes' bunker, his face bearing the weight of the news he had just received as entered the bunker. The morning light cast shadows across his weary features as he approached Sgt. Holmes, who was standing watch near the entrance.

Holmes looked up from his vantage point, his expression a mix of concern and anticipation. "Sir, what's the word?"

Anderson took a moment, as if collecting his thoughts in the midst of the chaos around them. He glanced at the men huddled in the nearby foxholes, bracing against the relentless storm and the persistent threat of the enemy. Then, with a steadying breath, he turned to Holmes.

"The situation is tougher than we thought," Anderson began, his voice firm. "Resupply efforts are grounded due to the weather. The Germans have tightened their grip on Bastogne, and now we've got two Panzer divisions bearing down on us from multiple directions."

Holmes exchanged a knowing glance with Anderson, a shared understanding of the direness of their predicament. "So, we're truly on our own then," Holmes said, his voice steady despite the gravity of the news.

Anderson nodded; his jaw set in determination. "We are, but we cannot falter. We've held them off so far, and we'll continue to do so.

Holmes offered a grim smile, a mixture of respect and resolve in his eyes. "Yes, sir. We won't let them take this town."

As they stood there, surrounded by the forest's cold embrace and the echoes of battle, their commitment to each other and to their mission burned stronger.

"I have to go back this evening," said Lt. Anderson. "General McAuliffe is holding a briefing each evening so can move troops around as needed to reinforce areas where we have taken heavy casualties. I've heard several other platoons in Easy sustained losses up to fifty percent. That's a lot of men to lose in one evening. What is our status?"

"Our status is holding, sir," Sgt. Holmes replied, his voice carrying a mix of fatigue and determination. He shifted his gaze from Lt. Anderson to the men stationed in their defensive positions, their eyes weary but resolute. "We've managed to fend off their attacks, but it's been tough going. We've lost a few good men and have several wounded. I've redistributed our forces to cover the gaps, but it's stretching us thin."

Lt. Anderson's brows furrowed, concern etching lines on his face. "I hate to ask, but how bad is it?"

Holmes's gaze remained steady; his unwavering determination evident in his eyes. "We've lost about a quarter of the platoon, and a few are wounded to varying degrees. Those who can still fight are giving their all, but we need reinforcements and supplies."

Anderson's eyes met Holmes's, a shared understanding passing between them. "We can't afford to let them overrun us. I'll do my best to convey the urgency of our situation to command."

Holmes nodded, a renewed sense of responsibility settling on his shoulders. "Thank you, sir. The men are gritty and determined. We'll hold the line."

Over the next 24 hours, the forest seemed to become a relentless battleground, the clash of wills echoing through the trees. The Germans launched repeated assaults, each one more determined than the last, their artillery fire shaking the ground and their infantry attacks sending waves of tension through the American ranks. The platoon's foxholes bore witness to the ebb and flow of battle, the men hunkering down as mortar shells exploded and bullets whizzed overhead.

Casualties mounted, and the platoon felt the weight of loss as they mourned fallen comrades and cared for the wounded. Each dawn brought a renewed sense of purpose, as the soldiers emerged from their foxholes, faces set with determination. Sgt. Holmes's voice resonated with orders, the backbone of their defenses, and Lt. Anderson's unwavering presence provided a rallying point amidst the chaos.

The weather, unrelenting in its fury, seemed to mirror the soldiers' struggle. Snow and wind continued to lash the forest, gnawing at their resolve as they fought to stay warm and alert. Short supplies further tested their endurance, and the camaraderie that had grown among them deepened as they shared meager rations, cigarettes, and stories of home.

Through it all, the forest became a battleground not just of physical warfare, but of endurance and resilience. The soldiers pressed on, clinging to the hope that reinforcements would arrive, that the tide of battle would turn in their favor. As they faced each new wave of attack, they did so with a spirit unyielding, a testament to the unbreakable resolve that had come to define the men of Easy Company.

On the afternoon of the 22nd, Lt. Anderson returned from command, his face bearing the weariness of many trips back and forth. He sought out Sgt. Holmes amidst the foxholes and quickly relayed the news, his voice carrying a glimmer of hope. "Sgt. Holmes, the parachute drop of supplies has begun. It'll be spread out over the next several days. The 969th Artillery Battalion stationed around Bastogne is helping gather those supplies and they'll be sending them our way. Finally, some relief."

Sgt. Holmes's eyes sparked with a mixture of relief and determination. "That's good news, Lieutenant. Our boys could use some resupply after all this."

Lt. Anderson nodded, his expression grave but resolute. "Absolutely. The situation might be tough, but we've faced worse."

As they conversed, the distant thud of artillery fire continued to punctuate the air, a somber reminder of the ongoing struggle. But the news of supplies rekindled a sense of purpose among the platoon, a renewed belief that they could hold their ground and withstand whatever came their way.

Within the next days, the skies above Bastogne were transformed into a lifeline. The parachute drops, while not without their challenges due to the turbulent weather, brought much-needed sustenance and ammunition to the besieged defenders. The 969th Artillery Battalion, once limited in their ability to provide support, now focused their efforts on collecting the dropped supplies and distributing them to the platoons scattered in the woods.

For the soldiers in Jack's Forest, the sight of supplies parachuting down from the heavens was a sight to behold. The crunch of snow underfoot mingled with the excited murmurs of men; their spirits lifted by the tangible proof that they were not forgotten. As crates were opened and distributed, faces lit up with a mixture of gratitude and renewed determination.

And it was amidst this flurry of activity that history unfolded. On the 22nd of December, General von Lüttwitz presented his demand for surrender to the American forces in Bastogne. The demand urged the American forces to surrender and avoid further bloodshed. However, the response from Brigadier General Anthony McAuliffe was swift and unyielding, capturing the defiance that had come to symbolize the defense of Bastogne: "Nuts!"

The word resonated not just within the forest, but across the hearts of the soldiers. It was a rallying cry, a declaration that they would not back down, that their resolve was unbreakable. As the winter sun cast long shadows through the trees, the platoon in Jack's Forest stood united, determined to weather the storm, and emerge victorious.

FOY AND THE FALLEN

The bleak winter landscape around Bastogne had become an arena of courage and endurance, where the 101st Airborne Division stood resilient against the relentless onslaught of German forces. Yet, as hope flickered dimly in the hearts of the weary soldiers, a glimmer of salvation was about to appear on the horizon.

In the midst of the bitter cold and the roar of artillery, the unmistakable sound of engines growling through the snow-soaked earth reached the ears of the beleaguered defenders. It was General George S. Patton, and with him came the 3rd Army, pushing eastward with indomitable resolve.

The arrival of Patton's forces marked a turning point in the battle. Like a whirlwind, they had executed a daring 90-degree pivot, breaking through German lines, and cutting their way towards Bastogne. Their sheer audacity and unyielding determination had shattered the encircling grip of the enemy, and the skies above Bastogne seemed to echo with the rumble of tanks and the thunder of artillery as Patton's forces drove the Germans eastward, relentlessly pursuing them across the Rhine.

For the soldiers of the 101st, the sight of Patton's tanks and the sound of his battle-hardened troops was a beacon of hope. The arrival of reinforcements and the relief that washed over them carried a renewed sense of purpose. It was a testament to the strength of the human spirit and the unbreakable bond between those who fought side by side.

The 101st Airborne Division and Patton's 3rd Army began to reshape the fate of Bastogne. The once-impenetrable ring of German forces was now fragmented and scattered, their onslaught broken by the resolve of those who stood firm in the face of adversity.

And so, the men who had weathered the storm in the forest surrounding Bastogne could finally catch their breath, knowing that their sacrifices were not in vain. With Patton's arrival came a glimmer of triumph, and a new task, to push forward and take the town of Foy.

Foy was a small French town nestled within the Ardennes region and had bore witness to the tumultuous events of World War II. As an integral part of the theater of war, Foy became a setting of historical significance during the Battle of the Bulge.

The town's architecture reflected its age-old history, characterized by quaint stone buildings that lined narrow streets, giving it a rustic charm. The houses, some dating back centuries, stood as silent witnesses to the passage of time and the trials of war. Cobblestone streets wound through the town, meandering past homes, shops, and other structures.

However, the serenity and quaint look of Foy was shattered during that winter when it found itself at the crossroads of conflict. Foy's strategic location northeast of Bastogne made it a key point of interest for both Allied and German forces.

The town's buildings, once symbols of continuity and stability, had been transformed into battlegrounds. Ruined structures, crumbled facades, and the scars of war marred Foy's landscape.

Sergeant Holmes moved with purpose through the scattered remnants of 3rd Platoon, his voice a clear command in the crisp morning air. "Alright, boys, gather your gear and prepare to move out," he directed, his eyes scanning each tired face. The news of the platoon's impending departure was met with a mix of weariness and determination, a silent acknowledgment that the time had come to leave behind the familiarity of the forest's embrace.

John exchanged a tired but knowing look with Guppy as they began to secure their belongings. "Seems like the forest's finally letting us go," Guppy remarked, his voice carrying a hint of both relief and nostalgia.

"Yeah," John replied, his tone tinged with a mix of exhaustion and reflection. "We've made our mark here, but it's time to move on."

As the platoon members methodically gathered their equipment, Evans and Jackson engaged in a hushed conversation nearby. "Can't believe we're leaving this place," Evans muttered, his breath visible in the cold morning air.

"Better than waiting around for another German attack," Jackson replied, his voice carrying the weight of experience. "We'll be alright."

Sergeant Holmes' voice cut through the air again, issuing instructions that reverberated through the ranks. "Pack up, boys, and do it quickly. We've got a path to clear."

The soldiers moved with a practiced efficiency, shouldering their packs, securing their weapons, and ensuring that they were ready for the march ahead. Amid the bustle of activity, the platoon's camaraderie shone through in the occasional exchange of jokes and knowing glances. There was a sense of unity, a shared understanding that they were all in this together.

As John finished securing his gear, Sergeant Holmes approached him, his expression a mixture of concern and determination. "Keep your head up, John," he said quietly. "We've weathered worse, and we'll get through this too."

John nodded, a grateful smile playing at the corners of his lips. "I know, Sergeant. Just taking it one step at a time."

The sun began to rise, and with their equipment in order, the platoon fell into formation, ready to face the challenges that lay ahead on the move towards Foy. Conversations murmured among them as they marched, a mixture of anticipation, apprehension, and determination to continue pushing forward. Their task, take the town of Foy and push the Germans out of Belgium.

The forest, once their battleground and sanctuary, gradually faded into the background as the platoon moved forward. Ahead, they could hear to rumble of artillery fire softening up the defenses of the German soldiers holding the town.

At the edge of the forest, the platoon came to a halt, their breath visible in the crisp winter air. The transition from the familiar cover of the woods to the exposed open field was palpable, a reminder of the shifting landscape of battle. Sergeant Holmes pulled out his radio, his expression focused as he keyed in a signal to reach Lieutenant Anderson.

Meanwhile, John and Parsons positioned themselves on a slight rise, their binoculars trained on the landscape before them. The hay field stretched out, patches of white punctuating the green expanse, evidence of snow clinging to the earth. "Take a look at those bales," John murmured, adjusting his binoculars for a clearer view.

Parsons followed John's gaze, focusing on the large hay bales strategically placed across the field. "Good cover," he noted, his voice low. "Could provide some protection as we advance."

John nodded in agreement, then shifted his attention to the outskirts of the town. His trained eye picked out the telltale signs of machine gun positions, a stark reminder of the formidable defenses they were up against. "We'll need to move carefully through that area," he said, his voice a mixture of caution and determination.

Parsons' gaze followed John's, settling on the distant shapes of tanks partially hidden among buildings. "Looks like they're prepared for us," he remarked grimly.

As they continued to survey the scene, Sgt. Holmes' voice broke through their observations. "Lt. Anderson, this is Holmes. We're at the edge of the forest, ready to move out. What's the situation on the offensive?"

John and Parsons exchanged a glance as they listened, the static of the radio momentarily filling the air. The tension was palpable as they awaited Lt. Anderson's response, aware that the success of their next moves hinged on the information they were about to receive.

"Copy that, Lieutenant," Sgt. Holmes responded, his tone steady. "We'll proceed with caution and maintain radio contact."

With the communication concluded, John turned to Parsons, a determined look in his eyes. "We've got our orders," he said. "Let's stay focused and work our way through this."

Parsons nodded, his grip on his binoculars tightening. "We've faced worse odds before. We'll get through this too."

Just before he was about to give the order to advance, Sgt. Holmes watched as Corporal Kincaid approached from the rear, the urgency in his expression evident even from a distance. He hand-delivered a message he carried that spoke of crucial developments unfolding on the battlefield. As Kincaid reached him, his breath slightly labored from the exertion, he extended the message to Sgt. Holmes.

Holmes took the message, his fingers tightening around the paper as he quickly scanned its contents. The words conveyed a sense of urgency, a call to hold their position while 1st Platoon, involved in a flanking maneuver, attempted to break through a heated firefight. The weight of the situation settled heavily on his shoulders, the responsibility of maintaining cohesion and communication within the platoon pressing upon him.

He exchanged a brief nod with Kincaid, an unspoken acknowledgment of the gravity of the task at hand. "I'll ensure this reaches Lt. Anderson," he said firmly, his voice carrying the resolve that had become a hallmark of his leadership.

Kincaid nodded in return, his expression reflecting both concern and trust. "We've got to push forward, Sgt. Holmes. 1st Platoon's success is crucial to our advance."

Sgt. Holmes' gaze shifted from the message to the landscape before them, his thoughts racing as he considered the fluidity of the situation. "We'll do what we can, just let us know when we can move forward," he affirmed, his words a silent promise to his fellow soldiers and the mission they were all committed to.

As he folded the message and tucked it securely into his pocket, Sgt. Holmes turned his attention back to the platoon. His voice carried across the clearing as he relayed the orders they had just received. "Hold your positions," he commanded, his tone a blend of authority and calm. "We're awaiting word from 1st Platoon. Stay alert and ready."

The platoon members nodded in understanding, their eyes reflecting a mix of determination and readiness. The forest edge around them seemed to hold its breath, the tension palpable as they awaited further instructions.

The platoon members huddled in their positions, their eyes flicking toward one another in the dim light of the forest.

Guppy leaned toward John; his voice hushed but edged with a touch of concern. "Hey, John, how's your ammo count looking'?"

John spared a quick glance at the belt of ammunition slung over his shoulder, then looked back at Guppy with a confident grin. "Got enough to keep these Germans at bay, I reckon. How 'bout you?"

Guppy's reply was accompanied by a wry smile. "Well, let's just say I'll take them all out, far cry from conserving ammo in forest the past few days."

Jackson, squatting behind a tree a few yards away, chimed in with a quiet chuckle. "You ain't the only one, Guppy. My grenade pouch feels like I am dragging around a bowling ball."

Evans, who was positioned a bit farther down the line, joined the conversation. "Don't worry, guys, I've got a couple extra grenades to spare if you need any."

Sgt. Holmes moved behind their positions as he checked on his them, catching wind of their conversation. He leaned in closer, his voice a low, steady presence in the midst of their exchange. "Listen up guys, keep an ear out for my voice. We should get word to advance within the next half hour."

John nodded, his respect for Sgt. Holmes evident in his gaze. "You got it, Sarge."

Holmes offered a brief, reassuring smile before moving back up the line to his former position.

As the tension thickened in the forest, the platoon members saw Corporal Kincaid approach once again, his face flushed with a mix of excitement and urgency. Holmes stepped forward, his eyes narrowing in anticipation.

"Alright, what's the word, Kincaid?" Holmes asked, his voice low but eager.

Kincaid's eyes gleamed with excitement as he began recounting the events that had unfolded in Foy. "Alright, listen up, boys. You won't believe what happened over in 1st platoon. They were sent to flank the town, just like before, and things took a turn."

The platoon members leaned in; their curiosity piqued. "What happened?" John asked, unable to hide his amusement.

Kincaid grinned, clearly enjoying the story he was about to share. "So, 1st platoon was told to halt and take cover, right? Lt. Dike ordered them to hold position, and they were basically sitting ducks out there."

Guppy let out a snort of laughter. "Oh man, I can only imagine how that went."

Kincaid nodded enthusiastically. "Oh, it gets better. Without any means of communication, they were stuck out there, waiting for orders to move. And that's First Lieutenant Speirs ran through the German lines, through the town and surprised the hell out of the Germans. Can you imagine their faces?"

The platoon erupted into laughter, the absurdity of the situation sinking in. John wiped away a tear from his eye, chuckling. "Wait, he ran through Foy, back and forth?"

Kincaid nodded; his excitement unabated. "You got it. He delivered the orders to 1st platoon, then ran back toward our lines, right through Foy again, and the Germans didn't even fire at him!"

Evans shook his head in disbelief. "That's like something out of a movie."

Kincaid nodded, his voice dripping with enthusiasm. "I know, right? And that's not even the best part. He did all that with a grin on his face. Apparently, the Germans were so shocked they forgot to shoot at him. They just stared at this lunatic running through the middle of town."

As the platoon members laughed and exchanged incredulous glances, Sgt. Holmes shook his head in amazement. "Well, I'll be damned. That's one way to make an entrance."

Kincaid nodded, a mischievous twinkle in his eye. "You bet it is. So, the orders are to push forward into Foy. The 1st platoon is making their move, and it's our turn to join the party."

"Relay the message that we will be moving in," said Holmes.

Kincaid headed back through the forest towards the Command station. The platoon picked up their gear and began moving into the outskirts of Foy from the south. Slowly moving through the hay field making sure to stay in line with a large barn that was hiding their advance. The artillery unit had softened things up a bit with a barrage of ordinance for well over an hour disorienting and causing the German troops to move indoors or underground.

As the 3rd platoon advanced into the outskirts of Foy, the air grew thick with tension. The once distant sounds of battle became a deafening roar as they entered the heart of the fight. Holmes led his men with a steady determination, their eyes sharp and senses heightened.

The buildings on the perimeter of the town provided ample cover, but also concealed hidden threats. The platoon members maneuvered with caution; their rifles ready. Bullets pinged off the walls as they returned fire, the crackling exchanges creating a cacophony of chaos.

"Stay low and keep moving!" Holmes shouted over the din, his voice a beacon of guidance amidst the turmoil. The men followed his lead, dodging and weaving as they advanced.

John and Parsons found themselves behind a crumbling stone wall, exchanging quick glances as they assessed their next move. "We need to clear those windows," John said, his voice tense. "Snipers could pick us off from there."

Parsons nodded, his expression resolute. "I'll provide cover fire; you take the shot."

As Parsons unleashed a barrage of shots toward the windows, John took careful aim. His heart pounded in his chest as he squeezed the trigger, and a moment later, a satisfying thud signaled a successful hit. Parsons grinned at him, a silent acknowledgment of their teamwork.

Meanwhile, tank movement rattled the ground, sending tremors through the air. The platoon members exchanged concerned glances, knowing they needed a way to neutralize the armored threat. Holmes swiftly surveyed their surroundings and gestured to a pile of discarded equipment nearby.

"Jackson, grab that bazooka and take aim!" Holmes shouted, his voice cutting through the chaos.

Jackson nodded and positioned himself, his focus unwavering. The rocket launcher roared to life as he fired, the explosive projectile hurtling toward the tank. A moment later, the ground shook with a thunderous explosion as the tank's demise was sealed.

With the immediate threat neutralized, the platoon pushed forward into the town square. Sniper fire continued to zip around them, prompting the men to take cover behind any available barrier. Holmes radioed for support, ensuring their position was communicated to the rest of Easy Company.

"We need to clear those snipers out," Holmes said, his jaw set in determination.

Guppy nodded, his grip tightening on his rifle. "Let's give 'em a taste of their own medicine."

The platoon members exchanged fire, systematically targeting the windows from which the deadly shots originated. With each precise shot, the snipers were silenced one by one, the threat diminishing as the echoes of gunfire filled the square.

As the battle raged on, buildings smoldering and the air heavy with the scent of gunpowder, 3rd platoon stood their ground. With every shot fired, every obstacle overcome, they moved closer to their objective, pushing back the enemy forces one building, one street at a time.

Amidst the chaos, the Germans mounted a fierce counterattack, their ranks swelling with additional soldiers. The situation grew precarious as the platoon found themselves temporarily outnumbered and outgunned. Holmes quickly made the call to fall back, directing his men to retreat to a more defensible position.

"Fall back, 100 yards! Move, move!" Holmes's voice rang out above the din, rallying his platoon as they withdrew.

In the disarray, Jackson's leg was struck by a bullet, and he stumbled to the ground with a cry of pain. The rest of the platoon continued their retreat, but John's instincts kicked in. Without a second thought, he abandoned his position and sprinted back toward Jackson.

Ignoring the hail of bullets around him, John reached Jackson's side and hoisted him over his shoulder. Adrenaline surged through his veins as he ran, the weight of his injured comrade driving him forward. He could feel Jackson's labored breath against his neck, a stark reminder of the urgency of the situation.

John's boots pounded against the pavement as he carried Jackson back toward cover. The crumbling stone wall offered a temporary sanctuary, and John deposited Jackson behind it with care. "You're gonna be alright, buddy," John assured him, his voice firm despite the chaos around them. "Medic!" he shouted. "Medic!"

Jackson's face was etched with pain, but he managed a weak nod of gratitude. "Thanks, John."

Bullets continued to whiz through the air as John hunkered down beside Jackson, his mind racing to assess their next move. He knew they couldn't stay there indefinitely – the counterattack was gaining momentum, and they needed to regroup with the platoon.

"Stay low, Jackson," John instructed, his eyes scanning the surroundings. "We're gonna make our way back to the others as soon as we get a chance."

Before John and Jackson could make their move to rejoin the others, a welcome sight unfolded before them. The rest of the platoon, joined by 2nd platoon in a coordinated flanking maneuver, launched another push into town. The combined effort breathed new life into the assault, catching the Germans off-guard and driving them back from their fortified positions.

The rhythmic cracks of gunfire reverberated through the air as the platoons advanced, moving with renewed determination. Explosions punctuated the chaos as grenades were hurled, and the streets of Foy became a battleground of grit and resilience.

Amidst the fervor of the assault, Corporal Smith, the platoon medic, arrived on the scene. He wasted no time in assessing Jackson's injuries, his skilled hands working swiftly to stabilize the wounded soldier. "You're gonna be alright, Jackson," he reassured, his voice carrying a calm confidence that provided a much-needed anchor in the midst of the storm.

John spared a quick nod of gratitude toward the medic before turning his attention back to the unfolding battle. He could feel the collective determination of his comrades, a shared resolve that pushed them forward even in the face of adversity.

As the platoons continued their push, the Germans began to falter, their defenses crumbling under the relentless assault. The combined effort of the two platoons proved too much for them to withstand, and the momentum began to shift in favor of the American forces.

The streets of Foy became a maze of chaos and combat, with buildings echoing with gunfire and plumes of smoke. The platoon moved up to the edge of the town square, the Germans pulling back to the northeast of the town.

The platoon pressed on; their advance marked by twosomes darting across the square with the precision of a well-coordinated dance. Each pair of soldiers moved with a mix of urgency and caution, using the chaotic landscape to their advantage as they sought cover and concealment.

First, it was Parsons and Smith, their rifles held at the ready as they sprinted from the protection of a crumbled wall to an overturned truck. Bullets ricocheted off the asphalt around them, the enemy's fire intensifying as the Americans closed in on their position. The truck offered a momentary shield, and they huddled behind its rusted frame before making a break for the relative safety of an abandoned shop across the street.

Sgt. Holmes yelled, "Sniper! Top floor window of the hotel!"

The platoon opened fire on the hotel window as Evans and John moved across the square. They weaved through the debris-strewn thoroughfare, relying on instinct and training as they moved. Reaching the overturned truck, they took a breath, their eyes locking in a shared understanding before they surged forward again, sprinting for the cover of the abandoned shop's shattered windows.

Two by two the platoon navigated the square across the street to the abandoned shop while the ones already across fired at the Germans hiding in the upper floors of the hotel from the broken shop's windows.

And finally, it was Guppy and Jenkins turn, their breaths coming in short bursts as they raced across the square. Guppy's eyes darted around, his keen awareness scanning for threats. They reached the overturned truck, a brief respite from the onslaught of bullets. But as they prepared to make their final sprint to the shop, tragedy struck.

A single shot rang out, the crack of a rifle cutting through the chaos. Guppy stumbled, a look of surprise on his face as his body jolted. He fell to the ground, his chest stained with a dark blossoming stain. Jenkins, unaware of the tragedy that had befallen his comrade, continued running, his eyes locked on the abandoned shop.

Sgt. Holmes, ever watchful, saw the horrific scene unfold. He reached out and grabbed John's arm, his grip firm. "Don't," he said, his voice laced with an unspoken truth. "He's gone."

John's heart sank, his eyes fixed on Guppy's still form in the street. He wanted to go back, to help, to save his friend. But Holmes' words held a weight of finality that he couldn't ignore. With a heavy heart, he tore his gaze away and followed Jenkins into the shop, the echoes of gunfire and the memory of Guppy's sacrifice haunting his every step. His best friend for the last couple of years now a victim of this terrible war. They would eventually lose the town to the Germans after briefly taking control over it.

The town of Foy, a seemingly unassuming collection of buildings and streets, became the epicenter of a relentless struggle between the US Army and the Germans that winter. Foy found itself caught in a violent tug-of-war that would span several more weeks, with its fate hanging in the balance.

The 506th Parachute Infantry Regiment of the 101st Airborne Division in their relentless push, inflicted the German forces with heavy losses—both in manpower and tanks—while the suffering significant casualties. The town's streets became a theater of conflict, echoing with the sounds of gunfire and the clamor of war.

The initial German victory was short-lived. Just a few weeks later, supported by the thunderous roar of artillery fire, they pushed the German forces back, inch by inch, in an effort to reclaim Foy. The bitter cold and the treacherous snowy terrain only heightened the intensity of the struggle.

However, the battle was far from over. The Germans launched a renewed effort to retake Foy, sending in tanks and a battalion to seize the town once again. The fighting escalated, house-to-house and street-by-street, as both sides fought for control. The American forces faced a formidable challenge, lacking the cover needed to shield themselves in the open and snowy fields surrounding Foy.

Despite the odds stacked against them, the American soldiers persisted. With the assistance of the US 11th Armored Division, they mounted a final counterattack on the determined German forces. The town's fate hung in the balance as the opposing sides clashed, their determination unwavering. The struggle culminated in a final push, and the Americans managed to reclaim Foy for the last time.

The price was high, many soldiers from the 101st lost their lives. Guppy's death weighed heavily on 3rd platoon, and especially on John, revealing the gravity of their situation and the reality of war.

Amidst the ruins of Foy, John and the remnants of his platoon found a brief rest from the turmoil that had consumed their last weeks. Perched on a pile of debris, they shared stories of Guppy, their fallen comrade, a mix of somber reflection and fond laughter at the memory of his antics. Guppy's wild spirit had been a source of both frustration and amusement, and now, as they sat among the rubble, they realized how much they missed his infectious energy.

Their conversation was suddenly interrupted by a faint figure emerging in the distance. As the figure drew closer, John's heart leapt in recognition—it was Jackson. A collective gasp of surprise rippled through the group, followed by a chorus of joyful exclamations. Hugs and pats on the back were exchanged as Jackson was warmly welcomed back into their midst.

"Jackson, you old son of a gun!" one of the platoon members exclaimed, slapping him playfully on the shoulder. "We thought you were a goner!"

Jackson grinned, his eyes reflecting the camaraderie and relief in the air. "Not that easy to get rid of me," he quipped, his voice carrying a touch of the lightheartedness that had endeared him to his fellow soldiers.

The story of Jackson's return was a remarkable one. After that fateful bullet had pierced his leg, he had endured through the pain and uncertainty of recovery. His determination paid off, and he was deemed fit to rejoin the platoon once more. The fact that he was back, standing among them, was a testament to his resilience and the unbreakable bond that united these men.

As they gathered around Jackson, the loss of Guppy was still fresh in their minds, one of the platoon members spoke up. "You know, it's moments like these that make you think we're going to be alright." The sentiment hung in the air, a silent acknowledgment of the strength they drew from each other and the hope that persisted even in the darkest of times.

LETTERS

In the quiet moments before their next engagement, the platoon found themselves on the outskirts of Drulingen, a town in the historically contested Alsace-Lorraine region. The air was heavy with anticipation as they prepared to face the Germans once more on this new battleground. The scars of war were etched deep into the landscape, and the soldiers felt the weight of their mission.

Sitting around their makeshift camp, the platoon members exchanged glances and words in hushed tones. The camaraderie that had carried them through the trials of Bastogne was still intact, even as they braced for the challenges that lay ahead. Amid the tension, Jenkins, ever the curious one, caught sight of John sitting apart, penning a letter.

"Hey, John," Jenkins called out, his voice breaking the stillness. "Is that a letter to your girl back in Soller?"

John looked up, a faint smile touching his lips. "Nah," he replied, his gaze shifting to the paper in his hands. "It's a letter to Guppy's parents."

Jenkins' expression softened as he nodded in understanding. Guppy's absence was still keenly felt among them, a reminder of the sacrifices they all made. "You're doing a good thing, writing to them," Jenkins said, his voice tinged with sympathy.

John nodded, his gaze dropping to the letter. "Yeah, I hope it brings them some comfort," he said quietly. "Guppy was a character, that's for sure."

Just as the conversation began to drift into somber territory, Jenkins leaned in, his curiosity piqued once more.

"What about that letter to Mary?" he asked, a knowing grin on his face. "I've seen you writing it before."

John chuckled, his features softening with a mixture of longing and fondness. "Yeah, it's in my knapsack," he admitted. "But there's no way to get it to her now."

Jenkins leaned back, a mischievous glint in his eye. "Come on, let me read it!" he urged. "I need something to keep my spirits up, you know."

John's smile widened, and he relented. He reached into his knapsack and pulled out the letter he had penned in the freezing cold of Bastogne. Handing it over to Jenkins, he watched as his fellow soldier eagerly opened it.

Parsons leaned over and said, "Read it aloud. If that's okay with you John. We sure could use the entertainment, of course I am kidding. Please?"

"Go ahead," said John as he put down his pencil to listen to his own words.

Dear Mary,

I hope this letter finds you well and brings a smile to your face. It has been far too long since we last saw each other, and not a day goes by that you are not on my mind. The memories we shared in Paris, walking along the Seine, have remained etched in my heart, and I long for the day when we can create new memories together.

As I sit here, surrounded by the chaos of war, I find solace in our love and the dreams we shared. Your question about my experiences on D-Day reminded me of the courage and sacrifice of so many men who fought alongside me. The beaches of Normandy were a battleground unlike any other. The Germans had fortified the coastline, and the beach was a deadly stretch of sand, littered with obstacles and enemy fire.

I vividly remember the fear and anticipation as we landed, the deafening sounds of gunfire and explosions, and the camaraderie that kept us moving forward. It was a day of both triumph and tragedy, as so many lives were lost on those shores. But through it all, I held onto the hope that we were part of something bigger, something that would change the course of history.

Mary, you were my strength during those trying times. Your love and support fueled my determination to fight for a better future. I often thought of you as I navigated the challenges of war, drawing inspiration from the dreams we shared. You asked about my dreams after the war, and I can tell you that they revolve around a peaceful life with you, filled with love, laughter, and the simple joys of everyday moments.

I yearn for the day when I can hold you in my arms again, when the war is just a distant memory, and we can build a life together. Until then, know that I carry you with me, your presence guiding me through the darkest of days. Stay strong, my love, and keep faith in our future. We will endure these trials and emerge victorious, for our love is a force that can conquer anything.

With all my heart,

John

Listening to his own words, John's gaze drifted to the horizon. The memories of Bastogne, the camaraderie of his platoon, and the enduring love he held for Mary all converged in that moment. Jenkins read the letter with a mix of reverence and understanding, and as the last words were spoken, he looked up with a smile.

"Mary's a lucky girl," Jenkins remarked, handing the letter back to John. "And you're a lucky guy to have something like that to hold on to."

John nodded, his fingers tracing the words he had written. "Yes, I am the lucky one. One day, I'll be at her side, and I can lay down this rifle forever."

John sat alone in the dim light of the camp, his hands clutching the letter he had written to Guppy's parents, Mr., and Mrs. Lake. He closed his eyes for a moment, taking a deep breath before he began to read the words, he had carefully penned for them.

"Dear Mr. and Mrs. Lake,

I hope this letter finds you as well as can be expected in these trying times. I wanted to take a moment to write to you and share my thoughts about your son, George, or as we all came to know him, Guppy. His nickname might have come from his last name, but it was a name that suited him perfectly.

Guppy was a presence that could light up even the darkest of days. His laughter was infectious, and his sense of humor kept our spirits high during moments when it felt like the world was falling apart around us. He had a way of bringing us together, creating a bond among the platoon that was unbreakable. His stories, his jokes, they were the threads that wove us into a family.

But beyond his humor, Guppy possessed a courage and strength that inspired us all. In the midst of the battle in Bastogne, when the world was chaos and danger seemed to lurk around every corner, Guppy stood tall. He faced adversity head-on, and he did so with a smile on his face. He reminded us that even in the bleakest of moments, we could find a reason to keep fighting.

I want you to know that Guppy's sacrifice was not in vain. In the heart of battle, when the odds seemed insurmountable, he never faltered. He fought with everything he had, alongside his fellow soldiers, his brothers. His dedication to our mission was unwavering, and his loss is felt deeply by each and every one of us.

I can't begin to understand the pain of losing a child, and I know that no words can ease the ache in your hearts. But please know that Guppy was not alone in his final moments. He was surrounded by his platoon, and he will forever be remembered as a brave soldier who gave everything for the cause he believed in.

As we move forward, as we continue to fight for our shared purpose, Guppy's spirit lives on in each of us. His memory will be our driving force, a reminder that in the darkest times, even the smallest glimmer of light can guide us home.

With the deepest condolences and respect,

Corporal John Reynolds, 3rd Platoon, Easy Company, 10st Airborne Division"

John folded the letter and placed it carefully back into its envelope. He looked up at the stars above, feeling a mixture of sadness and gratitude. Guppy's absence was a heavy weight on their hearts, but his presence would forever be a guiding light, inspiring them to carry on with courage and determination.

As the evening sun dipped behind the hills of the countryside, the mild glow of the campfire flickered off the tents in the camp. Jenkins and Parsons were enjoying a chocolate bar that they got from the re-supply while in Bastogne. Sgt. Holmes was quietly cleaning his rifle while sitting up against one of the many Ash trees that covered the landscape in Alsace-Lorraine.

"Hey Sarg." asked Evans. "Do you ever write home to your parents?"

"Nah," he replied. "My ma and pa don't read that well, especially since their eyesight has started to fail. I am sure they follow the war from the radio and don't worry too much about me."

"I'm writing a letter back to my parents in Lubbock," said Evans. "My dad will be furious if he doesn't get at least one letter from me."

"What are you going to say to him," asked John.

"Well, here is what I have so far," replied Evans.

"Dear Mom and Dad," began Evans. "I hope this letter finds you both well. I know it's been a while since I wrote, but things have been a bit chaotic here, to say the least. Let me tell you about the rollercoaster ride we've been on lately.

So, remember when I told you I was shipped off to Europe? Well, I didn't exactly mention that I would be spending Christmas in a snowy forest with a bunch of guys, fighting off Germans like it's some kind of winter vacation. Yeah, Europe's a bit different than Lubbock, that's for sure.

We were in this place called Bastogne, and let me tell you, it was colder than a cow's nose in a blizzard. But don't worry, I bundled up like a champ. I've never seen so much snow in my life. It's like they're trying to make up for all those years of drought back home.

Anyway, we were holding our ground and doing our best to keep those Germans at bay. You wouldn't believe the stuff we went through – bullets flying, snowstorms, and even a couple of snowball fights in between. Yeah, you read that right, snowball fights in the middle of a battle. It's like we were all kids again, except with rifles and grenades.

And then there was Foy. We were going back and forth like a game of tag with the Germans. One day, they had the town, the next day we had it, and so on. It was like a real-life version of that cat-and-mouse game we used to play on the farm. Except instead of a mouse, it was a whole bunch of Germans. Not exactly the kind of chase I was hoping for, but you gotta make do, right?

I'll tell you one thing though – those Germans don't mess around when it comes to shooting. Bullets were whizzing by like they were in a hurry to get somewhere. But don't worry, I've been practicing my dodging skills, just like I did with that bull back home. Although, I have to admit, this is a little more life-threatening than dealing with ol' Bessie.

Oh, and speaking of dodging, you should've seen me during a close encounter with a grenade. I swear, I did a move that would put any football player to shame. It was like I was doing the world's most intense dance move – the "Evans Shuffle." I might patent that when I get back home.

But enough about my antics. I know you're probably worried sick reading all this. Just want to let you know that I'm hanging in there. We've got a great bunch of guys here, and we're looking out for each other.

I hope you're both taking care of yourselves and looking after each other. I can't wait to be back and share all these crazy stories in person. Until then, stay strong, keep the Texas spirit alive, and remember to save some of that good ol' BBQ for me."

"That's a good letter Evans," said Sgt. Holmes. "Enough information to let them know our troubles without worrying them too much."

"I am not so eloquent with my words like John or light-hearted but serious like Evans," said Parsons. "I would probably end up worrying my parents."

"You have to write something," said Sgt. Holmes. "At least let them know you're alive and have a group of guys around you to help protect you. It's the least you can do. "

"I will," replied Evans. "I'll try to pen something tomorrow."

The evening settled over the camp like a heavy blanket, muffling the sounds of war momentarily. The flickering glow of the campfires painted dancing shadows across tired faces. The day's events had taken their toll, and as the men settled into their makeshift beds, exhaustion mingled with a quiet sense of calm.

In the distance, the occasional hum of aircraft could be heard, reminding them that even in moments of calm, the battle was far from over. The snow-covered ground beneath them seemed both unforgiving and strangely comforting, a reminder of the harshness of their reality but also a shared experience that bound them together.

The news about the 4th Armored Division's spread across Drulingen and Pfaffenhoffen had circulated, and Easy Company knew their role along the Moder River was crucial. Positioned there to harass German patrols, gather critical intelligence, and aid in the liberation of nearby towns, the weight of responsibility hung heavily in the cold night air.

Sgt. Holmes moved through the camp, his silhouette a reassuring presence in the dim light. He checked on his men, making sure they were as comfortable as they could be under the circumstances. Conversations were hushed, and the few laughs that escaped were both a welcome relief and a testament to the strength of their spirits.

John, sitting by the fire with his back against a crate, leaned against his helmet, its worn edges bearing the marks of battles fought and won. Beside him, Lt. Anderson pored over a map, tracing their positions and potential paths of action with a focused intensity.

Meanwhile, Parsons sat nearby, his pencil scratching against a piece of paper as he composed a letter home. The distant look in his eyes hinted at the weight of emotions that words alone couldn't capture. Each letter was a connection to a world beyond the battle, a link to the loved ones waiting for their return.

As the night wore on, the camp gradually succumbed to the lull of sleep. Tensions eased, if only temporarily, as the men sought refuge in dreams that offered a temporary escape from the harsh reality that surrounded them. In the midst of uncertainty and danger, they found solace in each other's company.

DESPERATE MESSAGES

Christmas Eve on the island of Soller was a time of quiet reflection and warm conversation. The small community had come together to create a pocket of joy amid the somber backdrop of a world at war. As the sun dipped below the horizon, Mary and her family bustled about, making the final preparations for the evening's gathering. It was typical in the region for one family to host a gathering for their neighbors. After such a bountiful harvest of grapes and olives, Maria and Miguel decided to host.

The modest cottage was adorned with flickering candles, casting dancing shadows on the walls. The scent of freshly baked bread and simmering stews wafted through the air, creating an atmosphere of comfort and unity. Neighbors and friends arrived one by one, each bringing a dish to share and hearts full of gratitude.

First to arrive was Luis and Carmen Andova and their three children, followed by Mara and Sofia Garcia, elderly sisters who had lived on the island their entire lives and brought a sense of tradition and wisdom to any event.

Next were Jesus and Illana Hernandez. Jesus was one of the few cattle ranchers on the island and like always, Illana was holding a platter of exquisitely roasted meats. Several other neighbors arrived including Jorge, the last of the soldiers that fought in the Spanish Civil war from the island, most notably, the Battle of Mallorca.

Mary's mother had spent hours in the kitchen, her hands deftly working to prepare a feast that would nourish both body and soul. The long wooden table was set with care, each place adorned with a simple cloth and a single flower plucked from the garden. The island's bounty was laid out for all to enjoy – olives, cheeses, and fruits from the nearby orchards.

The gathering was not just a celebration of Christmas, but a chance to express their thanks for the safety that their remote island had provided during these uncertain times. As they sat down to eat, the soft murmur of conversation filled the air.

"Any news of the war?" asked Mary, directed at Jorge, who always seemed to be up to date on current events.

After the Spanish Civil War, Jorge opened a trading and shipping business at the Port of Soller just northwest of the town. Jorge, a dedicated merchant with a discerning eye for trade, orchestrated a bustling trading and shipping business that linked the ports of Valencia, Marseille, Tangiers, and more. Based in Soller, Mallorca, he skillfully navigated the complexities of maritime commerce, ensuring that his customers could acquire a diverse array of goods from distant corners of the Mediterranean.

Jorge's expertise extended beyond mere merchandise. He was a facilitator, connecting cultures and markets, and fostering relationships that transcended borders. His reputation for fair dealings and his ability to bridge gaps between merchants of different backgrounds made him a sought-after figure in the bustling trade network.

"Lots of news coming in from the ships sailing from Marseille," he replied. "Not all of it good I am afraid."

Amidst the cozy ambiance of the gathering, Jorge's voice carried the echoes of distant shores and battles. As the dinner guests leaned in, eager to catch every word,

Jorge began, "You know, my friends, these are extraordinary times we're living in. Back in September, Calais was finally liberated from the Germans. The streets that had been under occupation for so long echoed with newfound freedom."

Nods of agreement rippled around the table as the significance of Calais's liberation settled in. "And then, in November, Strasbourg," Jorge continued, "that beautiful city nestled along the Rhine. The French and American forces joined hands in a powerful push, reclaiming the heart of Western Alsace."

The news of the triumph at Strasbourg's sparked smiles and a shared sense of pride among the guests. Jorge's narratives had a way of knitting their hearts closer to the pulse of the world's events. "And in December," he went on, "Ravenna, Italy. The Allies made strides through the Italian soil, driving back the combined German and Italian forces."

The collective hope in the room grew as the stories unfolded. But then, Jorge's tone softened, his eyes reflecting the gravity of the news he was about to share. "But my dear friends," he said, his gaze encompassing them all, "amidst these victories, there is a shadow that has fallen over the American forces. Last word from a Parisian who was traveling to Nice told me that news reached him that the American's 101st Airborne Division were themselves trapped in Bastogne, encircled by German forces in the harsh conditions of winter."

Mary's heart sank and her face, now a pale expression of fear, caught her mother's attention.

A hushed silence settled over the room, broken only by the crackling of the fireplace. Jorge's words hung heavy in the air, a reminder that even amidst triumphs, the toll of war was a stark reality. "Their situation is dire," he continued, his voice tinged with empathy. "With the winter weather, getting supplies to them is difficult. He only knows this because he conducts business in western France where the supplies are being brought in."

Around the table, gazes met, and unspoken thoughts seemed to pass between them. The faces reflected concern, empathy, and a shared sense of solidarity with those facing the crucible of battle. "Let us not forget," Jorge said softly, "that even in the darkest hours, the human spirit perseveres."

Mary, tears in her eyes, quickly excused herself and scampered out to the terrace. The cool evening breeze and soft moonlight exacerbating the emotions she felt when thinking about John. She leaned against the railing, gazing up at the starlit sky, lost in her thoughts. Her mother's footsteps approached softly, and a gentle hand touched her shoulder.

"Mary," her mother's voice was a soothing whisper, "I thought I might find you here."

Mary turned to her mother, her eyes reflecting the mix of worry and uncertainty that churned within her. "Mother, the news about Bastogne... It's just so troubling."

Her mother's eyes held a warmth that came from years of experience and understanding. She joined Mary at the railing, standing beside her. "I know, my dear. War is a harsh and unpredictable ordeal. But remember, John is a brave and strong young man. He's been through challenges before, and he has the heart of a fighter."

A tremor of doubt passed through Mary's voice. "What if... What if something happens to him, Mother? What if we never see him again?"

Her mother's hand gently cupped Mary's cheek, her touch a comforting reassurance. "It's natural to have such worries, my love. But dwelling on fear won't change the outcome. We must have faith and hope for the best."

Mary's eyes welled with tears, her emotions close to the surface. "And what of Diego? He's kind, he cares for me..."

Her mother's gaze held both tenderness and wisdom. "Diego is a good man, Mary. He's here, and he has shown his affection for you. He could provide you with stability and security. Consider him not as a replacement, but as someone who is here for you."

Torn between her emotions, Mary looked out into the night sky. "I can't, Mother. I can't give up on John. Our time in Paris, our dreams... I can't let them slip away."

Her mother's voice grew soft, soothing like a lullaby. "Mary, my darling, love is a powerful thing. It's what keeps us connected even in the darkest of times. If you truly believe in John, then hold onto that belief. Trust your heart."

Mary's tears spilled over, and her mother's embrace enveloped her, providing a refuge from the storm of emotions. "Have faith, Mary. And remember, love has a way of finding its way back to us."

In the quiet of the night, the two women stood together on the terrace, bound by the bonds of love, hope, and the strength that comes from standing by one another's side.

As Mary stood on the terrace, her emotions spilling out under the moonlit sky, the remaining guests inside exchanged knowing glances.

Back inside at the dinner table Carmen spoke, "Luis, did you see Mary's face when Jorge was speaking?" she whispered, concern evident in her eyes.

"I did, Carmen. I hope she's alright," Luis replied, his gaze shifting to their children who continued to enjoy the evening's feast.

Mara and Sofia, had seen their fair share of trials, exchanged a knowing nod. Mara leaned in and whispered to Sofia, "It seems young hearts are facing their own battles tonight."

Jesus and Illana were engaged in a hushed conversation as her gaze occasionally drifting toward the terrace. "It's not every day that we receive news like this," Illana murmured.

"I know, my dear. But we must remember that our island has seen its share of hardships," Jesus replied, his tone gentle.

Jorge, his eyes, usually filled with stories of the past, now held a hint of remorse. He had brought the troubling news to the gathering, inadvertently casting a shadow over the festive occasion.

"I'm sorry," he said. "I did not know my news would cause troubled hearts. Take heed, nothing is ever etched in stone and these news stories could change anytime."

Luis deep voice mingled with Carmen's soothing words. "Jorge is right, we mustn't let worry overcome us," Luis said, his eyes glancing toward the terrace.

Mara and Sofia shared tales of bygone days, hoping to uplift the spirits of the group. "Remember, hardships come and go, but our strength remains," Sofia said, her voice filled with wisdom.

Jorge cleared his throat, his gaze momentarily distant as he reflected on the weight of the news he had brought. He wished he could take back the sorrow he had inadvertently stirred, replacing it with the sense of unity and joy that had brought the neighbors together.

But in the midst of their conversation, a soft breeze seemed to sweep through the room, carrying with it a sense of hope. Despite the concerns and the news that had unsettled them, there was an unspoken understanding among the guests. They were here for one another, bound by a shared history and a resilient spirit.

As the night carried on, the guests continued to share stories, laughter, and a delicious meal that had been lovingly prepared. Jorge's gaze returned to the terrace, his eyes catching Mary's figure as she turned to rejoin them.

"I'm sorry to have unknowingly upset you, Mary. Said Jorge. He offered her a reassuring smile, hoping that the camaraderie of the evening would bring solace to her heart.

"it's ok, Jorge," she replied as she sat back down next to her mother. "The young soldier I met in Paris and fell in love with is in the American 101st Airborne Division. So, to hear news that they are in grave danger upset me. I have not had word from him from the post since we parted. I imagine it is difficult to get a letter across such a great distance during these times."

"You say he is a soldier in the 101st?" asked Jorge.

"Yes," replied Mary.

I have regular customers who travel between Marseille and France, and they say the American army encampment is in Mourmelon. If you want to write him a letter, I can see if Rodolfo, he's my customer, can get that letter to the American headquarters on his next trip to Paris."

Mary jumped up from her seat at the table and ran around to where Jorge was seated and gave him a hug and kiss on the cheek.

"Oh, thank you Jorge," she exclaimed. "That raises my spirits a bit. Thank you, thank you, thank you."

Mary quickly left the dining room and hurried down the hall to her room to quickly write a letter to John. Meanwhile, back in the dining room Mara looked over at Jorge and said, "You shouldn't get her hopes up Jorge. If she writes a letter to him that he never receives or does not hear word back from him, she will be crushed."

Jorge with one hand on his heart and the other in the air said, "Mara, trust me. Rodolfo is a man of integrity, and if she writes a letter, it will get to Mourmelon. What happens after that is a matter of fate."

"Just don't what you to promise what you can't deliver," she replied.

With a warm smile, Maria returned from the kitchen, her hands delicately balancing a platter laden with an array of tempting desserts. The air filled with the sweet aromas of the treats she carried, creating a delectable anticipation among the guests.

On the platter, a golden Tarta de Santiago took center stage, adorned with the iconic cross of St. James made from powdered sugar. Its almond-scented aroma wafted through the air, inviting everyone to indulge in its rich flavors.

Beside the Tarta de Santiago sat a plate of Buñuelos, those delightful fritters that were a beloved Spanish tradition. Golden-brown and lightly dusted with sugar, they held promises of a crispy exterior that concealed a tender, doughy interior. The mere sight of them elicited delighted murmurs from the guests.

Completing the trio was the Crema Catalana, a dessert known for its velvety custard base and a perfectly caramelized top. The delicate scent of vanilla lingered in the air as the creamy confection seemed to beckon to those gathered.

Maria's eyes sparkled with pride as she presented the desserts to the guests, each creation a testament to her culinary skill and the cherished traditions of the island. With grace, she placed the platter in the center of the table, allowing the warm and inviting scents to envelop the room.

"Please, enjoy these delights," Maria said with a gracious nod. "May they bring sweetness to our evening, reminding us of the joys we share."

As forks delicately cut into the Tarta de Santiago, Buñuelos were savored with satisfied smiles, and spoons dipped into the velvety depths of the Crema Catalana, the essence of the gathering was captured in every bite. The flavors spoke of comfort, togetherness, and the rich tapestry of the island's heritage.

Around the table, laughter and conversation flowed, a testament to the power of community and the bonds that held them close.

In her bedroom, Mary sat on her bed with pencil and paper, eager to write to John, but worried the news she heard would taint her words. She decided to just be herself and write what her heart felt.

"My Dearest John," she began.

"I hope this letter finds you, despite the distance that separates us. These words bear with them the warmth of our island, the whisper of the waves that caress our shores, and the gentle rustle of olive trees that stand tall as silent witnesses to our love.

As the days have passed, news of your safety has brought solace to my heart. To know that you navigate the perils of war with steadfast courage only strengthens my admiration for you. It is my fervent hope that you find moments of peace amidst war, where thoughts of our tranquil island can soothe your spirit.

This year's harvest brought with it an abundance of grapes and olives, a testament to the resilience of our land even in the face of adversity. The vineyards stretched their arms wide, as if reaching for the same sky that spans across our hearts. Our island is a symphony of colors, a mosaic of life and vitality, and I am reminded of your unwavering determination as I tend to each vine and tree.

Christmas, despite the trials that besiege the world, has graced us with a gathering of friends and neighbors who share their gratitude for the safety that has embraced our island. In their laughter and stories, I find echoes of the love and support that surround us, a testament to the bonds that endure even in the harshest of times.

John, my heart swells with a love that defies distance and time. It is a love that has grown from the moment our eyes met in the streets of Paris, and it has flourished through each shared conversation, stolen glance, and whispered promise. Our dreams, though seemingly suspended by the events of the world, remain etched in the fabric of our souls.

I yearn for the day when you will return, when we can walk hand in hand through the olive groves, bask in the golden hues of the sunset, and watch as the waves kiss the shoreline. Together, we will turn the pages of our story, filling it with new chapters of joy, love, and the hope that can only be kindled by the presence of the one who holds my heart.

Until then, please be safe, my love. May the winds that guide you be gentle and may your journey lead you back to me. With every sunrise and sunset, know that my thoughts are with you, carried by the winds and whispered to the stars that watch over us.

Until the moment when our hands once again find each other's embrace, and our lips meet, know that you are cherished, loved, and missed beyond words.

With all my heart,
Mary"

As Mary returned to the dining room, letter in hand, a soft smile played on her lips despite the concern that had drawn her to the terrace moments ago. She placed the letter delicately on the table, casting a glance over the array of desserts that adorned it. "It seems I missed dessert," she said with a playful sigh.

Her mother, who had been observing the scene with a watchful eye, smiled warmly. "Oh, don't worry, my dear. There's plenty left for you. Sit, enjoy," she reassured, her voice carrying the soothing cadence of a mother's comfort.

The guests around the table exchanged contented glances, their faces aglow with the afterglow of a shared meal and heartfelt conversations. One by one, they bid their host good evening, expressing gratitude for the hospitality that had enveloped them in warmth and unity.

"Thank you, Maria, for this wonderful evening," Luis Andova said, his wife Carmen nodding in agreement. Mara and Sofia Garcia, the wise sisters, offered their appreciation as well, their voices a chorus of gratitude.

Jesus and Illana who had brought the savory meats that had delighted the palates of the guests, stood up as well. "Your cooking always leaves us speechless, Maria. Thank you," Jesus said with a hearty laugh, his eyes twinkling.

Jorge, who had been part of the conversation earlier, rose from his seat. "It was truly an unforgettable evening, Maria. Thank you for having us."

As the guests began to depart, Mary approached Jorge with a sense of purpose. "Jorge," she began, her voice carrying a trace of urgency, "I wrote John a letter. Could you please deliver this letter to your customer, Rodolfo, when he returns to Paris in the next couple of weeks?"

Jorge's brows lifted in happiness as he took the letter from Mary's outstretched hand. "Of course, Mary. I'll make sure he receives it," he replied, his tone carrying a mixture of seriousness and understanding.

With a nod of gratitude, Mary watched as the guests bid their final goodbyes and made their way into the moonlit night. As the sounds of their footsteps faded, she turned her gaze to the letter now in Jorge's possession, a silent plea to the stars above that her words would reach the one they were meant for.

In the gentle embrace of the night, a promise hung in the air, carried by the winds that whispered through the olive trees and over the waves of the sea.

RETURN TO MOURMELON

The Ardennes-Alsace Campaign emerged as a turning point in the final stages of World War II. Hitler's last offensives, aimed at disrupting the Allied coalition, instead incurred heavy losses for the Germans.

Operation Northwind as it was called was the final significant German offensive on the Western Front during World War II. Launched to aid the failing Ardennes offensive, it targeted the thinly held front line of the U.S. 7th Army. The offensive drew upon almost 1,000 aircraft from the Luftwaffe to support it, known as Operation Bodenplatte. The U.S. 7th Army was stretched thin due to reinforcements sent to the Ardennes.

The 101st and many other armored and infantry divisions mobilized to support the 7th army and the region vacated by Patton's 3rd army as he pushed North into Germany.

After a long and arduous journey, 3rd Platoon of the 101st Airborne finally reached their target position near the intersection of the Moder River and the Rhine and hold positions on the south bank. The Germans held the north bank. Their anticipation was palpable, hoping that after their gallant efforts in Bastogne, they would have been relieved. However, upon arrival, they were greeted with a somewhat unexpected scene. The area was already bustling with activity, and it became evident that the U.S. 7th Army and several other divisions had already secured the location. Since they were not going to engage the Germans, they were held in reserve.

Mixed emotions swirled among the platoon members. While a sense of relief settled in knowing that the location was now under American control, there was also a tinge of disappointment that their expected role had been taken up by other units. The men had carried hopes of rest, perhaps a chance to rekindle their spirits after the grueling battles they had faced. Yet, the reality was different. They found themselves amidst a shifting front, where the Allies were steadily advancing, and the German forces were in retreat.

Despite the initial disappointment, the soldiers of 3rd Platoon understood the fluid nature of warfare. Adaptability was key, and they quickly adjusted their mindset to the new situation. They held their positions, assisting in the efforts to secure the Alsace region as part of the larger Allied offensive.

The atmosphere at Sgt. Holmes' encampment was a mixture of weariness and anticipation. The men of 3rd Platoon were scattered around, some sitting by the fires to stay warm, others cleaning their weapons, all finding a moment of rest from their duties. Suddenly, Lt. Anderson's figure emerged from the shadows, his steps purposeful as he approached Sgt. Holmes.

"Sergeant Holmes," he addressed, his voice carrying a tone of both authority and command. The platoon members instinctively turned their attention toward the scene unfolding.

Sgt. Holmes snapped to attention, acknowledging the lieutenant's presence. "Sir!"

"At ease, Sergeant," the lieutenant said, offering a reassuring smile. "I've got some news for you and the men."

A ripple of curiosity swept through the platoon as they awaited the announcement. The lieutenant took a moment to survey the faces before him, each one marked with the weariness of battles fought and the longing for home.

"We're being relieved," he declared, his words like a gust of fresh wind in the midst of exhaustion. Reinforcements are arriving from Paris later this evening. They'll take over the watch, and we'll be heading back to Mourmelon."

The announcement was met with a mixture of reactions. Relief and excitement danced in the eyes of some, while others exchanged knowing glances. The prospect of rest, a warm meal, and the comfort of familiar surroundings was enough to spark a sense of rejuvenation.

"Finally, a chance to catch our breath," Pvt. Evans muttered, a weary smile tugging at his lips.

Sgt. Holmes nodded, his expression a blend of pride and exhaustion. "We've done our part here, men. It's time for some well-deserved rest."

Pvt. Jackson chimed in, his voice carrying a touch of disbelief. "Mourmelon... I never thought I'd be so glad to hear that name."

Laughter rippled through the group, a moment of shared relief and brotherhood. For months, they had endured the challenges of the front lines, and now the prospect of leaving them behind was a bittersweet reality.

As the lieutenant addressed logistical details and the impending arrival of reinforcements, conversations amongst the platoon members continued.

"We made it through," Pvt. Evans mused, a quiet contemplation in his tone. "Bastogne, the Alsace... It feels good to know we held our ground."

Sgt. Holmes nodded, pride swelling in his chest. "We held strong, together. And we'll keep doing so."

The next morning brought a sense of purposeful activity to the camp as the 101st Airborne Division prepared to leave their positions along the Moder River and head back to Mourmelon. The sound of boots shuffling, equipment being stowed away, and the revving of engines filled the air as the platoon members packed up their gear and gathered around.

Sgt. Holmes stood at the forefront, his gaze sweeping over the assembled faces. The platoon had weathered battles, shared moments of camaraderie, and grown stronger as a unit. Now, they were about to transition into a different phase of their service.

"Alright, gather 'round, everyone," Sgt. Holmes called, his voice carrying its customary authority. The platoon members turned their attention to him, their expressions expectant.

"We've done our duty here," he began, his words firm yet laced with a touch of reflection. "We held the line, faced challenges head-on, and proved our mettle."

Nods and murmurs of agreement rippled through the platoon. They had faced adversity, and each one of them had played a vital role in the successes they had achieved.

Sgt. Holmes' eyes held a mixture of pride and determination as he continued. "Now, as we head back to Mourmelon, we'll be getting some well-earned rest and resupply. But that's not all. We'll also be training to keep us sharp, to refine our skills, and to prepare for what comes next."

The platoon members exchanged glances, curiosity flickering in their eyes. Sgt. Holmes' words hinted at a future beyond the battles they had been fighting.

"Occupation and governing," Sgt. Holmes said, his voice carrying a sense of gravitas. "Our mission isn't just about the fight. It's about building a better future, ensuring that the places we liberate have a chance to thrive."

Pvt. Evans raised an eyebrow, his curiosity evident. "Governing? You mean like, setting up governments?"

Sgt. Holmes nodded, a faint smile tugging at his lips. "Not Exactly, that's for the expert. As we move forward, our role will expand to include helping to maintain order, provide aid, and facilitate the transition to stability. It's a different kind of challenge, but one that's just as important."

Pvt. Jackson chimed in; his tone thoughtful. "So, we're not just soldiers. We're builders, too."

Sgt. Holmes' smile grew, a silent confirmation of Pvt. Jackson's observation. "That's right. We're building a foundation for peace, even as we continue to protect it."

The platoon members exchanged nods, a sense of purpose settling over them. The road ahead was still uncertain, but their commitment to the task remained unwavering.

"We've got a long journey ahead," Sgt. Holmes concluded, his gaze sweeping over the platoon. "But together, as we always have been, we'll face it head-on. Let's make our way back to Mourmelon, rest up, and get ready for the next phase of this journey."

As the platoon members boarded the box cars of the train, their gear in tow, they carried with them the knowledge that their responsibilities extended beyond the battlefield. With the sound of a whistle, the train headed east toward Mourmelon.

As the train made its way along the track, the platoon members noticed a change in the flow of traffic on the road next to the tracks. Ahead, the road widened, and the unmistakable silhouette of tanks and armored vehicles came into view. The convoy was passing an armored division, a formidable force heading toward the Rhine.

Sgt. Holmes leaned forward in his seat; his gaze fixed on the passing column of armor. It was a sight to behold—a display of might and determination as the armored division pressed forward on its own journey.

Beside him, Pvt. Evans whispered to Pvt. Jackson, "Wouldn't want to be on the wrong side of those tanks."

Pvt. Jackson nodded in agreement. "No kidding. They've got some serious firepower."

As the platoon's train continued to move alongside the armored division, Pvt. Parsons leaned over to John. "Think we'll be doing something like that?"

John shrugged, his gaze still fixed on the passing tanks. "Hard to say. Our path is our own, I reckon."

The convoy gradually left the armored division behind, and the platoon members settled back into their seats. The road stretched on, winding through the countryside they traveled reaching Mourmelon in mid-afternoon.

The train came to a halt alongside the familiar confines of Camp Mourmelon. The engines rumbled to a stop, and Sgt. Holmes's voice carried over the quieting sounds as he gave the order to disembark as he slid open the box car doors.

"Alright, men, back to the barracks," Sgt. Holmes called out, his tone a mixture of authority and relief. "Stow your gear and head over to the mess hall for dinner. Let's get settled in."

The platoon members wasted no time, moving with a sense of purpose as they gathered their belongings and made their way to the barracks. The barracks were a welcome sight—familiar bunks and the scent of well-worn wood greeted them.

Inside the barracks, Pvt. Evans grinned at Pvt. Jackson as they stowed their gear. "You believe it, Jack? Real beds again."

Pvt. Jackson chuckled, his exhaustion lifting slightly at the prospect of comfort. "Yeah, and a proper roof over our heads."

As they filed out of the barracks and headed to the mess hall, the men's footsteps echoed in unison. The mess hall buzzed with activity as soldiers lined up for dinner, the clatter of trays and the aroma of hot food filling the air.

Pvt. Parsons couldn't hide his excitement. "You know what this means, fellas? Actual food. Hot, edible food."

John nodded, a smirk playing on his lips. "I'd almost forgotten what that's like."

The line moved steadily forward, and soon enough, the platoon members were holding trays piled high with food. The sight of a well-cooked meal was a welcome change from the rations they had grown accustomed to during their recent engagements.

As they found a table and settled in, Pvt. Jenkins sighed in contentment. "I never thought I'd be this happy to see a plate of potatoes."

Sgt. Holmes joined them at the table, his own tray in hand. "It's the little things, Jenkins."

Around the table, laughter and conversation flowed freely. Stories from the past month's battles mixed with speculation about the future, and a sense of camaraderie permeated the air.

Pvt. Evans took a bite of his meal and closed his eyes in satisfaction. "You know, we might have been in the thick of it, but at least we're getting a decent meal now."

Pvt. Jackson raised his glass of water in a mock toast. "To actual food and a roof over our heads."

The platoon members joined in, clinking their glasses together with a shared sense of gratitude. The meal was more than sustenance; it was a reminder of normalcy.

As dinner drew to a close, the platoon members lingered a moment longer, savoring the company and the taste of real food. Soon enough, they would be back to training and preparing for whatever lay ahead. But for now, in this simple act of sharing a hot meal together, they headed back to their barracks, the sun still above the trees on the eastern horizon.

The late February winter still bit at the soldiers as they gathered around the crackling fire they had set up just outside their barracks. With the chill in the air, the flames provided a comforting warmth that helped to ward off the lingering cold. The men had arranged a makeshift seating area using wooden crates and whatever they could find, creating a circle around the fire. The flames danced and flickered and provided the perfect setting for storytelling.

Their breaths formed wisps of steam in the frigid air as they exchanged stories and laughter, a welcome contrast to the harshness of the battlefield they had recently left behind in Alsace. Some leaned against the crates, while others rested on folded blankets, finding comfort in the familiarity of their makeshift gathering place.

Sergeant Holmes sat on an upturned crate, his eyes fixed on the fire as he poked at the embers with a stick, stoking the flames to life. He was never one for long speeches, but his presence was enough to create a sense of unity among the men. The crackling of the fire accompanied their conversations, creating a soothing backdrop that seemed to muffle the distant sounds of the base.

Around the fire, the platoon members talked about their experiences in Alsace, the relief of not being needed on the front lines, and the prospect of the coming days of rest and resupply.

Lt. Anderson's footsteps crunched on the snow as he approached the scene, his breath visible in the chilly air. He stopped beside Sgt. Holmes, who had risen from his seat by the fire, and watched as the men acknowledged their superior's presence with a nod of respect.

"Good evening, Lieutenant," Sgt. Holmes greeted.

"Evening, Sergeant," Lt. Anderson replied, his gaze flickering toward the gathering before turning back to Holmes. "Sergeant, there's a man named Rodolfo Sanchez at the gate. He's asking for Corporal John Reynolds by name. Says he has urgent business with him."

Sgt. Holmes raised an eyebrow, his expression one of mild curiosity. "Rodolfo Sanchez? I don't recognize the name. Corporal, you know anything about this?"

Corporal John Reynolds looked up, his brow furrowing in thought. He shook his head, his expression mirroring the confusion in his eyes. "No, Sergeant, I can't say I do. I haven't been expecting anyone."

Lt. Anderson folded his arms, his gaze shifting between the two men. "It's quite peculiar. The man seems insistent. He mentioned something about having word from a woman named Mary."

John's eyes widened, a mixture of surprise and intrigue crossing his features. "Mary? Could it be..." He trailed off, his thoughts racing as he tried to make sense of the situation.

Sgt. Holmes exchanged a glance with Lt. Anderson, both of them catching on to the significance of the name. "Mary, huh?" Sgt. Holmes mused. "Well, Corporal, it seems like this might be something you should look into."

Lt. Anderson nodded in agreement. "Indeed. If it's connected to someone you know, it might be important. Best not to keep whoever this Rodolfo is waiting."

John stood up, his heart pounding with a mix of anticipation and anxiety. "You're right, Lieutenant. I should go find out what this is about."

With a reassuring pat on the shoulder, Lt. Anderson offered, "Go on, Corporal. Let's hope it's good news."

John nodded, his mind racing with possibilities. He excused himself from the gathering, leaving the warmth of the fire behind as he scurried toward the gate where Rodolfo Sanchez awaited.

Sgt. Holmes said, "I don't think I have ever seen him run that fast. Not even in Bastogne when we were being shelled by our own army."

"He's definitely moving fast!" said Jenkins.

As he reached the gate, he found Rodolfo Sanchez, a tall man with a serious expression. "Are you Corporal John Reynolds?" Rodolfo asked.

"Yes, that's me," John replied, his heart pounding with a mixture of curiosity and trepidation. "What's this about?"

Rodolfo's gaze softened, and he handed John a sealed letter. "I have a message for you, Corporal. A business friend of mine asked me to deliver a letter to you from a woman named Mary and that her name would immediately validate my presence."

John's fingers brushed against the paper, his heart racing as he recognized the familiar handwriting. With a mixture of excitement and hope, he looked up at Rodolfo. "Thank you," he said sincerely. "This means more to me than you know."

Rodolfo nodded, a hint of a smile on his lips. "You're welcome, Corporal. I'm glad I could deliver the message."

"Mr. Sanchez," John asked. "Are you planning to be back in Mallorca again?"

"As a matter of fact, I will be going there in a couple of weeks. Why?" inquired Rodolfo.

"I have two letters in my pocket I have written Mary, but we are unable to mail them to other places. Is it too much to ask that you take them with you for her?"

"I won't be seeing her," replied Rodolfo, "but I will see a family friend who can deliver your message."

"Oh, that's wonderful Sir, I am forever in your debt," said John.

With a final nod of gratitude, John handed the two letters from his jacket to Rodolfo and watched him walk away, disappearing into the twilight.

John walked back to the barracks, the letter from Mary held gently in his hand. The edges of the paper fluttered in the cold wind, but he kept his focus on the words written inside. As he read, a mixture of emotions washed over him—joy, longing, and a renewed sense of connection. Mary's words seemed to bridge the gap between the distant past and the present, bringing a piece of her world into his. She had heard news of their plight in Bastogne but not of the outcome. He was happy his letter would tell her he was still safe.

Arriving back at the fire outside the barracks, John found the platoon still gathered around, their faces illuminated by the flames. Their conversation and laughter filled the air, a contrast to the quiet intensity of the letter he held. As he approached, a few heads turned his way, and Jackson's voice rang out.

"Hey, Reynolds, what's got you all quiet and serious?"

John looked up from the letter, his lips curving into a small smile. He tucked the letter into his pocket before replying, "Just some news, fellas."

Evans arched an eyebrow, a playful grin on his face. "News, huh? Must be something big to put that look on your face."

John leaned against a nearby crate, his expression a mix of amusement and mystery. "Well, you know how it is. Some things are better kept secret for a little while."

Parsons, always one to jump into the conversation, chimed in. "Oh, come on, Reynolds! Don't leave us hanging. What's the news?"

Holmes, who had been quietly observing the exchange, gave a knowing smile. "Let the man have his secrets, Parsons. If he wants to share, he will."

John chuckled, the banter of the platoon playfully warming his heart. "Fair enough, Sergeant." He glanced around at his fellow soldiers, the firelight dancing in their eyes. "All I'll say for now is that it's a letter from Mary."

The mention of Mary brought a chorus of knowing nods and amused glances. Mary was a familiar topic among the platoon, her name carrying a sense of comfort and connection. John's mysterious smile only fueled their curiosity, but they respected his decision to keep the details to himself.

As the night went on, the platoon's laughter and stories continued to fill the air. And in the midst of it all, John found himself content, knowing that Mary's words were a source of strength.

The next few weeks were filled with training, many soldiers and officers felt that rigorous training was opposite of being held in reserve or getting rest. That is what base camp is for, not reserve camp.

One morning, Lt. Anderson barged into the barracks early to wake the platoon. "Sgt. Holmes," he shouted.

"Yes, Sir," replied Sgt. Holmes.

"Get your men to attention!" cried Lt. Anderson.

"Attention!" he shouted. "Attention!"

Then platoon popped to their feet, quickly putting on a pair of pants, but yet shirtless and standing tall, still wiping the sleepiness from their eyes. Lt. Anderson stood at the door and delivered the new of the surprise inspection.

The announcement of the surprise inspection by Lt. Anderson sent a ripple of excitement and anticipation through the barracks of the 101st Airborne Division. March 15th loomed ahead like a date marked by both pride and solemnity. General Dwight D. Eisenhower's impending visit was more than just a formal review; it was a recognition of the division's steadfast courage and sacrifice, particularly their unwavering stand in the heart of the Ardennes during the siege of Bastogne.

In the day leading up to the event, the barracks buzzed with activity. Uniforms were meticulously inspected and pressed, boots were polished to a shine, and equipment was meticulously arranged. The platoon members took extra care to ensure that every detail reflected their commitment and dedication to their duty.

As the sun rose on the morning of March 15th, a palpable sense of excitement filled the air. The platoon members gathered outside the barracks, standing tall and proud in their uniformed ranks. The sky was clear, a stark contrast to the battles they had fought in the freezing cold just months before. This day was a testament to their resilience and unwavering determination.

When General Eisenhower arrived, the entire division snapped to attention, their salute a symbol of their respect for his leadership and the significance of the moment. The reviewing stand was adorned with the flags of their nation and their division, fluttering gently in the breeze. As the troops marched past, the general's gaze moved over each soldier, a silent acknowledgment of their sacrifice and valor.

Among the visiting dignitaries was a sense of awe. The solemnity of the occasion was underscored by the memory of the battles that had been fought, the lives that had been lost, and the indomitable spirit that had carried them through. The platoon members held their heads high, their hearts filled with a mixture of pride and humility.

As they passed the reviewing stand, the platoon members saluted with unwavering precision. Each step they took was a tribute to their fallen comrades, a reaffirmation of their commitment to their country, and a recognition of their part in history. A tear fell from John's eye as he thought about Guppy. General Eisenhower's presence was a reminder that their sacrifices had not gone unnoticed, that their stand at Bastogne had earned them a place in the annals of valor.

And so, on that day, they were awarded the Presidential Unit Citation for their heroic stand in Bastogne. They embodied the spirit of their division, of their nation, and of the unwavering resolve that had carried them through the darkest of days.

KAUFERING

With the Germans pushed across the Rhine, the end of March brought forth new orders for the 101st Airborne Division. The call was to deploy to the Rhine, and the subsequent would see Easy Company moving southeast through Germany toward the Austrian border.

As the orders came in, Lt. Anderson's voice carried the weight of the situation, outlining the mission's importance and the challenges that lay ahead. The platoon members gathered their belongings and supplies, each man's face reflecting a mix of determination and readiness. The memory of Guppy's sacrifice in Foy was still fresh, a reminder of the stakes involved. The conversation among them hummed with a blend of anticipation and concern.

"Another move, boys," Lt. Anderson's voice rang out, his words a blend of authority and reassurance. "This one's taking us to the Rhine. We'll be traveling by train to Dormagen."

Sgt. Holmes exchanged knowing glances with his men. "You heard the Lieutenant. Let's get our gear packed and ready. Double-check your supplies. We don't know what's waiting for us."

John nodded, his face a mixture of resolve and contemplation. "It's been a journey, that's for sure."

Parsons chimed in, a touch of his usual humor lightening the mood. "Well, at least this time we know what to expect from those boxcars."

Jenkins shouldered his pack, his gaze thoughtful. "Yeah, and hopefully no surprises like Foy."

As they gathered their gear and loaded up, the weight of their experiences hung heavy in the air. The journey had tested them, transformed them, and now they were heading toward yet another chapter of uncertainty. The train station loomed ahead, the boxcars standing as a symbol of their resilience, the scars of battles past etched into their memory. With the Germans pushed back, the path to the Rhine lay open, and Easy Company stood poised to fulfill their duty once more.

The train's rhythmic clatter gradually slowed as it approached the station outside Dormagen. Easy Company and 3rd Platoon, with their gear and spirits in tow, prepared to disembark, their anticipation tinged with a mixture of weariness and curiosity. The doors of the boxcars creaked open, revealing a bright morning sky and a new destination.

Sgt. Holmes stepped onto the platform first, his gaze sweeping over the scene before him. The town of Dormagen lay ahead, its streets quiet but with a sense of life humming beneath the surface. As his men filed out behind him, there was a collective exhale, a moment of relief that they had made it to another point on their journey.

"Alright, listen up," Holmes called out, his voice carrying the authority of experience. "We're here in Dormagen. Keep your wits about you, and let's stay together. We're heading into town to set up and get our bearings."

Lt. Anderson nodded in agreement, his presence steady and reassuring. "Remember, we're here to do our duty and help wherever we're needed. The Germans pulled out a week ago heading east, there are a lot of evacuated people here and we need to protect them."

The platoon members shouldered their packs and weapons, the familiar weight grounding them in purpose. As they walked toward the town, their steps fell in rhythm, a collective march toward the unknown. The sights and sounds of Dormagen began to unfold around them—the war-torn streets, the crumbled architecture, and the hushed conversations of locals.

Conversations among the platoon members floated through the air, a mix of observations and speculation.

"Looks like a different kind of place compared to the other towns we've been through," Parsons mused.

John nodded, his eyes taking in the surroundings. "Seems quieter, but you never know what you might find."

Jenkins chimed in, his voice carrying a touch of optimism. "Maybe this time we'll actually have a chance to interact with the locals without all the chaos."

As they walked deeper into the heart of Dormagen, the town revealed itself in layers—a community still grappling with the aftermath of war, yet also striving to regain a sense of normalcy. The platoon members exchanged nods with the townspeople they passed, a subtle acknowledgment of their shared journey.

In the weeks that followed, Easy Company and 3rd Platoon continued their journey southward through Germany. The once-imposing German war machine was now a shell of its former self, and the 101st encountered little resistance as they moved from town to town. The citizens they encountered bore the scars of war, but also held onto a glimmer of hope for a better future.

As they traveled, the platoon's interactions with the locals became more frequent. In one small village, they came across a farmer whose horse and cart had become hopelessly stuck in the mud. Sgt. Holmes called for a halt, and the platoon immediately sprang into action. With coordinated efforts and combined strength, they managed to free the cart from the mire.

The farmer, his weathered face etched with gratitude, clasped his hands together and spoke in a heavy German accent. "Danke, danke!" he exclaimed, his eyes brimming with emotion. Then in English he spoke. "You are angels, yes? Sent to help in our darkest times."

John offered a smile and a reassuring pat on the farmer's shoulder. "No angels, just soldiers doing our part to help out."

The platoon continued their journey, their actions leaving a trail of gratitude in their wake. Passing through weary villages, they distributed chocolates to the locals—small tokens of sweetness amid the bitterness of war. Guarded smiles appeared on the faces of the citizens as they accepted the offerings, their eyes reflecting a mix of weariness and newfound hope.

In one such encounter, a young girl tentatively approached Lt. Anderson, her hand outstretched to receive a piece of chocolate. "Danke," she whispered, her eyes wide with wonder.

Lt. Anderson crouched down to her level, his smile warm and reassuring. "You're welcome, little one. Keep that smile shining." He had no idea if she understood him, but the look on her face inspired him.

Not all the citizens were happy to see the Americans, but they tolerated their passage as if they were the Germany army. The platoon hoped that acts of kindness would become a bridge between American soldiers and German citizens, only time would tell.

In late April, the 101st Airborne Division found themselves under the command of the US Seventh Army. Their deployment took them through the Rhineland's remnants of conflict until they finally reached the majestic Bavarian Alps. Along their path, the 12th Armored Division had already secured the town of Hurlach, marking a critical foothold in their journey.

As the 101st arrived in Hurlach, the town was now a scene of mixed emotions—evidence of both the horrors of war and the potential for renewal. The platoon, in close collaboration with the 12th Armored Division, began their meticulous surveillance of the surroundings, especially the nearby area of Landsberg.

But it wasn't long before this joint effort uncovered a chilling truth—the existence of Kaufering IV, one of the 11 concentration camps eventually discovered in the vicinity. The revelation was a grim reminder of the atrocities that had taken place under the veil of war, an indelible stain on humanity's history.

Sgt. Holmes led his platoon in somber exploration, their hearts heavy with the weight of the past. The scenes they encountered were harrowing evidence of suffering and cruelty etched into the walls of the camp. Their presence bore witness to the darkest facets of the war, urging them to remember the importance of their mission as they moved forward.

The camp was surrounded by barbed wire fences, creating a grim perimeter that seemed to encapsulate a sense of despair. Dilapidated and makeshift barracks, constructed with a cruel economy of materials, were scattered throughout the camp, each one telling a story of unimaginable hardship. The structures bore the scars of the past—crumbling walls, shattered windows, and roofs sagging under the weight of neglect.

As the soldiers cautiously entered the camp, the air was heavy with a mix of chilling silence and the lingering stench of human suffering. The ground was marked by the imprints of countless footsteps, as well as the remnants of personal belongings that had been discarded in haste. The soldiers saw tattered clothing, abandoned shoes, and meager possessions that bore witness to the lives that had been lived—and lost—within these confines piled up next to a building.

Upon entering the barracks, the true extent of the tragedy became apparent. The conditions were beyond deplorable—cramped living spaces with nothing more than a wooden plank to sleep on, the walls adorned with messages and prayers etched by desperate souls who clung to a glimmer of hope. The skeletal frames of bunk beds bore witness to the physical toll of malnutrition and illness of the men who were lying in them.

Outside, the discovery of mass graves revealed the horrifying extent of the atrocities committed here. The earth was scarred by the presence of shallow pits, each containing the remains of countless individuals who had perished in the most inhumane ways. The soldiers saw evidence of systematic brutality that had taken place—evidence that could not be unseen.

The discovery of the Kaufering IV concentration camp was a sobering reminder of the depths of human cruelty and the urgent need to ensure that such atrocities would never be repeated. As the soldiers stood amidst the ruins of this dark chapter in history, their hearts heavy with a mixture of grief, anger, and determination, they knew that bearing witness to this tragedy meant shouldering the responsibility to ensure that justice and humanity would prevail in the aftermath of such unspeakable horror.

While medical staff and units from the 7th and 12th Armies focused on providing care and aid to the liberated prisoners found within the grim walls of the concentration camps, the solemn duty fell upon Easy Company including

3rd platoon to confront yet another facet of the aftermath. The platoon's orders were clear—to return to Hurlach and order its citizens to join in the painful task of carrying away and giving proper burial to the remains of the departed. A task they would not enjoy.

The platoon's journey back to Hurlach was heavy with a sense of responsibility. The weight of the past lingered in the air, a palpable reminder of the atrocities that had transpired just miles away. As they reached the town's outskirts, the townspeople came into view, their faces turning away as if guilty themselves of the atrocity.

As the solemn task of burying the dead was immanent, Sgt. Holmes and his platoon handed over the citizens of Hurlach to 1st Platoon, who would now take on the responsibility of guiding them in their task. With this transition of duty complete, 3rd Platoon received new orders—to move through the city and take up positions guarding the rear.

The platoon walked through the streets of Hurlach, their footsteps echoing off the cobblestones. The atmosphere was a mixture of relief and lingering heaviness. The conversation among the platoon members flowed as they contemplated the uncertain future that lay ahead.

"Seems like things are finally shifting," John remarked, glancing at the picturesque surroundings of the Bavarian town.

"Yeah," replied Pvt. Jenkins, "the Germans are retreating deeper into the Alps. Makes you wonder what their plan is now."

Sgt. Holmes nodded, his eyes scanning the surroundings as they walked. "It's hard to predict their next move. But one thing's for certain—we've come a long way from where we started."

Parsons chimed in, "Battling our way across Europe, and now we're here."

Jenkins looked up at the towering mountains that framed the horizon. "I've heard tales about the Bavarian Alps. They say it's as beautiful as it is treacherous."

"That might be true," Sgt. Holmes agreed. "But we'll take it one step at a time, just like we always have."

As they continued their walk through the city, a sense of resolution permeated the air. The platoon had faced the horrors of war and witnessed humanity's capacity for cruelty, but they had also glimpsed moments of unity, kindness, and strength. Now, with the Alps beckoning in the distance, they carried those experiences with them, ready to face whatever challenges lay ahead.

As they moved through the city, the sun cast long shadows on the cobblestone streets. The platoon's steps were marked by a shared understanding that their journey was far from over. The winding path through the Bavarian Alps awaited them, and with it, a future still shrouded in uncertainty. Yet, as they walked together, their resilience and determination were as unwavering as ever.

As the afternoon sun dipped below the horizon, casting a golden hue over the town of Hurlach, Sgt. Holmes and his platoon were gathered around a small building on the southeast side of town.

The platoon had found a brief moment for a smoke break. The soldiers leaned against the walls of the building, the smoke from their cigarettes dissipating in the cool evening air.

John exhaled a stream of smoke, his gaze fixed on the ground as he spoke, "Man, I wonder what's next for us. After everything we've been through, it's like we're always on the move."

Parsons nodded in agreement, a weariness in his eyes. "Yeah, but at least we're pushing those damn Germans back. Did you see the looks on their faces when we rolled through? Priceless."

Garcia, his cigarette glowing as he took a drag, chimed in with a grin, "Nothing like seeing the tables turn on them. They thought they had it all figured out."

Jenkins leaned against a wall, the smoke curling around his face. "I just hope we get a chance to catch our breath at some point. My boots have seen better days."

Amid the laughter, Smith, the platoon medic, spoke up. "Well, let's hope we're not too far from a place where we can finally get some rest. We all need it."

Suddenly, a shadow fell over the group as Lt. Anderson approached. The platoon fell silent, acknowledging his presence with nods of respect.

"Good evening, gentlemen," Lt. Anderson's voice broke through the quiet, his tone a mix of authority and familiarity. The platoon straightened, their attention fully on their commanding officer.

"Evening, sir," Sgt. Holmes replied, a sense of anticipation in his voice.

Lt. Anderson's gaze swept over the group before he continued, "I've just received new orders. We're on the move again."

The platoon exchanged glances, curiosity, and readiness in their eyes. It was a familiar pattern—the uncertainty of the unknown tempered by their trust in each other.

Sgt. Holmes met Lt. Anderson's gaze, his eyes reflecting a mixture of curiosity and readiness. "New orders, sir?" he inquired, his voice steady.

Lt. Anderson nodded. "Yes. We're moving out in 12 hours," he stated. "The 12th Army is securing this location while we proceed."

A murmur of conversation rippled through the platoon, each member exchanging glances and gestures of understanding. The news brought a renewed sense of purpose, a reminder that their mission was far from over.

"Where are we headed, sir?" one of the soldiers asked, his voice laced with a mixture of curiosity and anticipation.

Lt. Anderson's gaze swept over the group before settling on Sgt. Holmes. "We'll be moving southeast through the Bavarian Alps with the 7th Army," he explained. "Our path lies ahead, and we'll be facing new challenges. The Germans are on the run,"

Sgt. Holmes shared a knowing glance with his fellow soldiers. The rugged terrain of the Bavarian Alps promised to be a different kind of battlefield, one that required adaptability and resourcefulness. As the platoon members absorbed the information, a sense of determination settled among them.

Lt. Anderson's presence and his words underscored the gravity of their mission. "Rest up tonight," he advised, his gaze meeting each soldier's eyes. "We'll need our strength for the journey ahead."

With a nod of acknowledgment, the platoon members began to disperse, returning to their tasks and settling into their routines.

As the night settled around them, the knowledge that their next chapter was about to begin hung in the air. The quiet determination of the soldiers spoke volumes—their commitment to their duty, to each other, and to the shared goal of bringing an end to the darkness that had cast its shadow over Europe for far too long.

THE PROMISE

On a crisp, sunny morning in early spring, Maria stood in her kitchen, the windows open to invite in the gentle breeze and the melodious songs of the birds. The room was filled with the aroma of flowers and the soft clinking of utensils as she was cleaning up from breakfast.

Amid the rhythmic sounds of her bustling kitchen, another sound caught her attention—a rhythmic clip-clop of horse hooves approaching from the road. Her heart skipped a beat, and a smile tugged at the corners of her lips. She recognized that sound, that familiar rhythm.

"Maria!" A voice called out from outside, carried by the wind and wrapping around her like a warm embrace. It was Jorge's voice, and it held a certain eagerness that was unmistakable.

Her hands instinctively moved to dry her hands on her apron as she hurried to the window, peering out with a mix of curiosity and delight. There he was, Jorge, guiding his wagon behind a horse, on horseback, his figure framed by the rays of the morning sun. His hat shaded his eyes, but his smile was unmistakable.

"Jorge!" Maria's voice rang out, a mixture of surprise and joy as she opened the window wider to better see him. Her heart danced within her chest, the sound of his horse's hooves merging with the rhythm of her own excitement.

The horse came to a graceful halt, and Jorge dismounted from the wagon. He looked up at her window, his eyes locking with hers. As she stepped outside to greet him, a soft breeze tousled her hair, and the warmth of the sun flushed her cheeks. Their smiles mirrored each other's, longtime friends who had seen the best and worst of the history of the island.

Maria hurried to the door and stepped onto the porch, her anticipation evident in her expression. "Jorge, what brings you here today?"

Jorge's eyes sparkled with a hint of excitement. "Maria, I have news that will bring a smile to Mary's face."

A mix of curiosity and hope played across Maria's features. "Tell me, Jorge. What news do you bring?"

With a grin, Jorge leaned in slightly. "Remember that favor Mary asked of me some months back?"

Maria's eyes widened, realization dawning. "Oh, yes. Could it be...?"

Jorge nodded. "Yes, indeed. Rodolfo, my ever-traveling friend, made it all the way to Paris as part of his business ventures."

Maria's breath caught. "And did he find...?"

Jorge's smile deepened. "He found John."

Maria's hand flew to her mouth, emotions welling up within her. "John... He's alright?"

Jorge nodded again. "Yes, Maria. He's in Mourmelon, and Mary's letter finally reached him."

Tears of joy glistened in Maria's eyes. "Oh, Jorge, you've brought the best news!"

Maria quickly turned around and called Mary's name. The door from the veranda swung open, and Mary bounded into the room, drawn by the excitement in the air.

"What's happening, Mama?" Mary asked, her curiosity piqued.

Maria turned to her daughter, her face radiant. "Mary, Jorge has news about someone you've been waiting to hear from."

A hopeful light entered Mary's eyes. "Is it... Is it about John?"

Jorge nodded, his voice warm with reassurance. "Yes, Mary. Rodolfo successfully journeyed to Mourmelon and found John there."

A mixture of disbelief and elation surged through Mary. "John... He's... he's alright?"

Jorge's eyes twinkled. "He is, indeed. And there's something more, Mary. I have something for you."

Intrigued, Mary watched as Jorge reached into his jacket and produced two slightly worn letters.

"These letters were personally delivered by Rodolfo," Jorge explained.

Mary's hands trembled with excitement as she reached out to accept the letters. "Letters from John?"

Jorge nodded, a kind smile on his lips. "Yes, Mary. Take your time and read what he has to say. I hope these letters bring you some measure of comfort."

With heartfelt gratitude, Mary clutched the letters to her chest. "Thank you, Jorge. You've given me a gift beyond words."

Mary hugged Jorge and kissed his cheek, a light glowing in her eyes not seen in months. Not hearing word from John and the news of their conflict in Bastogne had troubled her to her core. The past couple of months just going about the everyday business of taking care of the vineyard, completing the arduous pruning process for the new season, wore on her mind.

Mary moved to the kitchen, her steps light with anticipation. She carefully prepared a cup of coffee, the aroma of the freshly brewed liquid mingling with the promise of the letters she held in her hand. With her coffee in one hand and the letters in the other, she retreated to the cozy couch on the veranda, where the sun's warm rays spilled over her.

Sitting down, she placed the cup on the small table beside her and gazed down at the two letters, neatly tied together with a cord. Her heart raced as she gently untied the cord, releasing the hold on the precious words that lay within. As the cord fell away, she noticed the dates on each letter—one from December 1944 and the other from March 1945. The span of time represented by those dates felt both distant and yet intimately close.

With a mix of trepidation and excitement, Mary decided to start with the letter from December. She carefully unfolded the pages, her fingers tracing the familiar handwriting that bore John's essence. As she began to read, the words transported her to another world—a world of battlefields, hardships, and emotions laid bare.

Tears welled up in her eyes as she read about the fierce battle, the struggles he faced, and the friendship that bound the soldiers together. She felt a mixture of pride and anguish, knowing the sacrifices he and his fellow soldiers had made. And then, amidst the accounts of the battlefield, her heart soared as she read his words of love and longing.

"I think of you often, Mary," the words on the page seemed to speak directly to her heart. "Your memory gives me strength and purpose amidst the chaos around me. I imagine the day when I can hold you in my arms again, when we can share stories of our separate journeys and build a life together. Your love guides me through the darkest of times, and I find solace in knowing that you are waiting for me."

Mary's tears flowed freely now, mingling with the words on the page. She could almost hear his voice in her mind, his words etching themselves into her heart. With each sentence, the connection between them deepened, transcending the miles that separated them.

As the last lines of the December letter faded, Mary took a deep breath, wiping away her tears with the back of her hand. She looked down at the second letter, the one from March, knowing that more of John's words awaited her. With renewed determination, she began to read, feeling the weight of time and distance once again dissolve in the power of their love.

"My Dearest Mary,

As I sit down to write you this letter, I find myself overwhelmed with a mix of emotions that have been building up within me over the past months. The journey we've been through since the siege in Bastogne and that fateful day in Foy has been filled with moments of triumph, despair, and everything in between. I want to share with you the truth of our experiences, of the battles fought and the sacrifices made.

The battle for Foy was intense, a trial that tested our courage and our unity as a platoon. We fought valiantly, facing challenges that pushed us to our limits. Through the smoke and chaos, I saw Guppy, my best friend, show the true measure of a soldier. His courage was unwavering, his dedication to our cause inspiring. But fate can be cruel, and Guppy fell, leaving a void that still echoes in the hearts of all who knew him. His absence is a wound that time may heal, but never erase.

The journey through Alsace brought its own trials, as we traversed unfamiliar terrain and engaged the enemy in strategic maneuvers. The Moder river marked a milestone, a testament to our perseverance and resilience. It was there that the course of history took a different turn, where the horrors of the war turned picturesque towns into rubble and rolling meadows into graveyards.

But amidst the darkness, Mary, your light has been my guiding star. Your face, and our love, have been a source of strength that sustained me through the toughest moments. Your love has been a beacon of hope that allowed me to keep moving forward, even when the world around me seemed to crumble.

And so, my love, let me make a promise to you. If fate should call upon me in its most somber tone, know that I will carry your love with me, a flame that will never extinguish. I will find solace in the thought of your unwavering love, and it will be the force that carries me through whatever trials I may face.

However, let me assure you that I remain steadfast in my determination to come back to you, to return to you in Soller. I dream of the day when I can hold you in my arms again, when this war is but a distant memory and our love can thrive without the shadows of conflict.

Until that day comes, Mary, take my heart with you and know that every sunrise and sunset, every moment of triumph and sorrow, is shared between us. I love you more deeply than words can convey, and I eagerly await the time when I can make good on my promise and call you mine once more.

Forever yours,
John"

Unable to contain her emotions, Mary found herself rushing to her mother, who was in the kitchen, busy with the morning chores. Her mother looked up, concerned, and asked, "Mary, what's wrong?"

Struggling to catch her breath between sobs, Mary managed to say, "It's... it's the letter from John." Her voice wavered with a mixture of happiness and sorrow.

Her mother gently placed a comforting hand on Mary's shoulder. "Oh, my dear, come here." She guided Mary to the couch on the veranda, allowing her to cry freely. "Tell me, my love, what does the letter say?"

Amidst sobs, Mary managed to share the contents of the letter with her mother. She spoke of the battles, the friendships, and the love that poured from every word. Her mother listened with a tender smile, understanding the depth of Mary's feelings.

"Oh, my darling," her mother said softly, wiping away a tear from Mary's cheek. "It's okay to miss him, to worry for his safety. Love is a powerful thing, and distance can never diminish it."

Mary nodded, allowing her mother's words to sink in. "I know, Mama. I just... I long for his return. I fear for him, but I also believe in him."

Her mother embraced her, holding her close. "That's the spirit, my dear. Love will guide him back to us, unharmed. And until that day comes, we'll keep him close in our hearts."

With a heavy sigh, Mary handed the letter to her mother. "Would you like to read it, Mama?"

Her mother nodded, taking the letter with a gentle smile. As she read the words that John had penned, her eyes filled with understanding and compassion. "He loves you deeply, my dear. His words are a testament to the strength of your bond."

Mary rested her head on her mother's shoulder, finding comfort in her embrace. "Thank you, Mama. I'm grateful to have you by my side."

"I'll always be here for you, my love," her mother whispered, pressing a tender kiss to Mary's forehead. "And we'll await John's return together, with hope in our hearts."

As the sun shined down on them, mother and daughter sat on the veranda, finding solace in each other's presence and the love that connected them to John, even across the miles.

Just then, another horse could be heard outside. Maria said, "That will be your father. He is due back today from his trip to Palma."

Miguel had taken a two-day trip to Palma to secure supplies for the upcoming year's harvest, Miguel returned to the island with a weary but satisfied smile. As he walked up the path toward their modest house, he was met with the sight of his daughter Mary standing near the gate, her eyes shining with excitement.

"Daddy!" Mary exclaimed, unable to contain her joy. She rushed toward him, her skirt billowing in the breeze, and threw her arms around his neck in a tight embrace.

Miguel chuckled warmly, wrapping his arms around her. "Ah, mi niña, how I've missed you."

As they pulled back, Mary's eyes sparkled with anticipation. "Daddy, you won't believe what happened while you were away. Jorge came by with a surprise for me."

Miguel raised an eyebrow in curiosity. "Oh? And what might that surprise be?"

Mary's smile grew even wider as she recounted the tale. "He brought me letters from John, Daddy! Letters that he delivered all the way from France."

Miguel's eyes softened with understanding. "Ah, yes, I saw Jorge on the road back home. He mentioned that he had something important to deliver to you."

Mary's excitement bubbled over as she clutched her father's arm. "You knew, Daddy?"

He chuckled, ruffling her hair affectionately. "I may not know all the details, but Jorge's face said it all. He had that look of a man carrying something precious."

Gently guiding Mary back toward the house, Miguel listened with rapt attention as she shared the contents of John's letters. He listened as she spoke of the battles and the challenges, her voice filled with pride and concern for her beloved. When she reached the part about John losing his best friend in Belgium, Miguel's expression turned somber.

"War is a difficult thing, my dear," he said softly, his eyes reflecting the weight of understanding. "It brings both triumphs and losses, and it changes those who experience it."

Mary nodded; her heart heavy with the realization of the sacrifices made during times of conflict. "Yes, Daddy, but John's love for his friend and his determination to honor his memory—it's something that touches my heart deeply."

Miguel squeezed Mary's hand gently, his fatherly affection evident in his touch. "It's a testament to the strength of their bond, and to the strength of John's character. These trials shape us, my love, and they teach us what truly matters."

They reached the veranda, and Mary sat down, her father joining her. As Mary leaned against her father, she felt a sense of security and love that only a parent could provide.

"Daddy," she said softly, "I long for the day when John returns."

Miguel wrapped his arm around her shoulders, his gaze fixed on the horizon. "And that day will come, mi niña. Until then, let his letters be a source of strength, a reminder that love can withstand even the greatest distances."

Mary nodded, a mixture of hope and determination in her eyes. She rested her head on her father's shoulder, finding solace in his presence and the shared understanding of the challenges that lay ahead. Together, they gazed out at the sea, a symbol of both separation and connection, as they held onto the promise of love and the unwavering bond that time and distance could never diminish.

BERCHTESGADEN

The early morning sun rose up against the picturesque Bavarian landscape as Lieutenant Anderson rubbed his eyes and slowly rose from his makeshift bed in the field. He glanced around at his fellow paratroopers of Easy Company, 506th Parachute Infantry Regiment, who were stirring to life, their faces smudged with dirt and fatigue. The news of the German retreat and the triumphant march of the Russians into Berlin had reached their company, and a strange mix of relief and anticipation hung in the air.

Anderson stretched his arms overhead and let out a deep breath. It had been a long and arduous journey for his company, fighting their way across Europe, from Normandy to the heart of Germany. The battles they had seen, the bond they had forged, all led them to this moment.

Suddenly, Lt. Anderson heard the sound of running boots as a lone messenger arrived at his tent in a rush. Breathing heavily, he delivered a piece of news that would resonate through the ranks - Adolf Hitler was dead. Lieutenant Anderson, his expression a mixture of solemnity and reflection, knew that this development would shape the course of their mission.

Lieutenant Anderson's voice rang out in the early morning air, cutting through the quiet of the camp. "Sergeant Holmes, gather the men," he called out, his tone carrying a sense of urgency and authority. Sergeant Holmes nodded in acknowledgement and began relaying the order, the words spreading from tent to tent like a determined wave.

Within minutes, the soldiers of Easy Company had assembled in a rough formation, their hands shielding their tired faces from the sun. Lieutenant Anderson stood before them, flanked by Sergeant Holmes, his expression a mix of seriousness and resolve.

"Men," Anderson began, his voice steady and commanding, "we've just received word of a momentous event. Adolf Hitler is dead." Murmurs of disbelief and surprise rippled through the ranks, expressions ranging from skepticism to outright relief. "This changes the landscape of the war," Anderson continued, his gaze sweeping across the faces before him. "But our mission remains. We are now tasked with a new objective - the Bavarian Mountain town of Berchtesgaden. We will be accompanied by the French 2nd Armor Division."

A hushed anticipation settled over the assembled soldiers. Berchtesgaden held a significance that resonated deeply with each of them. It was a symbol of the enemy's power, a fortress nestled within the mountains that had once played host to the architects of oppression.

As Anderson's words sunk in, the soldiers began to exchange whispers, their voices a mixture of determination and curiosity.

"I never thought I'd live to see the day Hitler kicked the bucket," said John.

"Berchtesgaden, huh? That's where they thought they were invincible," said Parsons.

Sergeant Holmes' voice rose above the chatter, his rugged features etched with experience and purpose. "Make no mistake, men. This won't be a leisurely stroll. Berchtesgaden is a stronghold, the home of the SS, but we've faced worse odds before. We've bled for this cause, and we'll keep bleeding until it's over."

The soldiers nodded, a collective understanding passing between them. As they were dismissed, groups began to form, conversations weaving a tapestry of emotions and thoughts.

"You think this is really the turning point?" asked Jenkins.

"We've been through hell together. One more push," replied John.

As the men of Easy Company prepared for the day's march, Lieutenant Anderson could see the mixture of emotions on their faces. The war had taken a toll on each of them, physically and emotionally. Yet, there was a sense of purpose, a shared understanding that they were marching toward a place of historical significance. This was their moment to be a part of something bigger than themselves, to mark their place in the annals of history.

Meanwhile, a few miles away, in the heart of the 7th Infantry Regiment's encampment, Colonel John A. Heintges was busy conferring with his officers. News had reached them that the 101st Airborne was also heading toward Berchtesgaden. The race was on - a race to reach the fabled retreat before anyone else could claim the prize. The orders were clear, and Heintges was resolved - the 7th Infantry Regiment would move out swiftly and decisively.

As the sun climbed higher in the sky, Easy Company set out on the road to Berchtesgaden. The men fell into step, their boots rhythmically pounding the ground, a physical manifestation of their determination. Lieutenant Anderson walked up front with Major Winters, his gaze fixed on the road ahead, his mind processing the gravity of the situation. He knew that this wasn't just about capturing a physical location; it was about capturing a piece of history, a symbol of the end of tyranny.

Back in the 7th Infantry Regiment ranks, the trucks rumbled to life, soldiers checked their weapons and gear, and a sense of urgency pervaded the atmosphere. The news of the 101st Airborne's advance had spurred them on, lighting a fire under the veterans of the 7th Infantry Regiment. They were determined to claim their place in history.

The journey towards Berchtesgaden was one fraught with both tension and moments of unexpected relief. The joint forces of the French 2nd Armored Division and the 101st Airborne Division wound their way through the Bavarian mountains, the towering peaks casting shadows over their advancing columns. As they moved deeper into the heart of the region, signs of the enemy's desperation became evident.

At a narrow mountain pass, the vanguard of the combined units encountered fierce resistance from a determined group of SS soldiers. The pass had been fortified with hastily erected barricades, and the SS troops, fueled by a mix of fanaticism and fear, unleashed a barrage of gunfire and grenades. The echoes of battle reverberated off the steep walls of the pass as both sides exchanged fire, the air thick with the acrid scent of gunpowder.

Amidst the chaos, Lieutenant Anderson led 2nd and 3rd platoons into a flanking maneuver, their rifles barking in unison as they targeted the entrenched enemy positions. The French armor provided crucial support, its heavy cannons pounding the SS positions and forcing them to retreat. After a fierce and relentless push, the combined forces managed to break through the resistance, the enemy soldiers either surrendering or fleeing into the mountains.

As the echoes of gunfire subsided, a tense calm settled over the pass. The soldiers took a moment to catch their breath, the adrenaline of combat slowly receding. Among the SS prisoners, there were expressions of defeat mixed with traces of relief, as if some of them were beginning to sense the impending collapse of the once-mighty Nazi war machine.

Yet, amidst the challenges, there were also signs of hope and a shared desire for peace. Along their route, pockets of German soldiers emerged from hiding places, their tired faces carrying a mixture of surrender and resignation. They handed over their weapons and, in broken English, expressed a longing for an end to the fighting. The language barrier seemed insignificant in the face of the shared understanding that the tide had turned. Parsons spoke fluent German, a product of his education and his mother's descent.

As a group of German soldiers approached, they tossed their rifles aside and held their hands high in the air saying, "Amerikaner gebe ich auf," over and over.

"What are they saying? asked John.

Parsons replied, "Americans, I surrender."

French and American soldiers cautiously accepted these surrenders, their wariness giving way to a realization that the common goal now was to end the bloodshed and rebuild. Conversations between the former enemies were stilted but revealing, hinting at the complexities of human experience during wartime.

As the combined forces continued their ascent through the mountains, each step brought them closer to Berchtesgaden. Through the trees at the edge of the Berchtesgaden Alps, a breathtaking panorama unveiled itself to the advancing soldiers of the 101st Airborne Division and the French 2nd Armored Division. Before them lay the town of Berchtesgaden, nestled in the embrace of the mountains. The town, known for its picturesque beauty, stood in stark contrast to the scars of war that marred its surroundings. Although heavily bombed in the spring, the sight of the town was a poignant reminder that amidst the chaos and destruction, there still existed pockets of serenity and civilization.

As they made their way into Berchtesgaden on May 5th, 1945, the combined forces could not help but feel a mixture of relief and anticipation. However, their arrival was met with an unexpected twist. The town, which they had expected to be a potential battleground, had already been secured by another American unit.

To their astonishment, they discovered that the 7th Infantry Regiment of the 3rd Armored Division had arrived a day earlier and successfully negotiated the surrender of the town. The 7th Infantry Regiment had acted swiftly, their presence and reputation prompting the German garrison to recognize the futility of further resistance. Berchtesgaden, once a stronghold of Nazi power and a retreat for Hitler, now stood as a symbol of the crumbling Reich.

Lieutenant Anderson and his men, along with their French counterparts, paused at the outskirts of the town, processing the turn of events. There was a mixture of emotions among them—disappointment at missing the opportunity to participate in the liberation of the town, but also a sense of pride in the efficiency of their fellow soldiers.

As they entered the town's streets, they were greeted by the surreal scene of German soldiers, once formidable opponents, now standing in lines with hands raised, their surrender made all the more poignant by the backdrop of the Bavarian mountains. The surrender was not just of arms, but of a way of thinking that had led to such devastating conflict.

The 101st Airborne Division and the French 2nd Armored Division joined forces with the 7th Infantry Regiment, exchanging stories and experiences, forging a bond among soldiers who had come from different directions to converge on this symbolic town. Conversations were marked by a mixture of weariness and hope, as the realization sank in that the war in Europe was approaching its end.

With Berchtesgaden secured, the combined forces of the 101st Airborne Division, the French 2nd Armored Division, and the 7th Infantry Regiment turned their attention to a particularly symbolic target: the Berghof, Hitler's mountain retreat and home. Perched on the Obersalzberg, the imposing structure had been a focal point of Nazi power, and its capture held immense significance.

The soldiers of the 7th Infantry Regiment led the way, moving through the lush landscape towards the Berghof. As they approached the grand estate, a mix of anticipation and solemnity hung in the air. The place that had once been a sanctuary for Hitler and his inner circle was now about to be reclaimed by the forces of democracy.

With caution but determination, the soldiers entered the Berghof. The aura of authority that once enveloped the place had dissipated, replaced by an eerie stillness. The grandeur of the architecture clashed starkly with the knowledge of the atrocities that had been plotted within these walls.

As they explored the rooms, they found themselves faced with relics of a dark past—portraits, sculptures, and furniture that had once been symbols of Hitler's ego and delusion. The soldiers moved through these spaces with a mix of incredulity and disgust, bearing witness to the remnants of a regime that had caused immeasurable suffering.

In the cellars and wine cabinets of the Berghof, the soldiers discovered a hidden cache of fine wines. Bottles from various regions and years lined the shelves, a collection that spoke of excess and opulence.

In an act that combined celebration with a touch of irony, the soldiers uncorked the bottles and raised their glasses to toast the downfall of Hitler and his regime. The taste of the wine mingled with the knowledge that they had played a part, however small, in bringing about this moment.

As glasses were raised, Sgt. Holmes spoke with a mixture of solemnity and reverence, "To Guppy, who gave his all back in Foy. He may not be with us in person, but his spirit and courage remain embedded in our story." The clinking of glasses resonated, and the men's eyes held a mixture of remembrance and respect. In that moment, Guppy's sacrifice was honored, a bittersweet undercurrent to the celebrations, a reminder of the cost of their journey. Their conversation shifted to the topic of what each of them planned to do once the war was finally over.

Sgt. Holmes, with his rugged demeanor, started the conversation. "Men, I've been thinking about what's next for all of us. Once we're back home, what's the first thing you're gonna do?"

Private Parsons, his face lighting up with a smile, chimed in, "Well, Sarge, like I said before, I can't wait to hold my little girl in my arms again. She's grown so much, and I want to be there for all those moments I missed."

John, with a determined look, nodded in agreement. "I'm heading straight to find Mary. She went back to her home in Soller."

Jenkins, his voice laced with enthusiasm, added, "You know what, guys? I've always had this crazy idea of opening up a small diner back home. Nothing fancy, just good food, and good company. My mom's recipes are the best, and I want to share them with everyone."

Smith, ever the thoughtful one, said, "I've been thinking about this a lot. I want to become a teacher. I've seen the power of education, and I want to make a difference in the lives of kids who need guidance."

Jackson, the jovial soldier, laughed heartily. "Well, I'm going to travel, my friends! There's a big world out there, and I want to see it all. Maybe I'll even write a book about my adventures."

Holmes nodded, his eyes reflecting pride in his men. "You all have some solid plans there. It's inspiring to hear how determined you are to make the most of the peace we've fought for."

Parsons turned to Holmes. "Sarge, what about you? You've been leading us through this mess. What's your plan?"

Holmes smiled, his gaze fixed on the horizon. "First, go home to my wife, then perhaps, I've always loved woodworking. I think I'll try my hand at building furniture. There's a satisfaction in creating something with your own two hands."

Lt. Anderson chimed in, "You know what, I think I may stay in the Army, make a career of it. I like leading great men as yourselves."

The conversation continued, weaving dreams and ambitions among the soldiers. They talked about reuniting with families, starting businesses, pursuing education, and exploring the world. The weight of the war seemed to momentarily lift as they shared their hopes with each other.

In the midst of these celebrations, there was a shared recognition that the journey was far from over. The war might be drawing to a close, but the aftermath—the rebuilding, the healing, and the establishment of a lasting peace—posed challenges that were just as monumental.

As the wine flowed and the sun set behind the Bavarian mountains, the soldiers took a moment to revel in the triumph of the present, the shadows of the past—a world where the lessons learned from places like the Berghof would guide them towards a brighter future.

TRIUMPH

The next morning while patrolling the city, the platoon heard Lt. Anderson's voice cut through the air, alerting the members of 3rd platoon to assemble at once. The news was electrifying – Major Winters had received word that the French 2nd Armored Division had stumbled upon a concealed entrance within the tunnels to the north of Berchtesgaden, leading to an unknown structure atop the Kehlstein peak. The possibilities churned in the minds of the men, a mix of excitement and curiosity.

As the platoon gathered, adrenaline coursed through their veins. The prospect of venturing into hidden passages and exploring unknown places held a unique allure. The platoon's gear was quickly collected – rifles slung over shoulders, ammunition pouches fastened, and backpacks secured. Anderson's words hung in the crisp mountain air, outlining the plan. The platoon would be hopping into jeeps and racing up into the tunnel entrance, chasing after the secrets that the war-torn land still held.

The jeeps roared to life, their engines echoing off the surrounding peaks as they sped along the winding road. The journey was exhilarating, the wind whipping through their hair and the anticipation palpable. Inside the jeep, conversation buzzed as the platoon shared their thoughts.

Holmes, gripping the side of the jeep, spoke up with a wry grin. "Can't believe we're off to explore hidden tunnels now. Just when we thought the war was all about trenches and foxholes."

Parsons, adjusting his helmet, chimed in. "Who would've thought we'd be chasing mysteries in these mountains?"

John, his eyes scanning the passing landscape, added with a chuckle, "Well, it beats trudging through mud in some forgotten forest."

Jenkins, sitting across from John, raised an eyebrow. "Just hope these tunnels aren't infested with Krauts waiting to pounce."

Smith, next to Jenkins, laughed. "I'd take a hundred Krauts over one more winter on the front lines."

Jackson, in the back seat beside the driver, trying not to fall off the back with four people sitting on the back, grinned, "Either way, it's a damn sight better than taking orders from ol' Hitler."

Laughter erupted, a release of tension and a reminder of the friendship that had carried them through the trials of war. Their banter continued as the jeeps hurtled towards the tunnel.

The jeeps rolled to a halt at the end of the tunnel, where a large ornate elevator stood. It was a remarkable sight. The men hopped out, their boots crunching on the gravel as they took in the scene. The narrow road led only forward; anyone departing from this point would have to reverse their way back, as there was no space to turn.

As the platoon disembarked from the jeeps, they noticed a group of French soldiers gathered around the elevator. Holmes, ever the vigilant sergeant, approached them, and his gaze met that of a French soldier who stood near the elevator entrance. Their exchanged words but Holmes did not understand what they were saying in French.

John, who had picked up a bit of French during their journey, stepped forward, acting as a translator. The French soldiers were excitedly discussing the elevator, and their words flowed like a dance of shared curiosity. They spoke of Hitler's secret hideout at the top of the peak, the hidden chamber that had eluded discovery for so long. The French soldiers were eager to ascend, not for any sinister purpose, but to retrieve some bottles of wine brought down by their compatriots who had ventured up earlier.

Holmes leaned in, joining the conversation. "Sounds like Major Winters and 1st platoon are already up there," he said, his voice carrying a mix of admiration and intrigue. "Seems like they're ahead of the game."

The French soldier nodded, a knowing smile gracing his lips. John translated, his voice carrying the excitement that hung in the air. The platoon exchanged glances, a shared sense of purpose driving them forward. They were on the precipice of something monumental, an opportunity to explore the enigmatic heart of the mountains.

With the French soldiers' voices echoing in their ears, the men felt a renewed sense of anticipation. The elevator would ascend to a place where they would uncover the mysteries that lay hidden among the peaks.

The elevator gently hummed as it ascended, carrying the platoon into the heart of Hitler's Eagles Nest. As the doors opened, they stepped into a realm frozen in time – a space that had once played host to the most powerful figures of the Nazi regime. The grandeur of the interior was both impressive and unsettling, a juxtaposition of opulence and the weight of history.

The main reception room lay before them, adorned with intricate tapestries that depicted scenes of heroism and conquest. The walls were lined with rich wood paneling, a testament to meticulous craftsmanship. The platoon gazed around, their eyes taking in the magnificence of the space.

In the center of the room, a grand fireplace dominated the scene. Crafted from red Italian marble, it bore intricate carvings that depicted mythical figures and scenes of power.

The mantle above it held artifacts of a bygone era – delicate porcelain figurines, silver candelabras, and other treasures that spoke of a life of indulgence.

The furniture was a masterpiece in itself – ornate chairs and sofas upholstered in rich fabrics, their elegance a stark contrast to the stark reality that history had come to represent. The platoon moved through the room, their fingers grazing the polished surfaces as they marveled at the craftsmanship that had gone into creating this haven atop the mountains.

Large Venetian mirrors adorned the walls, their surfaces reflecting the faces of the men who had ventured into this hidden sanctuary. The play of light and reflection gave the room an illusion of vastness, as if the very walls held secrets that stretched beyond their confines.

A sense of surrealism settled over the platoon. They had fought their way through battles, marched across lands, and now stood in a space that had once been a symbol of power and tyranny. The air felt heavy with the weight of history, a reminder that even amid such beauty, darkness had once thrived.

And so, the platoon explored the Eagles Nest, chipping off pieces of the Italian red marble as souvenirs, putting various porcelain trinkets in their pockets, pilfering that which they could put in their knapsacks.

Over the next several days, a sense of brotherhood between the American and French soldiers grew as they explored the Eagles Nest together. Stories were exchanged, bonds were formed, and a shared history was written in the halls of the once-dreaded fortress. However, as the days passed, the French soldiers received orders from American high command to rejoin their division. With heartfelt farewells, they bid their American counterparts goodbye, leaving behind a piece of their shared history atop the Kehlstein.

As the French soldiers departed, the 101st Airborne Division took charge of the Eagles Nest and Hitler's Berghof residence. Lieutenant Anderson and his men settled into their newfound role assisting 1st platoon as stewards of these historic sites, mindful of the gravity of the responsibility that had been placed upon their shoulders. They patrolled the area, safeguarding the remnants of a regime that had once threatened the world.

Then, on May 7th, 1945, news reached the platoon that Germany had officially surrendered. The war in Europe was over. A wave of jubilation spread through the soldiers, and Lt. Anderson's platoon gathered once more at the Eagles Nest and Berghof residence. The once-feared symbols of power had now become places of celebration and victory.

Amid the stone walls and echoing chambers, the soldiers raised glasses of wine that had once been part of Hitler's private collection. Laughter and cheers rang out as they toasted to the end of a brutal chapter in history and the dawn of a new era of peace. The wine, once a symbol of opulence and tyranny, was now a testament to the triumph of democracy and unity.

Press agents who accompanied the 101st took pictures of the soldiers drinking wine and celebrating the victory and the sense of accomplishment that it gave them. They posed by the grand fireplace, raised bottles of wine in mock toasts, and leaned against ornate furniture with a casualness that belied the weight of the world they had carried on their shoulders.

In the heart of what was once Hitler's inner sanctum, the soldiers found a way to rewrite history in their own terms. The Eagles Nest and Berghof were no longer symbols of oppression but instead markers of resilience, courage, and the unbreakable spirit of those who had fought to secure a brighter future.

As the sun set over the Bavarian mountains, the soldiers continued their celebration. They were not only commemorating the victory of their generation but also honoring the sacrifices made by those who had come before them. The echoes of their laughter and the clinking of their glasses reverberated through the mountains.

John stood up from his chair and walked around to face the men. He held his glass up, a single tear falling from his eye.

"Here's to Guppy," John cried.

"To Guppy!" exclaimed the platoon.

"May his funny laugh stay in our memories, and his memory in our heart," said John.

"Here, here," echoed the platoon.

As they drank to Guppy, an eerie silence fell across the platoon. Guppy had always imagined the day the war was over.

"I wonder if he knows? Said Jenkins.

"He does, he does," replied Sgt. Holmes looking skyward and holding up his glass.

John stood up and walked to the edge of the ridge. He looked across at the Alps, the clouds just barely covering some of its peaks. He thought about Mary. He thought about his parents' home in Texas. He missed them both.

Parsons walked up behind John and asked, "You look like you're in deep thought? What are you thinking about?"

"I was thinking about my parents and how much I miss them," said John. "I want to be with Mary, but how can I abandon my parents.' What would they say and think if I didn't come home first?

Parsons looked at John. "That's a hard decision to make," he replied. "On the one hand you want to see your parents and the life you led, but also start the life you want with Mary. I'm afraid I would not want to be in your shoes. My advice, do what is going to make you happy even it if means Mary has to wait just a bit longer, you will have the rest of your lives together."

"Yea," John said. "I'll think it over. We are not headed home yet; we still have work to do."

"That is for sure," replied Parsons.

The pair walked back over to where Evans and Jackson were sitting and sat down, the weight of the war in the past, the uncertainty of the future ahead of them.

HOMECOMING

Two weeks had passed since the 101st Airborne Division had moved out of the Eagles Nest, leaving behind the awe-inspiring view and the memories of their victorious campaign. The men of Easy Company had transitioned into new roles, participating in occupation duties, managing prisoners, and assisting the local Bavarian civilians. Amidst these changes, Lt. Anderson approached John, who had proven himself time and again, both as a skilled soldier and as a leader Lt Anderson was sporting his own new set of Captain's bars.

"John," Captain Anderson said, a proud smile on his face, "you've shown remarkable leadership and commitment throughout our time here. I'm promoting you to Sergeant, and I'm granting you a well-deserved three-week furlough back home."

John's heart swelled with a mix of gratitude and excitement. The prospect of returning home after the long and arduous journey across Europe filled him with anticipation. "Thank you, sir," he replied with genuine appreciation. "It's an honor to serve with this company."

At the same moment, Captain Anderson turned to Sergeant Holmes and continued, "And Holmes, your leadership and experience are invaluable to this platoon. I'm promoting you to Master Sergeant."

Holmes nodded, his weathered face breaking into a proud grin. "Thank you, sir. I'll make sure this platoon continues to do its best."

John walked over and sat down next to Parsons with a contemplative expression.

Parsons said, "What? You look relieved."

"Parsons, you know that dilemma I've been grappling with. Where to go once this is all over?"

Parsons nodded, his gaze steady. "Yeah, I remember our conversation very well."

"Well, I think I've figured it out," John said, a determined look in his eyes. "I'm going home on this furlough. Back to Austin."

Parsons raised an eyebrow. "Back to your ranch?"

John nodded. "Yeah, and I'm going to tell my parents about Mary. About us."

A slow smile spread across Parsons' face. "Sounds like you've found your answer."

"I have," John confirmed. "And after I'm released from service, I'm going to find her, wherever she is."

Parsons chuckled softly. "Well, it's about time, my friend. You deserve some happiness."

"Thanks, Parsons," John replied, gratitude in his voice. "It feels good to have a plan."

Parsons leaned back against a crate, looking up at the stars. "You know, John, maybe I'll find my own path once this is over."

John patted Parsons on the back. "You will. But for now, let's focus on getting through these days."

As they sat there, John felt a sense of relief and purpose wash over him. The uncertainty that had haunted him was replaced by a clear direction, and he knew that telling his parents about Mary was the first step toward a future beyond the war.

With the promotions announced and well-wishes exchanged, John began to prepare for his journey back home. He gathered his belongings, neatly folding his uniform and packing away the memories of his time in Europe. As he made his way to the train station, he couldn't help but feel a mixture of emotions. The brotherhood of the men, the challenges they had overcome, and the memories they had created were now etched into his heart.

The train ride to Reims was a chance for reflection. John's thoughts oscillated between the experiences of the war-torn landscapes and the anticipation of reuniting with loved ones. He could hardly believe how much had changed in the span of a few years. The flight from Reims to London was filled with a sense of wonder, as if he were stepping into a world that had been distant for far too long.

In London, John boarded one of the large cargo ships being used to ferry soldiers across the Atlantic. Upon arriving in New York, John felt a surge of excitement. The city's bustling streets and vibrant energy were a stark contrast to the war-torn landscapes he had grown accustomed to. Yet, amidst the chaos, he found a sense of purpose. His journey was not over; he still had one final leg to complete.

Arriving at Grand Central Station, he quickly wired his parents about his arrival as he boarded a train ultimately headed Austin, Texas. His heart raced as the train rolled through the Appalachians, winding through the Ozark mountains and across the vast Texan plains. The familiar landscape outside the window seemed to welcome him back with open arms. He remembered the rugged beauty of the land, the cattle grazing under the vast skies, and the fragrance of wildflowers that carried on the breeze and wafted through the train window.

Finally, the train pulled into the Austin train station. John stood up and put on his jacket, adjusted his tie, and put on his Beret. His chest adorned with the decorations laid upon him and the 101st in Europe. He stepped down onto the platform and scanned the crowd. His heart skipped a beat when he spotted them: his parents. His mother and father,

James, and Jessica Reynolds, were at the end of the platform. His mother's face covered in tears while his father was donning a smile that mirrored his own. The reunion was a mix of tears, laughter, and embraces that conveyed all the emotions words couldn't express.

"Welcome home, son," his father said, his voice choked with emotion.

"Oh, how I've missed you," said his mother. "I was so terrified when we heard about Bastogne. I am so glad you are safe."

John looked around at the familiar surroundings, the open plains stretching out before him. He had come full circle, returning to the place that had shaped him into the man he had become. The ranch, the open skies, and the gentle lowing of cattle were a testament to the values he held dear – hard work, perseverance, and the unbreakable bond of family.

"Let's head home," said his father.

John and his parents got into their brand new 1944 Cadillac Fleetwood. James opened the trunk and put John's knapsack into it before getting behind the driver's seat and firing up the willing engine.

"I see you got a new car dad," exclaimed John.

"Yes son," said James. "We still have the old truck back at the ranch, but your mama wanted something a little more sophisticated to drive into town. She's got her license now and is driving."

"Really?" exclaimed John. "You mama, driving. Amazing. A lot has changed around here."

The drive from the train station to the ranch was a journey through familiar landscapes that held a new sense of anticipation for John. As the car rolled along the winding roads, the scent of the earth wafted through the open windows, filling the air with a comforting familiarity.

As they approached the entrance to the ranch, the large wrought-iron gate stood open, inviting them in. The gravel road crunched under the tires, and the towering oak trees that lined the drive whispered tales of years gone by. The main house came into view, its white walls gleaming softly in the fading light. The wraparound porch stretched out like open arms, and the windows emitted a warm, inviting glow.

John's heart quickened as they pulled up to the garage next to the bunkhouse. He stepped out of the car, his boots meeting the familiar crunch of gravel beneath them. The ranch had a quiet majesty to it, a serene retreat from the tumultuous world beyond its borders. The bunkhouse, with its well-worn charm, stood to the side, a place that held countless memories of hard work.

"Home sweet home," John remarked, a grin on his face as he carried his bags up the steps of the porch and entered the house. The interior was a blend of rustic elegance, with warm wooden furnishings and photographs that told stories of generations past.

"It's good to have you home," Jessica said, her voice catching with emotion.

As they sat down for dinner that night, the ranch seemed to embrace John in its quiet embrace. The clinking of silverware and the gentle laughter of his family filled the air, weaving a tapestry of belonging that he had sorely missed.

As the evening settled into a comfortable rhythm, John found himself recounting his wartime experiences to his parents in the cozy living room of their ranch house.

He began with the momentous event of D-Day, describing the harrowing landing on the beaches of Normandy and the fierce battles that followed. He painted vivid pictures with his words, capturing the chaos that defined those days. His parents listened with a mixture of pride and concern, their expressions shifting with each twist of the narrative.

John's voice grew more somber as he spoke about Bastogne and the bitter cold that gripped the Ardennes. He talked about the courage of his fellow soldiers, the resilience in the face of overwhelming odds, and the unwavering determination that eventually led to victory. His parents exchanged glances; their hearts undoubtedly gripped by the reality of what their son had endured.

As he transitioned to the Battle of Foy, John's voice cracked with emotion. He described the fierce fighting, the loss of comrades, and the unbreakable bonds that formed among those who fought side by side. He spoke of Guppy, his friend and fellow soldier, with a mixture of sadness and reverence. He told them of Guppy's sacrifice, his unwavering spirit, and the profound impact he had on the platoon.

And then, John spoke of the horror of the camps they found and the Jews they helped to free. He recounted the unexpected turn of events that had led them to the Eagle's Nest in the Bavarian Alps. He described the awe-inspiring landscape, the capture of the mountain stronghold, and the brotherhood that had flourished among the soldiers as they reveled in their victory. He recounted the toasts they had made in Guppy's honor, the celebrations, and the shared moments of reflection.

He reached into his pocket knapsack and pulled out a porcelain doll, one that he had taken off the fireplace mantle in Hitler's hideout in the Eagles Nest.

His parents listened in silence, absorbing each word as if they were there themselves. Their faces reflected a mixture of pride, empathy, and a deep understanding of the sacrifices that had been made. When John finally fell silent, his mother reached out and gently placed a hand on his, her eyes filled with a mixture of love and admiration.

"John," his father began, his voice steady with emotion, "we couldn't be prouder of you and what you've done. Your strength, your courage, it's beyond words."

His mother nodded in agreement, her eyes shining with unshed tears. "You've seen and experienced things that most can't even imagine. Your father and I have been praying for your safety every day, and we're so thankful to have you back."

John swallowed hard, his throat tight with emotion. He knew that no amount of words could truly convey the depth of his experiences, but in that moment, he felt a profound connection with his parents. He reached out and squeezed his mother's hand, then turned to his father with a nod of gratitude.

"Thank you, Mom. Thank you, Dad. It means the world to me to have your support and understanding."

John's mother got up from the couch and disappeared into the kitchen, returning a few minutes later with a tray of coffee and some cakes. She placed the tray on the table in front of the couch. As each one poured a cup of coffee and sat back in their seat, John cleared his throat and looked directly into his mother's eyes.

"Mom," he said softly. "I need to talk to you and dad about something very important to me, someone very important to me."

His parents' faces expressed curiosity as he began to speak and tell the story about Mary.

He spoke of their time in Paris, the city of love, where they had shared moments that felt suspended in time. He described the way the city had come alive for them, as if each cobblestone street and café had been touched by their presence. His words painted a picture of a whirlwind romance, of stolen glances by the Seine and late-night conversations under the glow of the Eiffel Tower.

John's parents listened with rapt attention, their eyes fixed on him as he spoke of Mary's vibrant spirit and her unwavering support during the trials of war. He talked about his plan to go to her in Soller, Mallorca, Spain, and how the prospect of meeting her parents filled him with both excitement and nervousness.

"It's hard to put into words but being with her felt like finding a missing piece of myself," John confessed, his voice laced with emotion. "She's been my anchor, my solace in the midst of chaos. And I want you both to know her, to understand how much she means to me."

His mother reached out and placed a hand over his, her touch warm and reassuring. "John, it warms my heart to hear you speak of her this way. Love is a powerful force, and it's clear that Mary holds a special place in your heart."

His father nodded in agreement; his gaze filled with fatherly understanding. "Son, we trust your judgment. You've shown us that you're a thoughtful and responsible young man. If Mary brings you happiness, then go to her, perhaps one day we will get to meet her."

Tears glistened in John's eyes as he felt the weight of his parents' support and love. He knew that sharing his feelings with them had been the right choice, and their understanding meant more to him than words could express.

"Thank you, Mom. Thank you, Dad," he said, his voice choked with gratitude. "I want you to meet her, to get to know her as I do."

His mother reached for a tissue, her own eyes glistening. "We look forward to it, John. And we're here for you every step of the way."

As they continued to talk and share stories, John felt a deep sense of connection and belonging. He had brought Mary into his parents' world, weaving her into the tapestry of his life as he shared his journey from the battlefields of Europe to the warmth of his Texas home. And in that moment, surrounded by the love of his family, he knew his path. He was ready to take the next step.

It wasn't long before the short stay at home was over and he again boarded the train, as he did so long ago to go to training, back to New York and eventually Europe. He bid farewell to his parents with the promise of the next time they see him, they would see Mary if that truly was his destiny.

PREPARATIONS AND ENDINGS

John's return to his platoon was met with a mix of cheers and playful jeers. As he stepped back into the fold, his comrades greeted him with pats on the back, hearty handshakes, and a few good-natured jokes.

"Look who's back from his luxury vacation in the States!" Smith quipped, a wide grin on his face.

"Yeah, John, did you bring us back any souvenirs?" Jenkins chimed in, a mischievous glint in his eyes.

John chuckled, shaking his head. "Sorry to disappoint you guys, but I didn't have room in my bag for anything but memories."

"Memories of what?" Holmes asked, genuinely interested as he joined the banter.

"Of all the good food, the Texas sun, and my mom's never-ending questions," John replied, a smile playing on his lips. "But more importantly, I had a chance to catch up with my parents and talk about the war, about everything that's happened."

Parsons raised an eyebrow. "So, did you tell them about Guppy?"

John's smile faded slightly as he nodded. "Yeah, I did. It was tough, but I knew I had to."

Holmes clapped a hand on John's shoulder. "That couldn't have been easy, John. But it's important to share those stories."

Over the next two months, as the platoon's base shifted to the Austrian Alps, they found themselves in a routine of training, patrols, and rest. The stunning alpine landscapes offered a stark contrast to the battlefields they had left behind, and the platoon took advantage of the calmer environment to strengthen their bonds.

Sitting around the makeshift campfire one evening, John shared tales of his time back home, describing the vast Texas ranch, the endless skies, and the charm of Austin. The platoon listened intently; their eyes distant as they imagined the scenes John painted with his words.

"So, John," Smith began with a grin, "are you planning to head back to that ranch once this is all over?"

John nodded thoughtfully. "Not right away, that's not been determined. There's someone else I'm thinking about too."

Jenkins waggled his eyebrows suggestively. "Ah, the mysterious Mary, huh? You planning to take her back to that ranch?"

Laughter erupted around the campfire as John playfully rolled his eyes. "Maybe not the ranch, but yeah, I want to see her again. I do want to show her the Texas I grew up in, but we could end up where she is."

Holmes leaned back, a nostalgic smile on his face. "You know, John, life's a strange thing. War brings people together, and sometimes it takes them far away, only to bring them back again."

Out of the corner of his eye, John saw newly promoted Captain Anderson walking toward them with another officer. He quickly snapped to attention followed by the rest of the platoon.

"At ease men," said Anderson.

"Evening, everyone," Anderson greeted, his voice carrying over the camp. "I've got some news to share with you all."

He paused, his gaze scanning the faces before him. "First things first, I want you to meet Lieutenant Powell."

Anderson motioned to the young officer standing beside him. "He's going to be taking over as your platoon leader. I'll be moving on to report directly to Major Winters."

A mixture of surprise and understanding swept through the assembled soldiers. Lt. Powell offered a nod of acknowledgment, his expression a blend of determination and respect. The men exchanged glances, some giving nods of approval while others looked slightly wary of the new change.

"I know this might come as a surprise," Anderson continued, "but Lt. Powell is a capable leader. You'll find him just as dedicated to our mission as I am. He was previously a member of 1st platoon and has chewed the same ground as we have."

Lieutenant Powell stepped forward; his gaze steady as he addressed the platoon. "I'm honored to join your ranks and lead you through the challenges that lie ahead. Together, we'll continue to uphold the standards and principles that define the 101st."

Anderson's gaze returned to the men. "Now, before you start worrying, let me assure you that I'm not disappearing entirely. I'll still be around, but my focus will be on coordinating with Major Winters and helping to ensure the success of our operations."

He let that sink in for a moment before continuing. "Speaking of which, new orders have finally come through. It's time for us to move out once again."

A low hum of anticipation rippled through the platoon. The men had become accustomed to the ebb and flow of orders, knowing that each mission brought them closer to the end of the war.

Captain Anderson's voice held a note of gravity. "We've come a long way together, faced challenges that none of us could have imagined. But we're not done yet. There's still work to be done, and I know each and every one of you is up to the task."

The air was charged with a mixture of anticipation and a touch of trepidation as Captain Anderson stepped forward once again, his voice carrying over the camp. The soldiers had been used to the unpredictability of wartime orders, but the mention of returning to France and the potential for redeployment to the Pacific Theater introduced a new layer of uncertainty.

"Men," Anderson began, his tone steady and commanding, "we've received our next set of orders. It's time for us to leave the Austrian Alps and head back to France." He paused for a moment, allowing the weight of his words to sink in.

"We've been through a lot together, and I know this might come as a surprise," he continued, his gaze sweeping over the attentive faces before him. "But our mission is far from over. The war against Japan is still ongoing, and we might be called upon to join the fight in the Pacific Theater."

A murmur of conversations broke out among the soldiers, their expressions a mix of curiosity and concern. Anderson raised a hand, quieting them with a gesture. "I know this is a big change, and it's natural to have questions. But remember, we're a team. We've faced challenges before, and we'll face them again."

He allowed a moment of silence before delivering the final piece of information. "Be ready to move out at 0900 hours tomorrow morning. We'll be packing up our gear and heading out to return to France for training and potential redeployment."

As the significance of the orders settled in, the soldiers exchanged glances and nods. The prospect of transitioning from the European Theater to the Pacific Theater was a shift that required mental adjustment, yet their training and shared experiences had prepared them for adaptability.

"I won't deny that this is a new chapter for us," Anderson said, his voice resonating with conviction. "But we've proven time and again that we can rise to any challenge. Our commitment to each other and our duty remains unwavering."

He met their eyes, his gaze steady and resolute. "We'll face this next phase with the same dedication and unity that has carried us through. Get your gear packed and ready. We'll be ready to move as one."

With that, the platoons began to disperse, the conversations taking on a more determined tone. As the soldiers set about their tasks, Captain Anderson exchanged a nod with Lieutenant Powell.

As the sun began its slow descent behind the rugged peaks of the Austrian Alps, the soldiers of the 3rd and 4th platoons bustled with purpose. The camp that had been their home for the past months was slowly being dismantled, gear being packed with a mix of efficiency and nostalgia. Supplies were organized, and personal belongings were carefully stowed away.

John moved with a sense of practiced routine, folding his uniform with precision, and securing his equipment. Alongside him, Parsons neatly stacked his gear, a reflective expression on his face. It was a bittersweet task, packing up the remnants of their time in the alps, uncertain of what the future held.

As dusk settled in, the soldiers gathered around the crackling fire that had been a steady companion during their evenings in camp. Sure, it was summer, no longer needed for warmth, but it was their gathering place, their solace.

Holmes, sitting on a log near the fire, leaned forward, stoking the flames absentmindedly. "You think we're really gonna end up in the Pacific?" he mused, his voice carrying a mix of curiosity and concern.

John joined the conversation, settling down on a nearby log. "Could be. Captain Anderson seemed pretty certain about it. Japan's a whole different beast compared to what we've been dealing with over here."

Jenkins, who had been sharpening a knife nearby, chimed in. "Yeah, I heard they're talking about an invasion of Japan. That's no walk in the park, that's for sure."

The flames crackled and popped, their embers casting a solemn light over the group. Parsons leaned back against a tree, staring into the fire. "I never thought the war would take us there," he admitted, his voice tinged with a mixture of contemplation and worry.

John nodded in agreement. "None of us did. But we've faced the unexpected before. We'll adapt and do what needs to be done."

Smith, who had been quietly listening, spoke up. "If we're called upon to go to the Pacific, we'll go. That's what soldiers do."

The sentiment hung in the air, a shared understanding among the men that their duty would take them wherever the fight demanded. As the night grew darker, their conversation shifted to memories of their time in Europe, moments that brought smiles and occasional laughter.

With the fire out and the moon shining bright, the platoon retired for their last night in the field. John looked across the tent at Parsons and said, "Parsons, do you think the world will ever get back to normal? I mean, so much death and destruction; so many lives changed. I am glad we were part of history, but I just wonder what the future holds."

Parsons replied, "I often think about that too, liberating Europe is one thing, returning them to some sense of normalcy is another."

"Yea," said John. "Goodnight Parsons."

The night passed in a quiet hum of contemplation, with the sounds of occasional rustling and the distant call of an owl. The next morning arrived and with the platoon, now well-versed in efficient movements, was up and ready long before the 0900-departure time.

Gear was checked, backpacks were slung over shoulders, and rifles were shouldered as the soldiers fell into formation. The air held a sense of anticipation, a mixture of leaving behind one chapter while heading into another.

As the platoon boarded the trucks to the train station, the journey back to Mourmelon lay before them. Conversations ebbed and flowed among the soldiers as they sat on the train, discussing everything from their experiences in the Austrian Alps to the uncertainties of what awaited them in France.

John sat next to Parsons. The question from the previous night still lingered in his mind, and he turned to Parsons. "You know, it's strange to think that we were part of something so massive. And now, as we head back, it feels like we're leaving behind a piece of history."

Parsons nodded, his expression thoughtful. "It's like we're carrying the weight of what we've seen and done, even as we move forward. But we can't carry it alone. The world has to heal, rebuild, and move on. And we'll play our part in that too."

Upon reaching the camp on August 1st, 1945, the platoon settled back into the routine that had become their norm. Bunks were set up, gear was stored, and orders were received for what lay ahead. The uncertainty of the Pacific Theater still loomed, but for now, they had returned to a familiar place.

In the two weeks that followed, the platoon engaged in training exercises that seemed to encompass every aspect of their extensive skill set. The training grounds buzzed with activity as soldiers honed their abilities and prepared for the uncertain road ahead. The days began at dawn and stretched into the evening, the sun's journey across the sky marked by the soldiers' unwavering determination.

The training covered a range of critical areas. Additional firearms training ensured that every member of the platoon was a force to be reckoned with on the battlefield. The firing ranges echoed with the reports of rifles and the sharp cracks of handguns as soldiers practiced their accuracy and efficiency.

Jump training served as a reminder of the platoon's airborne roots. Parachutes unfurled against the backdrop of the open sky as soldiers leapt from planes, mastering the art of controlled descent. The thrill of freefall was matched only by the assurance that their training would keep them safe when the time came to deploy.

Survival skills took the platoon into the heart of nature's challenges. They learned to navigate dense forests, forage for sustenance, and construct shelters from the elements. The wild terrain became both a proving ground and a classroom, where resourcefulness and adaptability were paramount.

Emergency medical training ensured that every soldier could provide assistance when it mattered most. The platoon learned how to treat wounds, stabilize injuries, and provide basic medical care in the field. The mock scenarios were intense and realistic, fostering a sense of responsibility for one another's well-being.

As the training progressed, John found himself caught between the comfort of familiarity and the uncertainty of the future. Conversations with his fellow soldiers echoed his own thoughts—what lay ahead in the Pacific? The prospect of a new battleground, an unfamiliar enemy, and a different landscape weighed heavily on their minds.

One afternoon, as the sun started to set, John sat with Parsons near the edge of the training grounds. The sound of distant gunfire and the shouts of instructors filled the air. John looked at Parsons and said, "It's like we're preparing for a whole new war, a new set of challenges. I can't help but wonder how we'll adapt."

Parsons nodded, gazing out at the scene before them. "Adaptation has been our strength all along, hasn't it? From Normandy to Austria, we've faced the unknown and risen to the occasion. The Pacific won't be any different."

A moment of silence passed, broken only by the sounds of assembly from the bugler calling all soldiers to assemble. The platoons from the 101st and 501st PIR raced to the assembly area just outside the mess hall. Captain Anderson and Lt. Powell were standing tall under the flags of the United States, France, and the U.S. Army.

As Captain Anderson stepped forward, his gaze scanned the faces of the soldiers before him. His voice carried a weight that matched the gravity of the moment. "Men," he began, "I know the road we've traveled has been long and arduous. We've faced challenges that tested our resolve and shaped us into the soldiers we are today."

A collective nod of agreement rippled through the crowd, acknowledging the shared experiences that bound them together.

Anderson continued, his tone measured yet somber. "I bring news that will alter the course of history and signal the beginning of a new chapter for us all. On August 6th, we detonated a new type of bomb over the city of Hiroshima and then three days later on the 9th, another over the city of Nagasaki. The devastation that followed is a stark reminder of the power that mankind wields."

A murmur of realization swept through the soldiers, a mixture of shock and comprehension as they absorbed the weight of those words.

"Emperor Hirohito of Japan," Anderson stated, his voice steady, "announced the surrender of Japan on August 15th. bringing an end to the war in the Pacific."

A collective exhale seemed to fill the air, as if the weight of the war had been lifted from their shoulders.

"As we stand here today," Captain Anderson concluded, "we find ourselves on the cusp of a new era. While the Pacific Theater may call some of us to new horizons, many of you who have been here since the liberation of France will finally get to go home."

With those words, the platoon cheered uncontrollably. The news of Japan's surrender reverberated through the ranks of the 101st Airborne Division like a powerful wave. The weight of years of conflict and uncertainty lifted, replaced by an overwhelming mix of relief, joy, and a sense of accomplishment. With the sun leaving the sky, campfires flickered to life, their flames dancing in rhythm with the elation that filled the air. The sounds of celebration echoed through the night—cheers, songs, and the clinking of cups raised in toasts to the future.

In the heart of the camp, a makeshift stage was set up, adorned with flags and banners that symbolized the Allied victory. The mood was one of unity, of brotherhood forged in the crucible of war.

Captain Anderson, standing at the center of the stage, his face illuminated by the fires, raised his hands, calling for the attention of the assembled soldiers. The cheers gradually subsided, replaced by an eager anticipation as all eyes turned toward their leader.

"Tonight, my fellow soldiers," Anderson began, his voice carrying a mixture of pride and emotion, "we stand on the brink of a new era. We have faced challenges that few can comprehend, and through it all, we have remained unyielding in our dedication to freedom and justice."

The crowd erupted into applause, cheers, and the pounding of boots on the ground—a spontaneous ovation that echoed their shared sentiment. Amid the celebration, soldiers embraced, clinking cups, laughing, and some even rushed back to their bunk to write to their parents and loved ones. The tension that had defined their existence for so long melted away.

The next day dawned with a sense of calm that had become foreign to the soldiers of the 101st Airborne. The camp was alive with a different kind of energy, a mixture of relief and anticipation for what lay ahead. As the sun climbed higher in the sky, John found himself deep in thought, reflecting on the long and eventful journey that had brought him to this point.

As he was cleaning his rifle for inspection, John saw Lt. Powell approaching. The lieutenant's face wore a mix of formality and warmth, signaling that he bore important news. With a nod, John greeted him.

"Sergeant Reynolds," Lt. Powell began, his voice carrying a mixture of professionalism and familiarity, "I've received word from higher command. Your service in the 101st Airborne is coming to an end."

John's heart skipped a beat as his face bore a surprised expression.

"It's time for you to go home, son," Lt. Powell continued, his eyes meeting John's with genuine appreciation. "You've served with honor, and your dedication to duty has not gone unnoticed. You'll be receiving an honorable discharge," Lt. Powell added, his voice carrying a tone of finality. "Your country is grateful for your service, and it's time for you to embark on the next chapter of your life. Report to Lt. Johnson in Operations. He will process the necessary paperwork and travel instructions."

"Lt. Powell," John said. "Is there anyone else being discharged? I sure hope I am not the only one."

"Yes, Sergeant'", most of your platoon who have served since the beginning are being discharged. Replacements and new soldiers will carry on with occupation responsibilities until that ends."

"Thank you, sir," John said, his voice steady despite the swirl of emotions within him. "It's been an honor to serve."

Lt. Powell extended his hand, and John shook it firmly—a gesture of respect and mutual understanding.

"Take care, John," said Powell, his eyes reflecting the sentiment of their shared journey. "And remember, the lessons you've learned here will serve you well in whatever comes next."

As the Lieutenant walked away, John watched him for a moment as he delivered the same news to Parson, Jenkins, Holmes, and Evans.

Amid the bustle of the camp, John, Holmes, Parsons, Jenkins, and Evans found themselves gathered together, their gear neatly packed and their faces carrying a mixture of excitement and bittersweet nostalgia. They stood in a small circle. John walked up to the group.

"Well, John, I guess this is it," said Holmes, his tone both light and meaningful. "No more early morning drills or freezing foxholes."

John chuckled, the corners of his eyes crinkling with genuine amusement. "No more C-rations or sleeping in muddy trenches," he replied. "I'll miss the adventure, though."

Parsons chimed in, his voice tinged with a touch of sentimentality. "And the bonds we've formed, no doubt. We've been through a lot together."

Jenkins nodded in agreement, his usually boisterous demeanor tempered by the weight of the moment. "Yeah, it's been one hell of a ride, hasn't it?" he said, his gaze sweeping over his friends. "I'm proud to have served with you all."

As they exchanged knowing glances, the reality of parting settled upon them. They had become more than a platoon; they were brothers, bound by a unique bond that only those who had faced what they did could understand.

With a sigh, Parsons slung his pack over his shoulder. "Well, I suppose it's time to move on," he said, his gaze sweeping over the faces of his friends.

John nodded, his heart heavy with a mix of gratitude and anticipation. "We'll each carry a piece of this with us," he said, his voice carrying a note of quiet determination. "And wherever we go, we'll make the most of it."

As they exchanged farewells and promises to keep in touch, the group headed over to Operations to meet with Lt. Johnson. Each taking their turn signing papers, handing over their rifles, and receiving the discharge orders and travel vouchers.

"Lt. Johnson Sir," inquired John. "I am not going back to the States this time, I recently had furlough. I am headed to Spain to find my love, so I won't need any travel arrangements back home. I do have a letter I need to send to the Olive Trading Company in Paris, care of Rodolfo Sanchez."

"Sure Sergeant," said Lt. Johnson. "We have a V-Mail delivery headed to Paris this afternoon, I can have the Corporal drop the letter off at their local post."

"Thank you, Sir," replied John.

"Is there anything else Sergeant," asked Lt. Johnson.

"No Sir," said John.

"You are dismissed then soldier. Good luck," said Lt. Johnson.

John walked out of the operations building, his duffle bag across his back. He felt the warmth of the sun on his face as he walked to the gates to get a ride in a jeep from Corporal Jackson into Paris. Jackson, since he was a replacement well after the Normandy invasion, did not receive his discharge. He would continue with the rest of Easy Company in the future duties.

John looked back as they sped off away from Mourmelon, a last look at what for a time, had been home.

SÓLLER

As the afternoon sun spread elongated shadows upon the enchanting streets of Sóller, Mary stood at the train station, her heart echoing like a drum in her chest with anticipation. The air was a sweet symphony of blooming orange blossoms, harmonizing with the soft aroma of freshly baked bread wafting from a nearby bakery. The vibrant palette of the Mediterranean enveloped her – the sky a serene azure, rooftops adorned in terracotta hues, and the lush green expanses of vineyards stretching into the distance.

Clutching a worn letter, delivered by Jorge from John by way of Rodolfo's trading company, her hands trembled as she traced the familiar words etched into her memory. "I will return to you, my love, after the war. We will build a life together in Sóller, surrounded by the beauty of this place that you call home." John's promise was a constant echo in her mind, a steadfast light guiding her through the tempest of a world consumed by conflict.

In the distance, a low rumble crescendoed, signaling the train's approach from Palma. Mary's heart raced, a whirlwind of joy and nervousness mingling within her. This was the day she had yearned for, a day she had pictured in her dreams during the quiet nights when John's absence was a heavy burden.

As the train emerged from a bend, its wheels sang a screeching song against the tracks, sending a cloud of dust into the air. Mary's eyes searched eagerly for a familiar face among the alighting passengers. Her breath caught, her heart racing, but as seconds ticked by, her initial exhilaration transformed into quiet disappointment.

The train came to a halt, and travelers disembarked with weariness etched into their expressions. Mary's gaze flitted from one face to another, her hope diminishing with each fleeting look. She strained her eyes, yearning for that glimpse of the soldier who had written to her with promises of a future.

As the platform emptied, a sense of longing swelled within Mary. Tears shimmered in her eyes, threatening to cascade down her cheeks. Clutching the letter tighter, her fingers trembled with a cascade of emotions. The reality of war's capricious nature settled over her like a shroud, casting a shadow of doubt upon John's arrival.

Yet, amid the twinge of disappointment, Mary held steadfast. She wiped away a tear, her posture straightening as she whispered to the breeze, "I will wait for you, John. I will wait in Sóller, amidst the vineyards, orange groves, and olive trees, until the day you come back to me." Rekindled determination surged through her, as if the very air carried the strength of her surroundings. With a deep breath, she steeled herself for the uncertain journey that lay ahead. For tomorrow, she vowed to return to the train station, her hope an unextinguished flame, waiting for John's return.

The train slowly started to move again, Mary turned around in the direction of Bella, the family horse, ready to begin her trip back home. Just as she was about to take her first steps, she heard the distant whistle of the train pierce the cool breeze, followed by the unmistakable hiss of the brakes as it abruptly came to a stop.

Her heart leaped, a wild hope taking root. Could it be? She turned her gaze back towards the train, her eyes straining to see. And then, emerging from the last car, a figure descended the steps. A duffle bag swung at their side, and they wore a soldier's dress uniform, a beret resting atop their head. Her heart raced, her breath caught, as she recognized the familiar yet slightly weathered face. It was John.

A surge of emotion overcame Mary, her feet moving almost of their own accord. She began to run towards him, her pulse echoing in her ears, her steps echoing the beat of her heart. The duffle bag dropped to the ground as John, too, recognized her presence. With a wide smile spreading across his face, he opened his arms, and Mary flung herself into his embrace.

Time seemed to stand still in that moment, the world around them fading away as they held each other. Tears of joy welled up in Mary's eyes as she nestled her head against John's shoulder. His familiar scent, the warmth of his embrace, and the steady rhythm of his heartbeat were all the proof she needed – he was here, he had returned to her.

In a voice choked with emotion, John whispered into her ear, "I told you I would come back to you, Mary. Nothing could keep me away." And as they stood there, locked in an embrace that transcended words, the bustling train station faded into the background, leaving only the two of them in a moment that marked the end of a long journey.

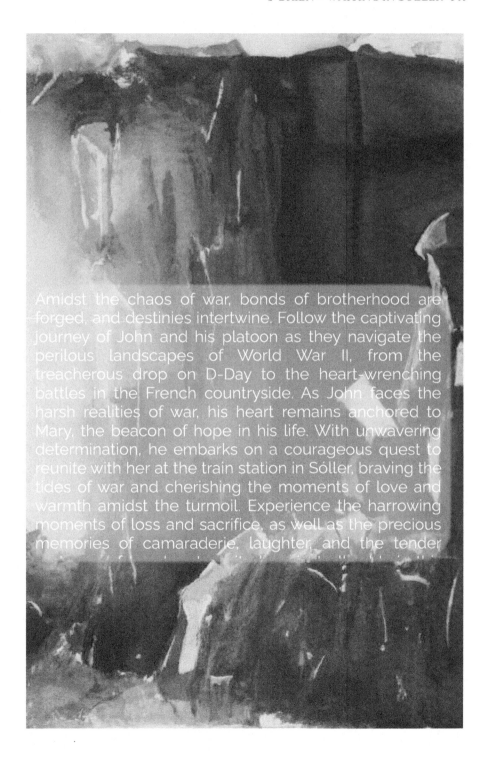

Amidst the chaos of war, bonds of brotherhood are forged, and destinies intertwine. Follow the captivating journey of John and his platoon as they navigate the perilous landscapes of World War II, from the treacherous drop on D-Day to the heart-wrenching battles in the French countryside. As John faces the harsh realities of war, his heart remains anchored to Mary, the beacon of hope in his life. With unwavering determination, he embarks on a courageous quest to reunite with her at the train station in Sóller, braving the tides of war and cherishing the moments of love and warmth amidst the turmoil. Experience the harrowing moments of loss and sacrifice, as well as the precious memories of camaraderie, laughter, and the tender